TROUBLE IN THE SADDLE

Center Point
Large Print

Also by Arthur Henry Gooden and available from Center Point Large Print:

Call of the Range
Death Rides the Range
Valley of the Kings

TROUBLE IN THE SADDLE

Arthur Henry Gooden

CENTER POINT LARGE PRINT
THORNDIKE, MAINE

This Center Point Large Print edition
is published in the year 2025 by arrangement with
Golden West Inc.

Copyright © 1947 and 1948 by Arthur Henry Gooden.

All rights reserved.

The text of this Large Print edition is unabridged.
In other aspects, this book may vary
from the original edition.
Printed in the United States of America
on permanent paper sourced using
environmentally responsible foresting methods.
Set in 16-point Times New Roman type.

ISBN: 979-8-89164-397-0

The Library of Congress has cataloged this record
under Library of Congress Control Number: 2024944863

TO THE VALIANT

CONTENTS

1. PURSUIT — 9
2. BELOW THE RIO GRANDE — 17
3. A HOSTILE COUNTRY — 34
4. THE PRISONER — 54
5. TRAIL NORTH — 63
6. BORDER TOWN — 79
7. ALLIES — 91
8. AT THE CANTINA — 106
9. DARK CANYON — 121
10. MR. BERREN — 140
11. WILD HORSE PASS — 152
12. MARSHALL MEN — 165
13. ACTION BY NIGHT — 177
14. TERROR — 190
15. DARK HOURS — 209
16. DAWN IN DOS RÍOS — 224
17. BLIND TRAIL — 242
18. THE CLOSING TRAP — 267
19. DEATH WHISPERS — 277
20. TRAIL'S END — 290

1
PURSUIT

The upthrust of rock stood off the trail about a hundred yards below the ridge and cut a long black shadow down the bright sunlight that lay on the steep slope. It offered the shade and temporary cover that Adam Marshall needed at that moment.

He slid from the saddle and stood for a brief space, eyes on his sweat-lathered horse. The fast ride up the sun-baked slope had taken the big buckskin's wind.

His look went thoughtfully to the trail, a short stone's-throw beyond the concealing brush. The buckskin was a speedy climber and it had taken all of twenty minutes to top the ridge. He could safely count on that much time before his pursuers reached the vicinity.

He knew that he was close to the Rio Grande. Another mile or two would put him in the brakes. He could give the horse five minutes and still retain his lead over those men who so strangely sought his life.

He turned and scrutinized the towering crag under which he stood. A narrow shelf-like ledge drew his eyes and he scrambled up, found he could see down the slope to the river-brakes.

Sunlight drew steely glints from the river where it showed between the trees.

His slow, thoughtful gaze moved across to the Mexican side. The country looked much the same over there, low-lying brush, a panorama of soft gray-greens and browns and yellows against a background of bleak desert hills.

He continued to study the landscape, fingers busy with tobacco and cigarette paper. Once he was down in those concealing reeds he could hide out from his mysterious pursuers, elude them until they gave up the chase, and then continue on his way north to El Paso.

Adam lit the cigarette, his expression suddenly grim as his thoughts back-trailed events of the past few days. It was his first trip to this corner of the Texas border. A useless trip that had wasted his time. He might have known something was wrong with those 7V cattle. The price was too low for decent stuff. His only consolation was that he had had the sense to insist on a personal inspection. It hadn't taken long to discover the reason for that attractively low price. Being Texas stock, the cows themselves were fairly immune to the fever, but there would have been hell to pay if he'd gone through with the deal and thrown that tick-infested bunch on his own JM range. Also every cowman in Arizona would have cursed him, and for good cause.

He had reason to believe that he had been

followed from the moment he had left Presidio. The bullet hole in his sombrero was proof that the gang had been uncomfortably close. The buckskin's burst of speed had put him beyond range of their guns, but the dust drift told him they still clung to his trail.

The reason for the pursuit mystified him. He could make no sense of it. He was a stranger in this remote fringe of Texas. It was unthinkable that the 7V outfit was back of this attempt to murder him because of his refusal to buy tick-infested cattle.

Adam snubbed the cigarette under his boot heel and climbed down from the ledge. The solution must wait. There was pressing need to be on his way.

The few minutes' rest had freshened the buckskin and they were soon down the steep slope and within several hundred yards of the river. The terrain here was thickly covered with clumps of bunch grass that made fast riding dangerous for a less sure-footed horse.

He kept to the narrow trail that twisted through the hummocks and had covered half of the distance when a shout faintly touched his ears. A backward glance showed a horseman sky-lined on the ridge.

More riders quickly appeared. He counted half a dozen forging at reckless speed down the slope. Gunfire crackled.

He made his decision instantly, left the trail, and sent the buckskin into a fast run across the narrow strip of bunch grass that lay between him and the willow-brakes. It was the quickest way of removing himself as a target for the rifles of those down-pouring horsemen.

The buckskin stumbled, recovered footing, jumped a yawning five-foot crevice, and suddenly the low-growing trees closed around them.

Adam halted the blowing horse, listened for a moment to the distant pounding hoofs. His position was not much improved. Once they reached the brakes his pursuers would scatter, stalk him like beasts of prey. They would be familiar with the country, forestall his every move.

It was slow going through the interminable swamp. He had to keep his eyes sharp for quicksands, his ears keen for any warning sound. He knew that the men trailing him would be equally on the alert. Movement meant sound, but he had to keep moving.

As best he could he pointed straight for the river. If the worst came he could attempt to make for the Mexican side.

A gigantic longhorn steer went crashing noisily through the willows. An old-timer, judging from the wide-spreading horns, a wary outlaw that had learned to evade the roundup.

Others had heard the telltale threshing in the

willows. A man shouted, was answered by other shouts. Adam kept his horse moving. There was nothing else to do. The circle thrown around him was shrinking.

He caught the flash of sunlight on water and turned to investigate. Quickened hopes fell, and for the first time he was conscious of something like panic, a despair as black as the waters of the slough that had flashed the momentary gleam of sunlight. Worse still, the slough lay like a great bent arm, a wide, muddy backwash, a bottomless pit of quicksands.

Adam reluctantly swung to the left, followed the hook of the slough toward the river. The half-circle would put him close to the searching men. If they knew about the slough they would also know that they had him trapped. They would be watching the river at the mouth of the slough.

A new sound touched his ears. The river. Hidden from view by cottonwoods and willows, but very close now, a hundred yards, perhaps less.

Other sounds came, the crackle of brush off to the left, yells, curses, a man's angry voice.

"Hell—it's that damn steer ag'in!"

The searchers were behind him. The old mossy-horn outlaw steer had given him the chance he needed.

Adam waited to hear no more. He sent the buckskin into a dead run over that treacherous ground. More shouts told him they had heard, were in full chase.

He knew now that his one hope was the river. The slough cut off escape to the right and his pursuers were closing in from the left. He had to keep going and the only way left open was the wide Rio Grande.

It was a thin chance. In fact no chance at all. He would make a target hard to miss.

Adam's jaw set in grim lines. Anything was better than falling into the hands of these men. They intended his death. He preferred death in the river to finding himself dangling at the end of a rope.

He was still in the lead, perhaps a couple of hundred yards, and hidden from sight by densely growing trees that now held his horse to a walk.

He was through the jungle growth at last. It seemed an eternity, was perhaps a matter of seconds, and then he was racing downstream. His wits were functioning smoothly. The only chance was to delay immediate discovery, gain time enough to get well out into the river.

He splashed through the shallows until he found the spot, well concealed by willows that would cover him from questing eyes. They would not think him crazy enough to attempt the long swim across to the Mexican side, would lose a few minutes combing the thicket. The shallows would effectually wipe out the last twenty yards of the trail.

The water deepened quickly. He dallied his loosened rope around the saddle-horn and slipped from the saddle, felt himself sliding through the water as the buckskin forged ahead.

The current dragged them downstream, which was what he wanted. He swam low, head barely above water. The opposite shore looked miles away.

He had no fear that the horse would attempt to circle back. The buckskin was river-wise, and now freed of his rider's weight was making good time.

Adam's hopes took an upward leap, as quickly dropped to zero. Loud shouts from the receding bank told him he had been spotted, and he was still within easy range for a good rifleman.

A bullet whined overhead. He heard the crash of guns and more bullets buzzed over him like vicious bees. He felt a hammer-like blow on his arm.

The force of it flung him sideways, still clinging desperately to the rope. The speed of the horse jerked his trailing body flat on the surface and he felt another blow on one of his legs, a sharp, searing pain. The next instant he was dully aware that the horse was no longer moving forward.

He was still clinging desperately to the rope when the dead horse sank. He felt the lifeless body roll against him, let go his hold on the rope, and rose to the surface.

Something brushed against him, pushed him gently, and he realized that he was caught in a tangle of floating branches.

There was still enough sense left in him to grasp with his good hand and draw himself up cautiously until his head was barely above water.

It was a huge limb, recently torn by some wind from an overhanging cottonwood, and its leafy branches made a screen that hid him from the killers on shore.

Careful to keep his head behind the covering leaves, he drew his good leg over the main limb and worked his body into the crotch. Even if he lost his senses for a time, the cradling branches would hold him secure above the water.

He lay there, content to drift with the current. At least he was no longer a visible target. His pursuers would be scanning the river for some sign of his body, would presently decide that he was in the clutches of the quicksands. They would ride away, report his death to whomever it was had wanted him dead.

Anger stirred in him as he thought of the slain buckskin. He had an account to settle with these ruthless men.

2
BELOW THE RIO GRANDE

Catalina looked at the branch with appraising eyes. She knew that the current would soon drift it away from the sandbar. A fine big limb, too green for immediate use, but a few months would make seasoned wood of it.

She hastily tucked up her skirt, kicked off her rawhide sandals, and waded into the shallows. She must work fast. Already the pull of the current was swinging the branch back into the stream.

Something she saw suddenly held her motionless. "*Madre de Dios!*" She crossed herself. It was a man, lying there in the crotch of the tree and almost hidden behind the thick green leaves.

The pull of the stream was slowly swinging the big limb free of the sandbar. Catalina came out of her trance and grasped the nearest branch with both hands.

"Juan!" she screamed. "Quick—"

Already the river was proving too strong. Inch by inch the great limb slid away from the sandbar. Catalina dug her toes into the soft mud, leaned her weight against the pull of the current.

She screamed again, and heard her husband's answering shout.

He ran up, splashed into the water, a lean old man with a seamed brown face under a steeple-crowned straw sombrero. He carried a coiled rawhide *reata* and in a moment he had his loop over the broken stub of the limb.

It took their combined strength and much splashing in the water that now came above Catalina's bare brown knees before the branch was at last securely grounded on the sandbar.

Catalina's husband dropped his *reata* and gazed incredulously at the man wedged in the green tangle. "*Por Dios!* A gringo!"

Catalina wasted no time in surmises. She bent her head for a close look. "He is not dead!" she exclaimed. "Quick—do not stand there like a stupid."

It was her face Adam saw bending over him when he opened his eyes a few minutes later. He tried to sit up, felt the press of her hand. "No, señor. You are hurt."

"He is a gringo," her husband pointed out. "He will not understand what you say."

"Listen—" Catalina gestured for silence. "He speaks—" She bent her head closer and a pleased smile spread over her face. "He understands—"

Adam grinned up at her. "*Sí, hablo Español.*" His look went to the man who was eyeing him doubtfully.

Catalina, watching him anxiously, smiled reassurance. "We wonder about you, señor, but do not worry. You are safe with us." She stole a glance at his leg, added significantly, "This is the Mexican side of the river, señor."

He nodded, and for a moment weakness held him silent, and then, his whisper hardly audible above the murmuring wash of the river, "You have saved my life. I am very grateful."

"It is the Good God you must thank," declared Catalina. "The good God said to me, 'Quick, Catalina, pull that fine branch from the river.'" She crossed herself. "A blessed miracle, señor."

Adam smiled up at her. He liked this friendly woman. He looked again at the man, silent, obviously perplexed, inclined to suspicion. His gaze moved on, noticed the long shadows crawling down the sandy beach. He must have been unconscious for hours, floating down the broad Rio Grande.

His look came back to the man on whose swarthy face suspicion was darkening. He said, holding the Mexican's look, "Some men, strangers, tried to kill me. My one chance was to escape across the river. They shot my horse."

The doubt continued in the Mexican's eyes. "I do not like this—" His tone was hostile. "Why should strangers try to kill you?"

"I don't know the answer to that one." Adam

managed a grin. He was feeling sick, growing more keenly aware of his wounds.

The man pursed his lips, shook his head dubiously. "I do not want trouble, señor—"

His wife interrupted him. "Such talk!" she flared. "Have you no heart, Juan Ortiz? This poor man needs our help."

The old *ranchero* glowered. "*Por Dios*," he grumbled, "I do not like to be mixed up with the affairs of these gringos. He may be a wrong one."

"With that face?" Catalina's tone was scornful. She was years younger than her husband. "When were you ever a frightened sheep that you fear trouble?"

A glint appeared in Juan's eyes, as if her words stirred memories of long-gone and violent days. His expression softened. "You are right, Catalina. We must help him—and quickly—"

A faintness laid hold of Adam and as from a long way off he heard the woman's frightened cry, "*Madre de Dios*, he dies in front of our eyes!"

When his eyes opened again it was the woman's face he saw, close to his own. He was lying on a bed, he vaguely realized.

Catalina smiled, exclaimed softly and put a glass to his lips.

Adam obediently took a swallow of the medicine. She smiled again, nodded satisfaction and replaced the glass on a table.

She leaned over him. "The doctor has been. He says you will not die, señor." She saw his bewilderment. "You have been unconscious half the night, señor. Juan rode to San Carlos for the doctor. He has put your broken leg in splints and a bandage on your arm. You are a very sick man, he says, but also a very strong man and will not die."

His aghast look drew a sympathetic nod from her.

"Do not worry," she comforted. "The leg will soon be as strong as ever."

A door softly opened and candlelight threw vague moving shadows on the wall. Adam turned his head, saw Juan Ortiz looking down at him.

The old Mexican's smile was friendly enough now. He asked courteously, "You are comfortable, señor?" He went on, not waiting for an answer. "You are welcome, señor. The house is yours . . . all that I have is yours." His gesture was grandly eloquent.

"*Gracias, señor.*" Adam's mind was functioning again. It was going to be a long time before his leg would allow him to sit in a saddle. He must manage to get word of the accident to the JM. His grandfather would worry. He said to Juan Ortiz, "I must tell you my name, señor, Adam Marshall of the JM ranch in Arizona, near Dos Ríos."

Relief passed like sunlight across the old *ranchero*'s face. It was plain that any lingering doubts in him were banished. He bowed polite acknowledgment. "You wish to send a message, señor?"

"If you can manage it for me," smiled Adam.

"*Sí,*" assured the Mexican. "I will send it to a friend in Juarez and he will take it across the border to the post office in El Paso." He turned to the door. "I will bring paper, a pen—"

"No," demurred Catalina. "No more talk tonight. Señor Marshall must rest. Out with you, Juan. The letter can wait until morning."

She picked up the candle, stood for a moment, her gaze on him. "I will say a prayer for you," she told him softly.

The door closed behind her and darkness filled the little room. Adam was suddenly acutely aware again of his hurts. He began to wish Catalina had left him the candle. He felt miserably helpless, lying there in that darkness, unable to move.

His thoughts went back to the men who had chased him into the Rio Grande. Whoever they were, or whatever their purpose, they would be thinking him dead, at the bottom of the river. They had no way of knowing he had escaped them, was at that moment under the protection of a humble Chihuahua *ranchero*.

It was obvious that his attackers had trailed him from Presidio, which indicated that his identity was known to them. The purpose behind the attack was a complete mystery. He could make no sense of it.

Adam scowled into the darkness. There was one possible explanation. Some long-forgotten affair that involved his grandfather. Old John Marshall was a Texan in the days of his youth before he had trailed his herd of longhorns into Arizona and founded the great JM ranch in the Dos Ríos country. It was not improbable that a dominating personality like John Marshall should have left behind him smaller men who still hated his memory.

He would give his grandfather a full account of the affair. He would ask for information that might explain things. There would be plenty of time to get an answer back before he could have the use of his leg again.

Adam reflected with grim amusement on his grandfather's reaction to the news. Old John Marshall would do more than sit down and write a letter. He would likely order out the whole JM outfit. At the very least he would send Bill Clemm, and probably old Celestino Baca who was a native of Chihuahua and familiar with the country. Celestino had been with the JM outfit since his youth and had an almost paternal affection for Adam. In fact, Celestino and his wife, Rosa, had virtually raised Adam from cradle days after the accident that took the lives of his own parents.

Drowsiness overtook his racing thoughts, and presently the door quietly opened and Catalina Ortiz, candle in hand, peered at him. She saw that he was asleep, nodded contentedly, and returned on soundless feet to her husband.

"In the morning his letter must go to the post office in El Paso," she said.

"*Sí*," assented Juan Ortiz. "I will send Mateo on our fastest horse to Juarez. He will give this letter to our good friend Porfirio Servera who will take it across the river to the post office in El Paso."

The days lengthened into weeks but no word came in answer to the letter. At Adam's request Juan again sent Mateo to Juarez to ask if the letter had been taken as agreed to El Paso. Mateo returned with a message from Porfirio Servera swearing by all the saints that he had personally delivered the gringo's letter to the *Americano* post office.

It was plain that Juan Ortiz was not liking the situation. Adam was uneasily aware of a change in him. The old suspicion was back in the *ranchero*'s eyes.

"This gringo tells us lies," Juan complained to his wife. "It is not true that he has a great *rancho* in Arizona. He is a wrong one and will bring us trouble. I do not like this business, Catalina."

Catalina's belief in the red-headed gringo remained unshaken. A letter was such a little thing, and easily lost in a big country like *Los Estados Unidos Del Norte.* It signified nothing that no answer had come. She was sure that Señor Marshall was not a wrong one, or else the good God would not have floated the big cottonwood branch to the sandbar for her to save from the river.

"He is beautiful," Catalina declared, "*Un grande caballero,* and when his leg is strong again for the saddle you will lend him your best horse for the journey to his home."

Juan was impressed. He had respect as well as admiration for his comely young wife.

"*Verdad,*" he said. "I will be patient, *chica.* You are always right." He smiled indulgently. "Only be careful, or I may be jealous."

"*Loco!*" she laughed.

Adam hobbled up from the corral on the crutches Juan had fashioned for him. He was frowning, and the worry plainly visible in him drew their startled attention.

"Men coming," he said briefly.

"You mean the doctor?" Fear put a shrill note in the Mexican woman's voice. "It is his day for a look at your leg."

"He would not bring men with him," Adam said. He added grimly, "They carry guns, and they ride down the hill like soldiers, two abreast."

"*Ay caramba!*" moaned Catalina. "The *rurales.*

Dios mio—that doctor has betrayed us, and he promised to say nothing about you."

The visitors rode into the yard and reined to a standstill in front of the door. Despite the dust that powdered their uniforms they were trim-looking men, and there was quiet efficiency in every line of them.

The dapper young captain in command broke the silence, his gaze hard on Adam, but addressing Juan Ortiz.

"We hear of a stranger living with you, Señor Ortiz. Is this the man?"

"*Sí.*" The old *ranchero* flung his wife a despairing look.

The *rurale* studied Adam intently for a brief moment. He said courteously, "I have orders to take you to San Carlos, señor."

Adam looked back at him, looked at the riders grouped on either side. He read a hardness in their unsmiling faces, a cold hostility.

He shook his head. "I do not understand, Captain. Why must I go with you to San Carlos?"

The young officer drew a paper from a pocket, glanced at it briefly, returned the paper to his pocket. He said in a toneless voice, "You are under arrest, señor. My orders are to take you to San Carlos."

Adam grinned. "I still don't understand—"

The *rurale* interrupted curtly. "The description

tallies, señor. Tall, red-haired, eyes gray-green. There can be no doubt."

"No doubt of what?" Adam was no longer smiling.

"Of your identity," replied the captain. "The description fits the man known as Brazos Jack, cattle thief, border bandit—and murderer."

"*Válgame Dios!*" exclaimed Catalina indignantly. "That is the big lie! This man is Señor Adam Marshall and comes from Arizona where he owns a rancho and many thousands of cattle."

The *rurale* heard her out politely, smiled, shook his head. "It is possible, señora, but not probable. I must take him to San Carlos. It will be for him to prove that he is not Brazos Jack."

"You seem very sure about it," Adam said. "What makes you think that I'm this Brazos Jack?"

"You were recognized in the town of Presidio on the American side of the river," explained the captain. "A posse pursued you and when you attempted to cross the river you were shot, seen to sink with your slain horse." The *rurale*'s voice hardened. "You were thought to be dead, and word to that effect was sent to us at San Carlos. Brazos Jack was much wanted in Mexico for the murder of two of my brave men."

"You've got the wrong man," Adam said. He was conscious of a cold prickle between the shoulder blades.

The *rurale* ignored him, looked sternly at Juan Ortiz. "Is it not true that you found this man drifting on a broken tree limb and pulled him from the river?"

"*Sí*," mumbled Juan. "It is true."

"The doctor told you," cried Catalina.

"It was his duty to report the man," reproved the captain. He returned his attention to Adam. "The facts fit too well to be mere coincidence. When word reached us of your presence here we quickly realized that Brazos Jack was not lying dead in the quicksands of the Rio Grande." Bitterness crept into his voice, a hint of fierce satisfaction. "You escaped American justice, señor, but it was a mistake for you to seek refuge in Mexico where you are wanted for murder and where the law is swift and sure."

Adam said desperately, "Señora Ortiz told you the truth. I can prove it!"

He saw that his protests meant nothing to these grim-faced men. They were convinced that he was the desperado they wanted for the crime of murder. He could hardly blame them for the mistake. It was going to be difficult to make them believe the truth—that it must have been Brazos Jack who had trailed him from Presidio and not a sheriff's posse, that it was Brazos Jack who left him for dead in the Rio Grande.

It was an answer that only partly explained his present predicament. It did not explain why

Brazos Jack had tried to kill him. Apparently his physical resemblance to the bandit had been used to spread the report that it was Brazos Jack who had died in the river. Adam could understand the bandit's purpose in spreading a report that would call the law off his trail. The baffling part of the picture was the fact that the bandit apparently knew of the physical resemblance. He had never heard of Brazos Jack, but it was obvious that the man had known plenty about Adam Marshall.

The captain's eyes signaled his men and two of the *rurales* slid from saddles and approached the prisoner.

The captain said, "Search him, and don't forget—he is dangerous."

"*Loco!*" scolded Catalina. "A cripple—and you call him dangerous!" Her dark eyes flashed. "You will be sorry for this business, Captain Gomez."

"Hush," begged Juan. "Do not interfere." He smiled apologetically at the officer frowning down at them from his saddle. "Her heart is too big."

"Fool!" Catalina tossed her head. "I'm afraid of no man, in uniform or out. I will say what is in my mind." Hands on hips she faced the captain. "For all that little mustache you wear your lips are still wet with your mother's milk, or you would show the good sense of a grown man and know that this gringo is not your wanted desperado."

His suddenly red face betrayed the handsome

captain's confusion, otherwise he appeared not to have heard her tirade. He rapped out another order, and two more *rurales* dismounted, hurried into the house.

The officer looked at Catalina's agitated husband. "You will go with them, Señor Ortiz, and help collect any articles belonging to the prisoner."

Juan gave Adam an unhappy glance and trotted after the *rurales*. Catalina, though, was not done with her protests. She flung the captain an outraged look. "*Dios mio!* You think to make him ride to San Carlos and his leg not yet healed?"

"The doctor permits the journey," replied the captain stiffly. His chin lifted haughtily. "I beg of you, señora, not to try my patience too far."

"So my pretty young soldier dares to threaten me!" she stormed. "*Madre de Dios!*"

Adam interrupted her fulminations. "It is no use, señora." He spoke gently, his look warm on her. "You have been my good friend. I owe you my life, and many kindnesses. I will not forget."

"But they will shoot you," she wailed. "I cannot bear this thing!"

"It is nothing," Adam assured her. "I will get the proof that will convince them." He looked at the captain. "I will demand that you send word to my grandfather who lives near Dos Ríos in Arizona. He will send men who can satisfy you that I speak the truth—identify me."

The officer bowed. "It shall be permitted.

Mexican justice does not seek to condemn an innocent man."

One of the *rurales* came quickly from the house. He carried Adam's belt, the gun in its holster. He held it up in both hands, and there was black suspicion in the look he flung at the prisoner.

"See, my captain—a forty-five Colt!" He spoke hoarsely. "The bullets that killed our comrades came from a gun such as this one."

A muttered curse broke the stillness that followed the man's words and a *rurale* spurred his horse into a jump toward the prisoner.

"I will have his blood!" he shouted. "Murderer of Felipe and Pablo!"

Captain Gomez barked a sharp command and two of the dismounted *rurales* sprang forward, seized their infuriated comrade's horse.

"You forget yourself, Pedro Nuñez," the captain rasped. "We represent the law of Mexico. Be careful, or you will find yourself in much trouble." His look went to Adam and he added gloomily, "These men feel bitter, and with cause, but have no fear, Señor Brazos Jack. You will be escorted to San Carlos in safety. You have the word of a Mexican officer." His trim black mustache lifted in a thin smile that showed a flash of white teeth. "I see by the look in Pedro's eyes that he will demand a place in the firing squad you will soon face."

31

Pedro Nuñez grinned malevolently at the prisoner. "*Sí,*" he growled. "My bullet will not miss the gringo's heart."

Adam leaned heavily on his clumsy crutches. He was longing just then for Bill Clemm and faithful old Celestino Baca. They could have saved him from this. It was obvious that John Marshall had never received his letter. There could be no other explanation for his grandfather's failure to send help.

He said quietly, "I don't blame any of you for this mistake, but it *is* a mistake. I am not Brazos Jack and I can prove it if you will get in touch with John Marshall who owns the JM ranch in Arizona. He is well known in the Dos Ríos country."

"Your request will be presented to the *jefe* for consideration," assured Captain Gomez.

Catalina was suddenly on her knees, arms lifted appealingly. "Have mercy on him. Grant him the time he needs."

"Do not kneel to me," snapped the young officer. He was embarrassed, annoyed. "I have promised he will reach San Carlos in safety."

The Mexican woman got slowly to her feet, fixed a penetrating look on him. "You evade," she charged. "You do not say how long he will live, once you have him in your *carcel.*"

He returned the look, and it was plain that anger grew in him. He said stiffly, "My duty is to take him to San Carlos for trial, Señora Ortiz. My duty in the matter ends there."

"No!" She shook her head, drew a silver crucifix from inside her dress, moved close to him. "Your duty does not end there, Captain Gomez. You will swear that you will make it your business to see that time is given for him to get this proof from Arizona." She lifted the cross high, held it to his lips. "Swear," she commanded, "swear that you will wait until Juan has time to go to this *rancho* in Arizona and bring men who can convince you that this man is Adam Marshall, and not Brazos Jack."

The captain hesitated, looked deep into her dark eyes. They were fine eyes, and he was young and found it hard to resist the appeal he read in them. The stern set of his face broke, warmed with a smile.

He said gently, respectfully, "I swear, señor. I swear that no harm shall touch him until your husband returns from this journey to Arizona." He took the crucifix from her fingers, pressed it reverently to his lips.

Catalina received the little silver cross back into her hands, turned a shining look on Adam.

Captain Gomez made a rasping sound in his throat, touched the waxed ends of his little mustache.

"Well," he barked. "*Vamos!* What are we waiting for?"

3
A HOSTILE COUNTRY

From the doorway of the ranch office John Marshall could see down the slope to the road that twisted through the mesquite until it disappeared around the bluffs a good mile away.

He stood there, a hint of excitement in him as he watched the distant dust drift, a big man, with a stoop to his heavy shoulders, and a grizzled-bearded face from which looked kindly eyes that offset an arrogant nose.

A man pushed through the yard gate and hurried up the walk with a noisy clatter of boot heels. John Marshall darted a brief look at him, gestured at the dust now trailing a long plume back to the bluffs.

"Looks like somebody is mighty anxious to get here," he said. "What do you make of it, Celestino?"

The Mexican came up the veranda steps and turned scrutinizing eyes on the distant horseman. He said in Spanish, slowly, as if reluctant to disappoint the unvoiced hope in the old cowman's question, "No, señor. It is not Adamito."

John Marshall nodded somberly. "I reckon

you're right, Celestino. Adam don't run a horse like that—" He broke off, eyed the Mexican sharply. "What's on your mind?"

Celestino gestured back at the yard gate. "A young woman, señor." A hint of uncertainty flickered across his lean brown face. "She has business with you, about sheep."

The cattleman's face darkened, and Celestino said hurriedly, "I will tell her to go away, no?" He turned toward the veranda steps. John Marshall's voice halted him.

"Is it that young schoolma'am?" His tone was fretful, impatient, his gaze again on the lone rider now halfway between the bluffs and the creek below the ranch house.

"*Sí*, señor." Celestino hesitated, gave the old cowman a sly look. "I t'ink she got beeg tr-rouble," he added in English.

Marshall was silent for a long moment, his attention obviously engrossed with the distant rider. He said, unhappily, "No Celestino, that wouldn't be Adam, riding his horse to death like that jasper is doing."

The Mexican came back to him, put a hand on the big, stooped shoulder. "Do not worry, old friend." He spoke in Spanish, his tone gentle, warm with understanding. "Adamito will return soon."

"I have bad dreams," muttered the owner of JM. He shook his head, gave the Mexican an embarrassed smile. "I'm getting old, Celestino, just a useless old man."

"*Loco* talk," grumbled the Mexican. He was himself perhaps in his fifties, a lean and durable-looking man with a deeply lined brown face and keen, watchful eyes. "You are a bull for strength, señor, and not a day older than when I came to this *rancho* more than thirty years ago."

"I'm going on eighty," reminded John Marshall. Nevertheless he showed pleasure, straightened the sag from his big shoulders. "Well, let's get it over with this schoolma'am," he added briskly.

The creak of the yard gate drew an ejaculation from the Mexican. "She does not wait to be sent for."

The old cattleman gave him a shrewd smile. "You don't fool me with that talk, hombre. You told her to give you a couple of minutes' start and then follow you."

Celestino's grin showed he was in no way abashed by the charge. "She is but a young girl. What else can a man do?" His look challenged the older man. "Would you have me set the dogs on her?"

"Don't be a fool," growled John Marshall. "If you'd sent her packing without a chance for a word with me I'd have had your ears."

His gaze was on the approaching girl, approval in his eyes. He liked the quick, sure rap of her boot heels on the flagstones, the high-held chin, the forthright look of her, and he was not insensible to her trim figure, the way the sunlight caught in the chestnut hair under the white Stetson. Something else about her pleased him less, put a hint of a frown in his eyes. He disliked to see a woman rigged out in a man's clothes, and this one wore faded blue overalls belted to slim hips.

He gave her a curt nod as she hesitated at the bottom of the steps. "You the Seton girl? You want to see me?"

His gruffness left her undaunted, and there was no hint of fear in the clear brown eyes that took him in from head to heel. "Yes," she answered, "I'm Linda Seton, and I do want to have a talk with you."

He motioned to a chair. "Sit down—" His eyes left her, went again to the lone horseman now close to the willows that fringed the creek. He said to Celestino, "Get back to the yard. I've an idea that man is bringing news, from the way he's making dust."

"*Sí.*" The Mexican hurried down the steps, and the girl was conscious of his warm, encouraging look as he passed her. She sat down in the indicated chair, looked up at the big man, saw with some surprise that he was smiling at her.

"You've got spirit," he said. "I like spirit in man or beast. Means you can fight, and if you want anything in this world you've got to fight for it." His arm lifted in a wide gesture. "I have had to fight for everything I've got—this ranch, my cattle, every foot of range I own in the Dos Ríos." His eyes took on a reminiscent gleam. "Had to fight for my life, too. Indians, floods, border renegades. Wouldn't be here now if I hadn't fought back. You've got to fight—keep on fighting, when there's trouble in the saddle."

He saw from her expression that she was rapidly revamping her ideas about him. "You've heard hard tales," he chuckled. "You've been told I'm a domineering, greedy old range hog."

"They say you don't like newcomers in the Dos Ríos country," Linda admitted. The hard defiance was gone from her face. Relief put a new brightness in her eyes as she looked at him.

"Nonsense," he fumed. "Honest folk are welcome. Men who make good neighbors, not cheap nesters who think to go into the cattle business at my expense, water-hole grabbers, scheming crooks, cow thieves, killers . . . all the worthless scum that drifts up from the border." He arched grizzled brows at her. "Where do you do your trading? In Dos Ríos?"

She nodded. "Some of it. We haven't been here long, and Dos Ríos is the nearest town."

"Keep away from that rustler's hangout," Marshall advised. "You'll find more bad hombres in that back yard to hell than fleas on a mangy pup." He shook his shaggy head like an angry buffalo bull. "Someday we'll have law and order in this man's country, but right now the only law we have is the law of rope and gun."

She was watching him closely, and the hard glint was back in her eyes. "Are you trying to frighten me away from the Dos Ríos, Mr. Marshall?" She gave him a faint smile. "I know cattlemen don't like sheep, but I'm here to stay and my sheep are going to stay."

"You won't be popular," grumbled JM's owner. "The Dos Ríos is cow country."

"I refuse to be frightened," Linda said. "We're not stealing anybody's water, and we're not nesters. We bought enough land to give us more than a mile frontage on the south bank of the Sombrio."

"You've big ideas for a schoolma'am." The old man's voice was unexpectedly mild.

She shook her head. "I'm not a schoolma'am any more. I've gone into the sheep business, partners with my father. He got just as tired of army life as I was of teaching. The sheep business seemed to be the answer." Her chin lifted. "Nobody is going to stop us."

"I'm not stopping you." The old cowman spoke gently. "There's plenty of good sheep graze in the high timber country."

"I'd like to believe you," Linda said.

His frown questioned her, and she went on quietly, "I'm told that Dos Ríos cattlemen will run me out of the country and that John Marshall of the JM will be the first to make trouble for us."

"Lies," rasped JM's owner. His face reddened.

Linda gestured wearily. "Your own foreman warned me only yesterday. He said you wouldn't stand for sheep on JM range."

The old cattleman chuckled. "Bill Clemm told you to get out, huh?"

"It's no joke!" she blazed.

There was sober approval in the look he bent on her. "I told you that I like your spirit, young woman. You've got the courage it takes for this country." Laughter was back in his eyes. "I reckon you said plenty to Bill."

"I told him what I've told you," Linda replied. "I don't scare easy and now you *both* know it."

"I reckon we savvy the way you feel," smiled Marshall. He spoke gently. "I'm glad you came and had it out with me. You get back home and tell your dad that you don't need to worry about JM. We're your friends, and if trouble hunts you out we'll side you, the whole damn outfit, including Bill Clemm. Ain't a speck of meanness in old Bill. He's a man to have along when trouble's in the saddle."

"I think—" Linda's voice was not quite steady. "I—I think I'm going to—like you, Mr. Marshall. You don't know what this—this means to me." She stood up from the big *manzanita* chair, impulsively reached out her hands to him. "I'm ashamed of all the horrid things I thought of you."

He squeezed her hands, a curious speculation in his eyes as he looked down into her upturned face. He said, almost wistfully, "You'll be liking my grandson, I'm hoping. He's due back from Texas any moment." Mirth crinkled his eyes. "You wait until he hears that he's going to be neighbor to a sheep outfit."

She was suddenly apprehensive again. "He—he hates sheep, you mean?"

"Adam is a cowman, born and bred," John Marshall said a bit grimly. "I reckon he thinks the same about sheep as any cowman." He chuckled, patted her shoulder. "It's going to be up to you to teach him a few things about sheep. Won't be easy, but I reckon you're still a right smart schoolma'am."

He was suddenly silent, stood there, shaggy head bent forward, and Linda saw that he was listening to the thudding hoofbeats of a fast-running horse. The sound drew up the avenue, dust drifted in the ranch yard, and the girl heard a sharp, demanding voice, the clump of booted feet, the quick rasp of dragging spurs.

John Marshall muttered uneasily, "Bill Clemm . . . that's Bill—"

The gate slammed, and Celestino and the foreman hurried up the walk. Their grim faces sent a chill through the girl.

The foreman halted at the foot of the steps, fixed a haggard look on the tall old man above him. "Got bad news, boss."

Marshall said quietly, "I figured you had, Bill—"

"Hate like hell to be the one to tell you—" The foreman's lean brown face was a mask of misery. "Got the word in Dos Ríos . . . about killed my horse gettin' here to tell you—" His voice cracked, and he gestured fiercely at Celestino. "*You* tell him—"

"*Sí.*" The Mexican mounted the steps, slowly, as if leaden weights held his feet. He put a hand on Marshall's arm. "Señor, it is news about Adamito—bad news—" Emotion made his voice husky.

"Dead?" The old cattleman was looking fixedly at the foreman. "Speak, man!"

Bill Clemm's face was pale. "That's right, boss." He was suddenly leaping up the steps.

Linda watched, frightened, shocked, while the two JM men gently eased the stricken cowman into a chair. Celestino straightened up. He was trembling. "I will get Rosa," he said in Spanish.

He lurched away and they heard his distracted shouts from somewhere inside the house.

Linda bent over the unconscious man, put slim fingers over his wrist. "He's not dead. . . . I can feel his pulse!"

Clemm's head turned in a look at her, and she

was uncomfortably aware of a hostility in him as she met his eyes. Their last meeting had not been pleasant.

It was more than she could bear. "He's my friend, too," she said, almost hysterically. "He was telling me just before you came that he was my friend, that all of you would be my friends. He said, 'Bill Clemm is a man to have along when trouble is in the saddle.'"

The harsh lines of his face relaxed, and after a moment he said slowly, "I'm believin' you, Miss Seton. You wouldn't be knowin' them words about trouble in the saddle. He's a way of talkin' like that."

She said faintly, gratefully, "Thank you, Bill Clemm."

The foreman straightened up, a long, lanky man with keen gray eyes in his range-weathered face and graying hair under the up-curving brim of his ancient sombrero.

He said sorrowfully, "He's an old man. I'm awful scared for him. Reckon it's what they call a stroke—"

Linda's gesture warned him, and he turned quickly, saw that Marshall was looking at them. His bearded lips moved, but no words came.

Tears filled the girl's eyes. She knew now that her new friend was paralyzed, that perhaps she would never again hear his kindly voice, encouraging her, counseling her with truths garnered from his own many years. She sank on her knees, clasped one of his big hands between hers.

"We're friends," she said to him. "Always friends." She saw that he understood, sent him a smile through her tears. "I'm coming again, soon, to see you," she added.

The quick rustle of skirts drew her to her feet and she saw Celestino, and a plump, elderly Mexican woman she guessed was Rosa.

The woman gave her a brief glance and bent over the stricken man. "We must get him to his bed," she said briskly in Spanish. She looked back at Clemm. "We must have a doctor—quick."

"I'll send for Doc Wills," the foreman said. He gave Celestino a nod. "All right. Let's get him inside."

Rosa drew back as the two men bent over the old cattleman. Linda met her inquiring look, sensed that she was not wanted.

She said hesitantly, "I'm Linda Seton. I—I'd like to help—if I can do anything."

The woman's stiffness relaxed a trifle. "*Gracias*, señorita." She shook her head. "I no need 'elp for look after the señor. Soon we 'ave doctor."

It was obvious that Rosa wanted her to leave. Linda went slowly down the veranda steps, reluctant to go, oppressed with a miserable fear that she would never see John Marshall again.

She rode in gloomy meditation down the slope, splashed across the shallows of the creek, and cut into the trail for Sombrio Canyon. A rainstorm had struck down from the high peaks and swept across the far end of the mesa. The air was fresh, faintly pungent with the smell of sage.

She kept the mare at an easy lope, her thoughts drawing away from the JM with the increasing distance and reaching now to her father. He would be anxious to hear the result of her visit.

The decision to go into the sheep business had taken a lot of courage, and all of their money, her own slim savings from three years of teaching school and every cent Captain Seton had realized from the sale of his mine to the New York syndicate. He had never been able to save anything out of his army pay.

The purchase of the land, the hundreds of ewes and the blooded rams, had already eaten alarmingly into their slender funds. They had staked their all, and they had to make a success. Anything else was unthinkable. Anything else would mean ruin, and Linda knew that her father was in no condition to face failure. He was far from well, which was one reason why they had chosen to make their new home in the Dos Ríos country.

The discovery that they were not wanted in this land of cattle had shocked them. It seemed that sheep were crawling vermin, a pest to be destroyed. Stories had come to her of others who had thought to run sheep in the Dos Ríos, grisly stories of ruthless raids by night, of entire flocks of sheep run over the cliffs, herders murdered, homes put to the torch.

She recalled Bill Clemm's visit the day before, his blunt warning that John Marshall would not stand for nesters. Linda had explained they were not nesters, but legal owners of the five sections. She had even shown Clemm the papers proving lawful ownership.

"Don't mean a thing," the tough old foreman had stubbornly asserted. "This land ain't never been for sale. It's JM range and always has been from the time John Marshall moved in from Texas with his longhorns. You folks will have to get out." And he added significantly, "Sheep and cows don't mix, not in the Dos Ríos country."

Linda pulled the mare to a walk. She was suddenly aware of returning doubts, a growing fear in her. Suppose old John Marshall never recovered from the stroke that had left him paralyzed, helpless.

The thought gave her a sinking feeling. She had counted so much on that fine old man's friendship.

Tears smarted in her eyes. She could have wept for the grief she felt for him, for her own bitter disappointment. He had promised to stand in friendship with her against the enmity of this hostile land, inspired her with encouraging words. For a few brief moments she had glimpsed hope's bright sunshine. And now, suddenly, terribly, this yawning and black abyss.

The trail lifted over a low rise, snaked through a growth of scrubby piñon trees, and came to the point where it dipped steeply down the canyon slope.

Linda drew the mare to a standstill and gazed for long moments at the panorama spread before her. The colors always took her breath, the reds, the blues, the deep purples, the lights and shadows. She loved this country. She found herself thinking again of old John Marshall, his words. *You've got the courage it takes for this country. . . . You've got spirit . . . means you can fight. . . . You've got to fight—keep on fighting, when there's trouble in the saddle . . . wouldn't be here now if I hadn't fought back.*

Linda sat very still, there in her saddle. She could hear that quiet, reassuring voice so plainly, steadying her, demanding from her the same high courage that must always have been his in the face of danger. There must be no faltering. She must keep her courage bright no matter how dark the prospect, or lonesome the trail. Old John Marshall had spoken profound truths, drawn from the deep wells of his many years.

She felt better, lifted from the black sinks of doubt and despair, and a smile touched her lips, quivered like sunlight across her face as she started the mare down the trail. It was up to herself to make good John Marshall's simple belief that she had what it took for this Territory of Arizona.

The trail dropped in a series of hairpin turns to the canyon floor. Linda kept the mare moving as fast as safety permitted. The place made her nervous. The towering draw-in cliffs that shut out the sunlight, the incessant roar of the falls. The vast gorge of the Rio Sombrio was well named, a canyon of darkness.

Five miles down the canyon widened, became a long, narrow valley with pretty groves of cottonwoods and alders and sycamores. Up here there were only great boulders choked with impenetrable thickets of thorny brush that clawed viciously at her legs. She wished she had thought to wear her leather chaps.

It was down in the little valley that her father had located five sections of land in the heart of the JM range. John Marshall had apparently neglected to obtain legal title to the property, thinking perhaps that his ownership would never be questioned.

The setup was ideal for their purpose, plenty of water for alfalfa and grain, the open range reaching across the vast desert plateau, and free access to the high timber country for summer browse.

She was again conscious of chilling doubts. If old John Marshall should die, or linger on a helpless invalid, it would mean a new management for the great JM ranch, perhaps new owners who would actively resent this invasion of the range. Young Marshall might have proved as friendly as his grandfather, but he was dead, drowned in the Rio Grande, and the news had stricken the fine old man whose friendship would have meant so much.

The tall cliffs drew apart and they were suddenly down in the sunlit valley and the mare was again moving at her easy lope along the trail that meandered through the trees.

The sound of a gunshot startled her, and she halted the mare, sat rigid, tense, sudden alarm in her.

She tried to reason with herself. She was unduly apprehensive. The affair at the JM ranch had left her nerves jumpy. It was senseless to be frightened by a distant gunshot. Martinez, their lone sheepherder, and her father, had shotguns . . . were always popping away at rabbits.

Her straining ears heard another shot, then two quick ones, and now she had the direction, up on the high bluffs that overlooked the little valley. She knew, too, the meaning of those three shots, first one and then the two in rapid succession. A signal, a call for help. Her father's idea for use if one of them needed the other. Martinez knew of the signal, too. Those shots meant that one or the other of them was in trouble.

Linda swung the mare from the trail and rode at a fast lope toward the bluffs, and as she cleared the trees she saw a man, crouching on a ledge and waving his hat to draw her attention.

Her heart turned over. The man was Martinez, the sheepherder, and even at that distance, a hundred feet above her, she could sense the terror in him.

She reined the mare to a quick standstill, and now she heard the Mexican's voice, stammering, frightened.

"Señorita—eet ees bad tr-rouble—"

"Was that you—shooting?"

"*Sí*, señorita. I 'ave watch for you . . . shoot gun w'en I see you." Martinez pulled the hat back on his head. "*Por Dios*—eet ees bad tr-rouble. You coam queek for see."

"You mean it—it's my father?" Linda fought to keep her voice steady. "Something has happened to him, Martinez?"

"*Sí*, señorita—" He gestured tragically.

She knew then, that her father was dead, and the horror of it left her limp in the saddle. Her father dead. She could not believe it. Martinez was lying . . . he was drunk—and seeing things.

She gazed up at the frightened brown face peering over the ledge at her. No, he was not drunk, not lying. He was telling her the truth.

She found her voice. "Where is he, Martinez?"

The Mexican gestured over his shoulder. There was compassion in the look he bent down on her.

Linda waited to hear no more. She sent the mare scrambling up the first trail she saw. It was a perilous climb and the mare's hoofs started slides of loose shale.

The Mexican ran to her, and she sat very still in the saddle, conscious of the mare's heaving sides, and conscious too of a tightness in her throat.

He sensed the question her lips refused to put into words, and with a gesture for her to follow, headed into the greasewood.

They topped a low rise. Linda glimpsed the small band of sheep browsing in the distance under the vigilant care of the Mexican's dog. Something else she saw drew a choked little cry from her.

She tore past Martinez, the mare on the dead run, pulled to a sliding standstill, and in a moment was bending over the motionless body of her father.

Martinez hurried up, breathless, stood watching her worriedly. She guessed what was in his mind. He was afraid she would faint, perhaps go into hysterics.

She said, between stiff lips, "I'm not going to faint. . . . I *won't* faint—"

The sheepherder looked relieved. He gestured at the dead man's horse, tied to a near-by bush, head drooping, tail switching at the flies. "I t'ink señor fall from saddle . . . the 'orse mooch scare . . . go loco . . . drag señor over rocks."

She was too heartsick just then for words. She could only nod in agreement. The dreadfully battered head was proof enough. Her father had had several minor heart attacks. It was quite possible that a seizure had caused him to faint—fall from his saddle. She could only hope that he was dead before the horse ran away with him.

"You found him lying here?" she asked Martinez.

The Mexican explained that he had noticed the riderless horse, realized that the thing dragging from the stirrup was a man.

"I catch 'orse queek." He lifted an expressive shoulder. "No good . . . too late for 'elp señor."

She continued to crouch there. She felt too sick to move, too dazed to think clearly.

The sheepherder's voice aroused her. "We put señor on 'orse, across saddle . . . take señor back to *casa*."

Linda got to her feet. "Yes," she said. "We— we'll take him home—" Her voice broke, and limp, helpless, she watched Martinez while he untied the horse and led the animal alongside the body.

Thoughts began to churn in her. *Of course it was an accident . . . a heart attack . . . he had fallen . . . the horse had taken fright and run away, dragged him to death.*

For some reason she felt dissatisfied. Suppose it was *not* an accident. *Suppose it was murder—made to seem like an accident.*

The possibility put a hard brightness in Linda's eyes. They were not wanted in the Dos Ríos country. They had been warned to leave . . . told to get out. Those words had been said to them only the day before. *Bill Clemm had said them.*

"Martinez—" Her voice sounded strangely shrill in her ears. "Have you seen anybody around today? Strangers?"

"No, señorita."

"Not even that—that JM man who was here yesterday?"

"No, señorita. No hombres come."

Linda went slowly to her mare, began to loosen the coil of rope from the saddle. She was allowing dark fears to confuse clear thinking. It was an accident. There was no other explanation. *Not murder . . . an accident.*

She felt dissatisfied. Her father had been dragged over rough country. A bullet wound would not easily show in his poor, battered head. He *could* have been shot from ambush, the murder made to look like an accident.

4
THE PRISONER

Early sunlight lanced through the bars of the window set high in the adobe wall. Adam gazed at it reflectively. It was a small window, too narrow for the shoulders of a grown man. An undersized ten-year-old boy could squeeze through—if the bars were removed. And they *could* be removed. He had tested them, made cautious experiments with the sharp-pointed spike he had found concealed under the pile of dirty straw that was his bed. Some other prisoner had planned a break for freedom. Apparently time had run too swiftly for his unfortunate predecessor. A firing squad must have got him before he could put the spike to good use.

Adam got up from his pile of straw and moved close to the window. He had done the work well, been careful to replace the crumbled bits of adobe and smooth and pack the dust with water from his drinking cup. His jailers would not suspect that he had tampered with the bars. They looked solid enough to the casual glance.

It only remained to pry out a few adobe bricks to make the opening wide enough. This must wait until the moment of escape. He hoped such a crisis would not come. He was confident there would be no need to complete his work on the window. A few more days would bring the proof of his identity. Bill Clemm would soon have him out of this Mexican jail. Action would be fast and furious when the news of his predicament reached the JM.

These were the thoughts, the hopes, with which he fed his courage during the long weeks of waiting. Of course there were certain unpleasant possibilities. Juan Ortiz might break a leg, or run into some trouble that would prevent him from reaching the JM. It was a long journey from San Carlos in Chihuahua to the little cowtown of Dos Ríos in Arizona. A lot of things could happen to Juan Ortiz.

It was these possibilities that Adam kept in the back of his mind. Optimism was a good thing, but he did not believe in shutting one's eyes to the darker side of the picture, which was why he had found a vast satisfaction in the discovery of the useful spike. If the worst came he would still have a fighting chance.

The Mexican doctor had done good work. The broken leg had mended, was as good as ever, a fact that he kept from his jailers for the reason that he wanted to retain the crutches. He had a hunch the crutches might prove useful in a way that would surprise his swarthy captors. Juan Ortiz had fashioned them from mountain mahogany. They were strong, heavy enough to crack a man's skull. It gave him a secret and grim amusement that he was able to fool his jailers, make them believe that he was helpless to walk without his crutches. They had taken everything else from him, even his pocket knife. It had not occurred to them that the crutches could prove deadly weapons in the hands of their quiet-voiced prisoner.

He was suddenly aware of the quick tramp of feet outside. Soldiers—approaching the *carcel.*

He returned quickly to the pile of straw and flung himself down, and now he heard the rasping command of an officer. It was a voice he recognized. Captain Gomez.

Cold prickles chased up and down Adam's spine. Only bad news would bring the *rurale* captain and his troopers. Perhaps he had waited too long to complete his job on the window.

He heard the rasp of a key in the lock, the click of the heavy bolt. The door opened and Captain Gomez swaggered into the cell. Six troopers filed in, lined up against the wall, and last came the jailer, a look of concern on his friendly brown face.

There was frost in the captain's eyes, and frost in his voice. "*Buenas días, señor.*"

Adam grinned up at him. "Hello, Gomez. Turning me loose? Sure am sick of your jail."

The *rurale* twiddled his little mustache,

frowned, shook his head. "I am here to conduct you to the *jefe*, señor."

Adam reached for his crutches and got awkwardly to his feet. He stood there, leaning on the crutches, and his lazy smile gave no hint of the perturbation in him. "I reckon I can hobble that far, captain." He flicked an amused glance at the stolid-faced troopers. "I seem to be honored that you bring so many to escort me."

Gomez flushed. "Silence!" he barked. "You forget that you are a prisoner, señor."

"I forget nothing," retorted Adam. He was watching one of the *rurales*. The man's face was familiar—Pedro Nuñez. The same Pedro Nuñez who had promised himself the pleasure of putting the first bullet into Brazos Jack's heart. He saw with growing alarm that the man was staring fixedly at the little window in the opposite wall.

"*Capitan mio!*" Nunez blurted the words. "See—" He pointed at the window. "There is mischief here—"

Captain Gomez looked, muttered a startled ejaculation, and now Adam's own shocked eyes saw what had attracted the *rurales* attention. One of the bars was slightly out of line with its mates.

Sickening dismay drained through him as he watched the captain stride quickly to the window and grasp the bar. He gave it a sharp tug, muttered another exclamation as the bar came away in his hand.

Gomez shot Adam a malevolent look, seized another bar, jerked it from the crumbled adobe. In rapid succession he snatched out the remaining bars, hurled them on the mud floor, and then, his face stiff with anger, he strode back to Adam.

"So!" he spluttered. "You have been industrious, *Señor* Brazos Jack!"

Adam forced a careless grin. "Sorry. Only I'm not Brazos Jack."

"Your bluff has been called," sneered Gomez. "We are not fools, as you will soon discover."

He barked out a command. Two of the *rurales* dived at the pile of straw and in a moment had uncovered the long spike.

Captain Gomez glared at the jailer. "How did this thing get in here?"

The horrified man flapped his hands in frantic protest, swore by his saints that he had never seen the spike before. His terror at the captain's suspicions drew on Adam's sympathy. After all, the man had been kindly disposed, done certain little favors in the matter of food.

"I found it under the straw," he informed Gomez. "Some poor devil you had in here, I reckon."

Captain Gomez nodded, thoughtfully, obviously harking back in his mind to the cell's previous occupant. "It is possible." He gave the frightened jailer a menacing scowl, gestured at the door. "Well," he barked. "*Vamos*! What are we waiting for?"

Adam dismally recalled the last time he had heard Gomez use that expression. More than two months ago, when they had dragged him away from the *ranchito* of Juan Ortiz, near the banks of the Rio Grande. And now they were taking him to the office of the *jefe*, and by all the signs, for no good purpose.

The *jefe*, a shriveled little man with a sallow face and the beady eyes of a rat, sat stiffly behind a flat desk. Adam hardly more than gave him a glance. His delighted smile fastened on Catalina Ortiz who sat primly in a chair against the wall under a large picture of Porfirio Diaz. Slumped in the adjoining chair was her husband, and it was plain from the scowl he wore that he was thinking hard things of the prisoner.

"Señor—" Tears welled in Catalina's fine dark eyes. "Mooch beeg tr-rouble—"

"Silence!" The *jefe* rapped hard on the desk, gave Catalina a reproving frown. "It is for me to do the talking, Señora Ortiz. And if you *must* speak, it is to be in our own language." He looked intently at Adam, his eyes bright and hard. "Señor Ortiz has returned from a long journey, and the news he brings is bad for you." He nodded. "*Very, very bad.*"

Adam said nothing, waited for the *jefe* to continue. He heard a sob from Catalina, turned his head in an encouraging look at her. The *jefe* again rapped for attention.

"I will give you Señor Ortiz' report," he said. "Señor Ortiz made this journey to the town of Dos Ríos in Arizona at your request. He found this *rancho* known as the JM and owned by Señor Marshall—"

"That's the place," interrupted Adam. "What's wrong with that?" He threw the *ranchero* a puzzled look.

"Everything is wrong with it," purred the *jefe*. His voice took on a rasp. "It seems you are a very big liar when you told us you are Señor Marshall's grandson."

"I don't understand," Adam said. His temper was thinning, he realized. It was no time to lose his temper. Something was indeed wrong, very wrong. "If Señor Ortiz spoke with my grandfather he must know that I haven't lied. I am John Marshall's grandson."

The *jefe* shook his head. "You are a bold rascal, with your lies . . . stupid lies—" He paused, looked down at a paper spread open on the desk. "I have here a deposition made by Señor Juan Ortiz—"

He began to read in a flat, toneless voice:

"I found the *Rancho* JM, owned by Señor Marshall, and there talked with a young man who said that his name was Adam

Marshall, the old señor's grandson. The young man was greatly surprised at the reason of my journey from Chihuahua and said that he had never been in the town of Presidio in Texas and that the man now in our San Carlos jail must be an impostor and no doubt was the much-wanted criminal known as Brazos Jack."

The *jefe*'s eyes lifted in a penetrating look at Adam. "Your stupid bluff is finished, Señor Brazos Jack. The evidence is conclusive. More lies from you can do you no good. You must stand immediate trial for murder."

"Somebody is crazy!" exploded Adam. He turned his head in an imploring look at the *ranchero*. "You are telling a lie, Señor Ortiz. You have not been to Dos Ríos, or you would not say these things. You could not have talked with Adam Marshall at the JM because I am Adam Marshall, and as you know, have been a prisoner here for more than two months—" He stopped, sickeningly aware of the cold hostility in the *ranchero*'s eyes, and looked at Catalina.

She said brokenly, "I believe you, señor. The devil is at work—" She gestured tragically. "Do not blame my poor Juan. He speaks the truth about his journey to the rancho in Arizona."

"It's not possible," muttered Adam. He fixed

puzzled eyes on Juan. "Who told you the man you talked with was Adam Marshall?"

"He told me." The *ranchero*'s tone was sullen.

"Describe him. What did he look like?"

"A tall man, like yourself. Red hair—" Juan hesitated, his expression thoughtful. "Like you, but different."

"How do you mean—*different?*" Adam asked sharply.

"A scar on his upper lip, and he seemed heavier—older." Juan was staring at him intently. "I do not remember the scar on your lip, señor. And now it is hard to see, with all those whiskers on you."

"I have no scar on my lip," Adam said. He rubbed his hairy face. Since his imprisonment he had not been allowed a razor. Two months had put a heavy beard on him.

"Take these whiskers off and you can see I have no scar," he fumed. "Somebody is lying like hell."

The *jefe* banged on the desk, and his eyes took on an ugly glitter. "No more talk! It is finished. Captain Gomez, you will conduct the prisoner back to the jail."

5
TRAIL NORTH

Viewed from any possible angle the outlook was more than desperate. Adam made no attempt to cheer himself with false hopes. The signs grimly indicated that he would soon be a dead man.

He stared morosely at the small window set high in the grimy wall of his new cell. Captain Gomez had made certain the iron bars were firmly in place, and taken other precautions. The usual litter of dirty straw had been removed from the mud floor, the walls examined for possible weaknesses, or concealed aids to escape left by some previous occupant. The *rurale* was taking no chances on losing his prisoner.

Adam was fully aware that his stay in the place would be short. A speedy farce of a trial, a swiftly approaching early dawn—the firing squad.

He faced the unpleasant facts coolly. It was no time to let fear sap his strength, dull his ability to examine the problem from all sides. His grandfather had drilled in him the necessity of coolness in the moment of crisis.

The old cattleman's deep, kindly voice was with him now as he stood there, somber gaze on the patch of blue sky beyond the iron-barred window.

Never lose your head, boy, when trouble's in the saddle. Keep your mind sharp, your nerve steady. There's always a fighting chance if you don't let panic ride you down.

Wise counsel, though hard to take at that moment with death reaching so close. Counsel that must be heeded for that very same reason, or else it would indeed be the finish, as the *jefe* had said with such relish.

He felt a stir in him, a hardening of muscles, a fierce resolution that found expression in the stern set of his face, put a hard, bright light in his eyes. He was ready for the worst, and ready too for that one fighting chance. There must be no fear in him—no faltering.

It was all very confusing. He could make no sense of it. One fact alone stood clear in his mind. Somebody wanted him dead.

A new worry grew in him as he thought about Juan's incredible story of the man he had met at the JM and who called himself Adam Marshall. Juan's description indicated that the impostor was Brazos Jack. The man's presence at the ranch offered grisly possibilities. Not even his striking resemblance to Adam would for an instant deceive old John Marshall, or Bill Clemm, or Celestino Baca. The thing had a bad smell. Adam's uneasiness mounted the more he pondered and speculated. Anything could have happened at the ranch—even *murder.*

Horror sent chills up and down his spine. He was beginning faintly to see a pattern in the jumbled pieces of the puzzle. He had been marked for death from the time he had left Presidio. He had eluded the would-be murderers on the trail, again eluded them in the waters of the Rio Grande. Unaware that he had escaped to the Mexican side they had spread the news of Brazos Jack's death, and the outlaw had assumed the name of Adam Marshall and headed for the Marshall ranch in Arizona.

Adam scowled. He was doing a lot of guessing, but the guesses seemed to make sense, indicated that a shrewd brain was responsible for the evil train of events. His grandfather was in great danger, was perhaps already dead.

The thought sickened him. He had to break out of this Mexican jail. He was needed at the JM. He was not going to let them stand him against a bullet-pocked mud wall and shoot the life out of him. He had to escape and get to the bottom of this dark and sinister mystery.

The soft pad of feet approaching up the corridor made him reach quickly for the crutches he had leaned against the wall. He drew them under his armpits and swung awkwardly to face the door. He must still keep them thinking him a helpless cripple. Deception, fast thinking, were his weapons now, and unfaltering courage.

He recognized the nearing footsteps. The

friendly jailer. His eyes narrowed as his furiously working mind examined—rejected—possibilities. *Not this man . . . And it was too early . . . Must wait for the dark . . . The night jailer.*

Bolts scraped and the door swung open, revealed the jailer, eyes blinking against the yellowing sunlight that streamed from the window in the opposite wall. He held a gun in one hand, a tin pan of cold beans in the other. He stood there for a moment, his expression wary, but not unfriendly.

Adam gave him a grin. "Same old *frijoles*, huh?"

"*Sí.*" The jailer's watchful face relaxed. He grinned back. He placed the pan of beans on the floor. The cell was bare of any furnishings. "I am watched, señor, or I would bring you better than cold *frijoles*."

"That's all right, *amigo*," Adam said. "Sorry I got you in bad with the captain."

The jailer shrugged. "I do not blame you for trying to get out, señor. It is bad for you. I think they make a big mistake. You have my sympathy." He gestured. "But to watch you is my job."

"*Gracias.* You're a good hombre." Adam spoke gratefully. "I suppose I'd kill you on the spot if it would help me to escape." His smile was grim. "Not much chance for a cripple—with that gun in your hand."

"Don't try, señor—" The jailer's smile was thin. "I would be forced to shoot you." He hesitated, drew a crumpled piece of paper from a pocket. "Señora Ortiz is my friend, señor. I do this for her. It can do no harm, so I give it to you." He dropped the paper on the floor, backed into the corridor. The door closed, the bolts scraped, the sound of his padding feet faded into silence.

Adam waited for a long moment, eyes lowered in a questioning look at the crumpled piece of paper lying near the plate of beans. *It could do no harm.* That was what the jailer had said. Meaning he could not expect a secret offer of help from Catalina. The man had read it, knew its contents, was satisfied it was safe for the prisoner to have it.

He leaned the crutches against the wall and reached for the paper, read the few scrawled words:

> Señor—The Good God will not allow this thing. I pray for you and He will hear.

Adam's fingers tightened over the note, and he was conscious of an odd lump in his throat, a sudden glow in him. The Mexican woman's simple faith moved him profoundly, stirred in him an iron determination not to disappoint that faith.

He slowly pushed the little piece of paper deep into a pocket. The chances were slim. He would need Catalina's prayers. She would know by morning if they had been answered.

He looked thoughtfully at the window. The twilight was fading fast. Another hour, and then darkness, and the night jailer. It was going to be hard to wait, to keep his nerves steady.

The plate of beans caught his restless eyes, and he grinned, picked up the plate, and began to eat, using his fingers. No spoon, or fork. They were taking no chances with him. Even a spoon might be a deadly weapon in his hands. It was obvious that the notorious Brazos Jack had put the fear of death into these Mexicans.

He swallowed the last mouthful and wiped greasy fingers on his legs. Two months in the smelly jail had been hard on him. He had been allowed no change of clothes. He felt filthy, horribly unwashed, a shaggy-haired, be-whiskered savage.

He moved restlessly around the cell, his feet soundless as a panther, his ears alert for footsteps in the corridor; and slowly darkness flowed in, blotted out the barred window. It was time for the night jailer to make his customary inspection. A repulsive brute of a man who had taken delight in inflicting humiliations on his prisoner.

The minutes dragged, and suddenly Adam heard the man's familiar limping step. He reached for the crutches and lay down on the mud floor, a little to one side and facing the door.

The footsteps paused, the bolts squealed, and he saw the jailer framed in the flow of the lantern he carried, an ugly leer on his pockmarked face.

"On your feet, hombre, or you will feel the toe of my boot against your ribs." The jailer took a step into the cell, his expression threatening. "Show respect, you lazy rascal."

Adam's hand lifted in a limp gesture. "Get me a doctor—" He spoke feebly. "I think I've broken my leg again."

The jailer hesitated, studied him with suspicious eyes. "I'll take a look first," he grumbled. He set the lantern on the floor, an action that took his attention for a brief moment.

It was the moment Adam needed. The crutch under his right hand shot forward with the lightning speed of a striking snake.

It was a heavy crutch Juan Ortiz had fashioned, and tipped with an iron cap that crashed with a sickening impact against the jailer's temple.

Adam leaped to his feet, ran to the door, and gently closed it. He turned, stared down at his prone victim. One look was enough. The man was unconscious, was likely to be for hours.

He stooped, removed the gun-belt with its cartridges and swiftly buckled it over his own lean hips. He picked up the lantern and the fallen bunch of keys and in another moment was in the corridor.

Adam pulled the door shut, threw the bolts, and, lantern in hand, went cautiously down the corridor.

As he had hoped the dimly lit office was empty. It was a small jail and he had been there long enough to know there were seldom more than two or three prisoners at a time, usually drunks. The night man now lying senseless in the locked cell was not due to be relieved until early morning. If his luck continued to hold he would be a long way from San Carlos before the escape was discovered.

He saw a machete in its sheath hanging from a peg. Adam strapped it to his waist. A knife might prove useful.

He blew out the lantern, set it in a corner, and took a cautious look into the night. Fortunately, the jail stood on a low rise between the hamlet and the creek that snaked back into the hills.

Lights glimmered from the little plaza some hundred yards to the right. Voices reached him faintly, and the muted strumming of a guitar from one of the *cantinas*.

He stepped outside, closed and locked the door, became a vague moving shape in the darkness, halting frequently to scrutinize other shapes that suddenly loomed out of the night. Boulders, clumps of cacti, trees.

His general direction was toward the creek, and gradually the tinkling of the guitar faded back into the distance. He was alone in a world of silence. Only the murmur of the creek now a few yards away.

The plan had been with him for weeks. He knew exactly what he was to do. The beginnings had been somewhat changed by the discovery of the loosened bars in the cell window. Otherwise the plan was working according to schedule. He was out of the jail—had reached the creek which he knew would be shallow at this time of the year.

Wading downstream was slow work. The soft sand sucked at his feet and he had to be careful of unseen holes. It was something he had to do. It was part of his plan. The *rurales* were among the best trackers in the world. Eventually they would pick up his trail from the jail, but the trail would end at the creek.

He kept at it for several hundred yards and finally decided he had waded enough when he noticed that the banks on either side were rising to sheer cliffs.

A ledge offered a foothold. Adam crawled up and took time to shake the water from his boots. He had stumbled several times and was soaked to the waist.

With an effort he resisted the urge to remove his clothes and take the bath he craved. The minutes were too precious. He must keep on traveling the long night, and only at night. He would have to put a lot of miles between him and San Carlos before he dared challenge the gaze of curious eyes.

Hour after hour he plodded doggedly on through the willow brakes that followed the course of the creek. He knew where he was going, knew that in time the creek would empty into the Rio Grande a short mile south of the *ranchito* of Juan Ortiz. It was all part of the plan that he had built from countless hours of thought.

The long confinement had left him alarmingly weak. He began to tire. His feet dragged, felt like lumps of lead, and he was finding it increasingly difficult to force his way through the dense brush.

The late moon came up, dimmed the scintillating luster of the stars that jeweled the vast bowl of the sky. He had kept track of the moon, knew that it was close on midnight.

The increased light made movement easier. He struggled on, frowning at his weakness, and presently, to his vast relief and some amazement, was aware of a new surge of strength in him, a freshening of spirit. His second wind, or perhaps it was the friendly moon and the knowledge that he had put several miles behind him.

He came to a small clearing with a scattering of cottonwoods and sycamores. Moonshine touched the trees with soft luminous veilings, mantled the scene with elusive lights and shadows. Instinctively he halted for a look before showing himself in that open and revealing space.

Satisfied, he took a step forward, again halted and crouched back into the deep shadow of a big boulder. The faint whiff of woodsmoke that came on the night breeze warned him that he was not alone here. Smoke meant a campfire.

It was difficult to identify motionless objects in that deceptive moonlight and it was several minutes before Adam's searching eyes fastened on the burro, a vague, almost invisible shape.

Somewhere near would be the animal's Mexican owner, wrapped in the *serape* and sound asleep. A charcoal-burner, or a wood-gatherer, Adam guessed.

He stealthily retreated into the thicket and worked his way around the clearing. The Mexican no doubt was harmless enough, but it was just as well not to be seen. If later the *rurales* should question the man he could honestly swear that nobody had passed that way during the night.

The lopsided moon dropped low to the west where lifted dark mountains. Little night creatures made rustlings in the underbrush. A coyote barked, was answered by a yipping chorus that tormented the night and as suddenly ceased.

A pale light pushed above the eastern horizon, the stars drew back, winked into oblivion, and a graveness veiled the moon now low to the western hills. Adam decided it was time to seek cover, but first there was the problem of food to be settled. The brush rabbits were numerous at this early hour, and after a little stalking he managed to knock over a couple with a stick. He could have used his gun, but feared to attract attention. It was a risk he dared not take.

He slung his catch on the stick and after a few minutes' scouting found the place he wanted, a tiny clearing a few yards from the creek and well screened by a thick growth of willows and alders.

Weariness laid hold of him and for a time he was content to lie motionless on his back, let tired muscles relax. He had been on the move for all of nine hours. Despite the slow going he must have done eight or nine miles. A long way yet to the Rio Grande. Perhaps another twenty miles if he continued to follow the windings of the creek. He could think of no other way that would bring him so surely to the Ortiz *ranchito*. He would be lost in a bewildering maze of gullies and would be certain to run into somebody who might report the presence of the shaggy-haired gringo. Nothing to do but stick to the creek, where he had cover from observation, and access to water.

He wondered if the Ortiz couple would have returned to the *ranchito* by the time he arrived. If they had stayed the night in San Carlos they would know of his escape by now. Catalina would rejoice that her prayers had been answered.

She would do some more praying to strengthen him on the way, perhaps would burn candles in thanks for his deliverance from the jail. He would never forget Catalina Ortiz. He wished he could have her at the JM. Rosa Baca would like her. The Ortiz *ranchito* was a poor place, and Juan would probably be willing to make the move to Arizona. He'd have to talk to them about it, Adam promised himself. Plenty of room in the Dos Ríos country for Juan to set up in the cow business. Those sections down on the Sombrio. Something would have to be done about that land. His grandfather was making a mistake, thinking he could hold it forever. Nesters would crowd in, undesirables who would be a nuisance to the JM. He'd talk to his grandfather about it, persuade him to let Juan Ortiz have those sections. Juan and Catalina would be fine neighbors. It was the least he could do for Catalina. She had saved his life.

Adam was suddenly conscious of a sick feeling in the pit of his stomach. *He was a fool . . . making his fine plans. Something was very wrong at the JM. . . . His grandfather was dead. . . . All of them—Bill Clemm—old Celestino Baca. How else could Juan's weird story be explained?*

He sat up, stared somberly at the rabbits lying in the grass. No sense giving way to weakening fears. He needed food—sleep. He had a job to do.

He took off his coat, shook it out and laid it on

a rock. He had hardly worn it while in the jail and it was still fairly clean. Also it contained nearly a hundred dollars in gold pieces he had sewn into the lining, using needle and thread borrowed from the friendly jailer on the pretense of mending a torn shirt. And in one of the coat pockets was a block of sulfur matches the same jailer had let him have, together with a packet of thin Mexican *cigarros*.

There were things he could do while he waited through the long day. He got to his feet, removed gun-belt and machete, stripped off his remaining clothes and carried them down to the creek.

He was nearly an hour, washing and scrubbing them as clean as he could without soap. Satisfied at last, he spread them on the rocks. The sun, already well up and blazing hot, would soon dry them.

The next thing was himself, and wading downstream a few yards he found a deep pool and dived in. The water felt good. He took his time, scrubbed his hard body from head to foot, washed his shaggy hair. The bath made him feel better, took the ache from his bones, and he was grinning cheerfully when he returned dripping to the rabbits. The machete had a razor edge, and in a few minutes he had the rabbits skinned and the choice portions broiling over a little fire.

The sun felt good on his nakedness. He was soon dry, glowing with restored energy—and ravenous for food. The thought of waiting until night before he resumed his journey began to fret him. He was in a fever of impatience to reach the Ortiz *ranchito*. He wanted to question Juan Ortiz about his visit to the JM, find out if he had noticed anything wrong at the ranch, ask him about the man who had claimed he was Adam Marshall. Also he was counting on being able to get a horse from Juan for the long ride to El Paso, from where he could continue his journey to Dos Ríos by rail and stage. He would offer the *ranchero* gold coin for a fast horse.

He thought regretfully of the buckskin, and again hot anger burned in him at the men who had shot that good horse, sent him to the bottom of the Rio Grande.

His meal finished, he got one of the jailer's *cigarros* from his coat pocket, sat on his bare heels, smoking, and gazed on his clothes spread out on the rocks.

Traveling by daylight was risky, but faster. He would gain precious hours, and he was needed at the ranch. The plan to travel only at night must be abandoned. But it would be at least another hour before his clothes would be dry enough to put on. Adam finished the *cigarro*, stretched full length on the grass, and closed his eyes. He would get an hour's sleep.

He awoke with a start, hand reaching for the gun at his side, and grinned as he saw a squirrel scurrying away from the remains of the rabbits. A glance at the sun told him he had slept more than an hour. His clothes were dry. Adam got into them hastily, buckled on gun and machete, and resumed his journey. The brief rest had taken the weariness from him. If his luck held he would make the Ortiz *ranchito* before the dawn of another day.

6
BORDER TOWN

Linda came to a standstill in the middle of the dusty road, a phantom shape in the eerie half-light of that early dawn. It was a narrow road, rutted deep by countless wagon wheels, and less than a quarter of a mile from where she stood it widened, became a street where sprawled a vague, dark blur of buildings.

The stars had lost their glitter, and beyond the dimly seen town a steely shimmer spread above the horizon and cut over the mountains. Light filled the sky, flowed across the landscape.

The girl continued to stand there, her gaze intent on the shapeless huddle of buildings. There was that in her that bespoke a weariness of mind and body hardly to be endured.

She was hatless, her hair in tumbled disorder, her blouse and skirt torn in a dozen places. Ugly red scratches marked hands and wrists, and as she stood there she fumbled a red-stained handkerchief from a pocket and cautiously pulled a long thorn from the upper leather of one of her brush-scarred boots.

She returned the handkerchief to her pocket and continued toward the town. She walked slowly, with a slight limp, and now and again she would pause and extract other thorns made visible by the swiftly brightening light.

The town of Dos Ríos presented a singularly unlovely aspect in that chill dawn. It had been much the same a hundred years before the Mexican War, and like most such border hamlets its buildings were adobe structures, some of them with overhanging balconies under which ran narrow, hard-packed paths instead of sidewalks. Here and there between crumbling mud hovels stood tawdry frame buildings with high false fronts, representing the American contribution to the town's architecture. In the center of the town the one dusty main street widened into a square dominated by an ancient church where bells hung in the ruins of a squat tower. Huge cottonwood and chinaberry trees made a grateful shade in the square, added a certain picturesque charm to the hoary gray walls of the church.

This early-morning hour showed no signs of life yet stirring. The girl halted at the beginning of a rough planked sidewalk and looked at the large livery barn set back from the street against high-fenced corrals. The big sign painted across the front of the building said:

SAM DOAN'S FEED STABLES
HORSES AND MULES
BOUGHT AND SOLD

She crossed over and went to a small door marked Office. She put a hand on the latch, then, drawn by the sound of voices, turned abruptly and made her way to the corral on the other side of the barn.

She saw huge freight wagons, and two men busy with a long string of mules. Her appearance drew startled looks from the men.

She addressed them impartially. "I'm looking for the sheriff's office," she said.

The taller of the two men, lanky, sandy-haired, evidently the wagon boss, continued to stare at her, his expression of surprise deepening to curiosity, suspicion. He moved toward her. "Sheriff, ma'am? You wantin' the sheriff?" He spoke with a Texan's slow drawl.

"Yes," the girl answered. "The sheriff—the law—"

"You a stranger in this town?" Her torn clothes, the scratches on hands and face put concern into his eyes.

She shook her head. "No—but I don't know where to look for the sheriff. There is a sheriff, I suppose."

Something like cynical amusement lay fleetingly on his lean, weathered face. "Ain't no sheriff in Dos Ríos, ma'am—" His soft drawl hardened. "Ain't no law in these parts, I reckon." His look shifted to the listening swamper. "Get the harness throwed on them mules, Pedro.

We've got to get these wagons rollin' pronto."

"*Si.*" The Mexican reluctantly resumed his work. The freighter's critical gaze watched him for a moment, came back to the girl. "Only feller that wears a law badge in this place is the town marshal. Kind of early to get hold of *him*."

"Where can I find him?" she asked.

The man gestured up the street. "The jail sets back in a clump of cottonwoods between the plaza and the crik. An old 'dobe. You cain't miss it."

"Thank you—" She turned to go. His voice held her.

"If you aim to see him right *now,* you'll most likely find him at the White House, whar he does his sleepin'."

"Thank you," she said again. She gave him an unsmiling nod.

The freighter watched her, his expression dissatisfied, uneasy. He sensed stark tragedy, and a courage that fought doggedly to survive an overwhelming disaster.

A man crossed the corral from a side door in the barn. He spoke softly to the freighter. "What's wrong with her?" He drew papers and tobacco sack from a shirt pocket and began shaping a cigarette, his gaze following the girl.

The lanky muleskinner eyed him intently for a long moment, apparently sizing him up. The newcomer gave him a slow, disarming smile. He was tall and lean, and there was an air of quiet competence about him. "Was just wondering," he drawled. His look went back to the girl. "She seems mighty upset."

The freighter's inspection satisfied him. He nodded, fished a plug of tobacco from a pocket, and gnawed at it reflectively. "Lookin' for the sheriff." He returned the tobacco to his pocket. "I'm tellin' you, mister, she's got me worried." His tone was somber.

The two men stared at each other. It was the freighter who broke the silence. "I've got to get my wagons rollin'," he said. "I'd like to stick around and keep an eye on that gal. She's in plenty trouble." He spat out a dark brown stream, shook his head gloomily. "This damn town ain't no place for a lone gal that's *her* kind."

Adam Marshall met his look with steady, understanding eyes. He nodded. "I savvy, pardner. You get your wagons moving. I'll stick around."

The freighter gave him a relieved grin, held out a hard brown hand. "That's white of you, feller. Sized you up right, I reckon."

"*Gracias.*" The younger man grinned back, gripped the proffered hand. "I'll ramble up the street, keep on her trail."

The lanky wagon boss watched him go, approval and liking in his eyes. There was an indefinable something about the tall stranger that he found reassuring.

Unaware of the protective interest she had aroused, Linda Seton made her way up the street. The clatter of her heels on the planked sidewalk was startlingly loud in that early morning hour.

A dog ran at her from a narrow alley between crumbling adobe walls. The fierce look she flung at him disconcerted the animal and he slid to a quick halt. She glanced back at him, came to a standstill, and the anger died out of her face. Her eyes softened, were suddenly misty with held-back tears.

The dog, tawny, wolfish, gazed at her intently. He seemed to sense an apology, an offer of friendship. A tremor ran along his tail and he approached, sniffed at her outstretched hand.

Some of the tenseness left the girl's tired face. She smiled faintly, rubbed the dog's ears, then continued on her way. The dog, after a moment's indecision, trotted along at her heels, tail waving contentedly.

Life was beginning to stir in the town. She heard the chatter of voices, and looking up, saw two Mexican women peering at her from a balcony across the street. The door under the balcony opened, revealing a man on the threshold. He was short and paunchy and he wore a tall steeple hat of plaited straw. He stood there, twisting a cigarette, an expression of mild surprise on his brown face. It was obvious that he recognized her.

She failed to notice him. Her gaze was on another man who was hooking back the wide doors of the store that stood on the next corner, a dingy red frame structure with a high false front.

The man straightened up and gave the girl an astonished look as she climbed the steps to the wide porch. He was a big man, with postlike legs and heavy shoulders. He wore a short, square-trimmed grizzled beard that added to the squareness of his high-boned face and his eyes were deep-set under a thatch of grizzled brows.

The girl halted, her face grave, unsmiling. "Good morning, Mr. Berren." The dog, pressed close to her knee, let out a low growl. She rebuked him with a touch of her hand.

The storekeeper reached a pair of horn-rimmed spectacles from a pocket and adjusted them to his nose. They added benevolence to his face. "You're in town early, Miss Seton," he greeted. The husky, whispering voice was not in keeping with the man's massive frame. He continued to look at her intently and the eyes behind the spectacles took on a shocked expression as if he read in her face the answer to his wordless question. He said, sorrowfully, commiseratingly, "So they've done it."

She nodded, continued to stroke the dog's head. Her dust-streaked face was pale.

"The scoundrels," muttered the storekeeper. He wagged his head. "I warned you, Miss Seton."

"They ran the sheep over a cliff . . . they're all dead, and they killed poor old Martinez and his dog." She gestured despairingly. "It's all so—so brutal."

"Cows and sheep don't mix in this lawless country," Berren said in his curious whispering voice.

"They burned the cabin, my hay—ran off my horses," Linda Seton told him bitterly. "I've been walking for hours through the chaparral." She touched the red scratch on her cheek. "It was so dark and frightening down in the canyon. I thought I'd die."

"Run into cat's-claw, by the looks of you," sympathized Berren. He jerked a big thumb at the dim interior of the store. "You'll be needing some things—" He paused, smiled benevolently. "There'll not be a cent's charge for anything you pick out, Miss Seton. I'm sick to the heart for what's been done to you."

"You are very good." There was gratitude in the grave little smile she gave him. "I'll be in later, Mr. Berren." She glanced up the street, at the hotel. "A man at the livery barn said I might find the town marshal at the White House."

The storekeeper looked dubious. "You'll not get much help from Al Deen," he said.

"He represents the law, doesn't he?"

Berren showed signs of uneasiness. He said slowly, cautiously, "He has legal authority to put folks in jail, Miss Seton. I suppose he represents the kind of law we have in these parts." His look went down to the dog under her hand. "Seems like he's took up with you for keeps," he added with a dry smile.

"He's somebody's good sheep dog," Linda surmised. "Poor thing—he looks half starved."

"He's a sheep dog, all right." There was a rasp in the storekeeper's whispering voice, an odd glint in his deep-set eyes. "Been hangin' around for most a week, waiting for the Mex herder that owns him to get out of jail."

"Jail?" The early-morning light picked up gold flecks in clear brown eyes now suddenly dark with anger.

"Sheepherders ain't popular in this town," Berren said laconically.

"I see—" Linda's fingers dug into the dog's furry neck. "Thank you, Mr. Berren. I—I'll be back later—for some things."

"Listen, Miss Seton—" His whisper held a warning note. "You won't like what I'm going to say, but if you've got good sense you'll clear out of this Dos Ríos country. I'm talking to you like you was my own daughter. I'm afraid for you. No telling what will happen if—if you stay."

She looked at him, and there was a stubborn lift to her chin. "My father and I came here to make a home." She spoke quietly, without resentment at him. "We put everything we had into that sheep ranch. I'm not going to let those JM cowards frighten me away."

The storekeeper looked shocked. "It's dangerous—naming names, unless you have proof," he warned.

Linda seemed not to hear. "After what happened last night I'm beginning to believe it was no accident that killed my father." Her hand tightened over the dog's heavy ruff.

"The JM does not like nesters." The storekeeper wagged his massive head gloomily.

"I'm not a nester." Her eyes blazed. "No, Mr. Berren, not all the cowmen in the Dos Ríos are going to make me run away. I'm fighting it out."

No answer came from the big man. He stood there, intent gaze on the slim, straight back as she went down the porch steps. The dog, padding close at the girl's heels, turned his head in a brief backward look, and there was a hint of a snarl in the lifted lip.

Mr. Berren removed and pocketed the horn-rimmed spectacles, and there was no hint now of benevolence in the eyes deep-set under their bushed and bony ridges. The gleam in them was ugly, an ugliness that spread over his square, bearded face and curled huge hands into knotted fists. He turned to enter the store, halted abruptly, and stared at the tall man sauntering under the balcony of the adobe house across the street.

The storekeeper's jaw sagged visibly and

his eyes widened, a look of incredulity stark in them. He seemed hardly to breathe. Only his head moved as his hypnotized gaze followed the stranger's slow progress toward the hotel that stood opposite the plaza.

The fat Mexican in the doorway of the balcony exhibited a similar interest in the man who had just passed him. The cigarette fell from his fingers. His eyes bulged and jerking off the high-peaked sombrero he agitatedly fingered badger-gray hair.

Berren saw the man's excitement, beckoned him over to the store. His own face had resumed its habitual and somewhat majestic serenity by the time the Mexican reluctantly climbed the porch steps.

The storekeeper smiled at him. "You know that man, Estrada?"

The Mexican's coffee-colored eyes took on a wary look. He shook his head, answered hesitantly, "No, señor."

"You seemed kind of startled—" There was a suspicion of a rasp in the whispering voice. "You wouldn't lie to me, Miguel Estrada."

"No, señor." Miguel's tone was sullen. "One leetle moment I theenk 'e ees hombre I see long time ago." The Mexican twiddled with the sombrero in his hands. "Thees hombre dead, so now I laugh for make beeg meestake."

Berren nodded, studied him for a moment with

eyes as sharp and hard as gimlets, then swung abruptly into the store.

Miguel let out a long breath, crammed on his sombrero, and clumped quickly down the steps. He seemed anxious to get away from there.

7

ALLIES

Linda paused on the hotel porch and glanced at the tall young man approaching from across the street. Fear darkened her eyes, vanished as another look told her that he was a stranger, also that he was unmistakably a cowman. She had no use for cowmen. They were ruthless wolves. She jerked the screen door open and slammed furiously into the untidy little lobby. The forgotten dog whimpered, nose pressed to the screen.

The elderly man behind the desk hastily withdrew his hand from the bottle in the top drawer. He closed the drawer, gave the girl a startled look, and got out of his chair. He was thin and stoop-shouldered, and the drooping grizzled mustache looked too big for his weazened red face. He said in a husky, whiskey voice, "In town some early, Miss Seton." He grinned, skinny hand scraped an unshaven cheek.

"I want to see the town marshal," Linda told him. She knew without looking that the tall stranger had paused in the doorway, was listening.

The clerk's pale, red-rimmed eyes were suddenly wary. He wagged his head regretfully. "The marshal ain't down yet," he answered. "He was up awful late last night." He rubbed his bald head, darted a brief glance at the man in the doorway.

"I've got to see him immediately," Linda insisted.

"He won't like bein' hauled out of bed," argued the clerk. His tone showed growing annoyance. "Sure am sorry, Miss Seton. Looks like you've got to wait."

Linda heard the tall stranger's voice and realized that he was standing close to her. She stiffened.

"Send up and tell Monte he's wanted in a hurry," the man said smilingly. "Tell him he has two customers waiting."

The clerk stared at him intently, brows drawn in a puzzled frown, then slowly, almost doubtfully, he said, "Reckon you're a stranger here, mister, or you wouldn't be askin' for Monte."

"If Monte is still town marshal here, I want to see him," drawled Adam.

The desk clerk shook his head. "Monte was killed most a year ago," he said. "Al Deen is town marshal now, mister."

"Killed!" Adam was shocked. "That's bad news." His face darkened. "A shooting?"

"Wasn't knowin' Monte myself," the desk clerk said. His look dropped longingly to the top drawer. "Ain't been in Dos Ríos but a couple of months and don't know how come Monte got killed." Curiosity returned to his eyes as he stared at the other man. "Seems like I've seen you some place," he added.

"*Quién sabé.*" The sudden chill in Adam's voice warned that personal questions were not welcome. He met the girl's resentfully impatient look, and when he spoke again the smile had gone from his eyes. He leaned over the littered desk, said with quiet emphasis, "You heard the little lady, didn't you? She's wanting that town marshal *now*."

"Sure I heard her," grumbled the hotel clerk. He fingered his huge mustache nervously. "Al's got a mean temper. He'll raise hell—" The clerk broke off, fascinated gaze on the suddenly bleak face opposite him. The menace in those unwinking gray eyes was unmistakable. He gulped, stammered, "Sure, sure—I'll go tell him he's wanted."

Adam gave him a wintry smile. "Fine. Hop to it, mister."

The girl was watching him uneasily. She seemed puzzled. The clerk's voice drew her attention. He was looking back at her from the foot of the stairs. "I reckon Al will want to know what you're wantin' him for," he said dejectedly. "What shall I tell him, Miss Seton?"

Linda's color was suddenly high. She said

fiercely, "Tell him my sheep camp has been raided . . . my sheep stampeded over the cliffs, my herder murdered, my house burned to the ground." Her voice was bitter. "That should be enough to wake him up."

The clerk's eyes bulged. He stifled an oath. "The damn coyotes! I'm sure sorry, Miss Seton." He wagged his head gloomily. "Any notion who done it?"

"Of course I know!" blazed the girl. "JM is the only outfit mean and cowardly enough to strike at a lone girl. I want the law on them . . . I want Al Deen to go out to the ranch with me and arrest them for murder."

The clerk gazed at her stupidly, bald head bent forward as though pulled over by the weight of his mighty mustache. Then, slowly, almost fearfully, he went stumbling up the stairs.

Linda heard the tall young man's voice, gentle, yet touched with a curious hardness. "When you say JM do you mean the Marshall ranch?"

She faced him, brows puckered in a faint frown. "Is it any of *your* business?"

Her animosity left him undisturbed. He stood there, looking at her, his eyes grave, friendly, a tall competent man. The strength in him seemed to reach out to her, a warming current that flowed through her tired body, took the hardness from her eyes.

He spoke again, gently. "I needn't have asked.

There is only one JM in the Dos Ríos country." He paused, added a bit grimly, "You see, my name is Adam Marshall, and I'm more than interested in this talk of yours about JM."

She swayed away from him, hands pressed against the desk, eyes wide with swift, unreasoning terror.

He gestured at the stairs, said in a quick, low voice, "Careful—"

Linda sensed urgent warning in voice and gesture, guessed that he was telling her not to divulge his name, telling her too, that she must trust him.

The night clerk's shuffling step sounded on the stairs. Linda got hold of her breath, said in a faint whisper, "I don't understand—but I—I'll do what you say—"

His look thanked her, reassured her, and he stood there, fingers busy with cigarette papers and tobacco sack, his eyes questioning the descending night clerk.

The clerk wore a surly grin. He slipped in behind his desk and shook his head at the girl. "Al says you got to wait. He ain't comin' down for nobody and he figgers your story don't make good sense."

Linda stared at him, defeat in the droop of her shoulders. The clerk fingered his heavy mustache, and there was something like concern in his rheumy eyes. He said suggestively, "Might be a right smart notion for you to mosey over to the Chinaman's place and get you a cup of cawfee. Dinin' room here ain't open so early, but the Chinaman don't never close his joint." The suggestion seemed to solve a problem for him. He nodded his head. "You look awful wore out. Do you good to set a while and rest while you're waitin' to see Al."

Adam Marshall made the decision for her. "That's right, Miss Seton." He smiled at her. "I could do with a cup of coffee myself."

Linda's eyes interrogated him. He was trying to tell her something. He wanted her to agree. Her mind in a daze, she nodded mute assent, turned and accompanied him out to the porch. The clerk's gaze followed them, eyes narrowed speculatively. His hand reached automatically to the top drawer and closed over the whiskey bottle. He pulled the cork, took a long drink, stood there, holding the bottle in lowered hand, his gaze still fastened on the screen door.

"Sure is queer about that hombre," he muttered to himself. "Got a look of Ad Marshall about him. Reckon that's why I got the notion I seed him some place. Got Ad's build, and same color of hair, only he ain't *really* like Ad . . . ain't got that ugly, mean face Ad wears."

He took another long drink from the bottle, pushed in the cork, and returned it to the drawer. Worried lines scored his face. He was wondering if he should have told Al Deen about the stranger who had not known that the town marshal's predecessor had been dead for nearly a year.

The freight outfit was moving slowly past the hotel when Linda and Adam emerged from the lobby door. The muleskinner saw them through the dust haze. He waved recognition, a wide grin on his face. They waved back, and Adam called out, "*Adios*, pardner—"

Linda gave him a thoughtful look. She was confused, wondering if she was mad putting herself in the hands of this stranger who had just admitted to a name she had every reason to regard with horror and loathing.

"You seem to know him," she said.

"Met him down at the corral," Adam told her with an enigmatic smile.

"That is where I met him," Linda said.

"I saw you talking to him," Adam confessed. "He was worried about you."

A hint of a smile played about the girl's lips. "Is that why you followed me?"

"Well—" Adam grinned. "I told him I'd keep an eye on you."

"Is that the only reason," she persisted. "You didn't know who I was—or anything?"

"Never saw you before, or heard of you," he assured her. He stared at the plaza across the street. "I think we can find something over there that will do us better than the Chinaman's."

She made no protest and they crossed the street. The dog followed close at the girl's heels. Adam gave him a brief glance.

"Yours?" he asked.

"He thinks he is." Linda's tone was compassionate. "Poor thing—his master's in jail, Mr. Berren told me." She gave Adam a sidewise look. "Do you know Mr. Berren? He's a very kind man," she added.

Adam shook his head. "Never heard of him."

"He owns that big store." She gave him another inquisitive look. "You said you knew that town marshal who was killed," she reminded. "You seem to know this town. I should think you'd know Mr. Berren."

"Pete Cline used to own the store. Pete was Monte's father. Pete must be dead, too, or else Berren bought him out. I don't blame you for being curious about me," he added grimly.

"You told me your name is Adam Marshall," she said in a low voice. "I can't help being curious."

The musical jangle of the mule team's bells now fading into the distance seemed to have aroused the street to sudden activities. Doors slammed, voices broke the stillness. Two cowboys pushed hastily from the hotel and went pounding along the board sidewalk toward a sign that said

GIN SING'S CHOP HOUSE
MEALS 25c

A slovenly-looking man in faded blue overalls emerged from the swing doors of the Ace High Saloon and began swilling the planked walk with buckets of water.

Dust swirled and a buckboard drew up in front of the big general merchandise store where Berren stood framed in the entrance, intent gaze on the girl and her tall companion crossing the little plaza.

The storekeeper's eyes took on an ugly gleam and he spoke curtly over his shoulder to somebody inside the store. A youth with frowsy straw-colored hair and dragging a big broom hurriedly joined him. He listened attentively to Berren's husky whispered words, nodded, leaned the broom against the wall, and ran down the porch steps in the direction of the hotel.

Unaware of the storekeeper's interest, Adam and Linda passed the worn steps leading up to the old church. The sun was well over the mountains that rose steeply in the distance. The sky was a clean, freshly washed blue, with snowy fluffs of cloud entangled in the higher peaks.

They passed the church and came to a clump of huge cottonwood trees that almost hid a low, rambling adobe building.

Adam Marshall said, "This is the place."

For some reason, Linda was suddenly apprehensive. Long hours of horror had frayed her nerves raw. She felt confused about this man.

She was not sure of him, his purpose in bringing her to this Mexican *cantina*. The desk clerk at the hotel had suggested the Chinaman's place. She knew Gin Sing, had more than once eaten at his restaurant. She would have felt quite safe at Gin Sing's.

She came to an abrupt standstill. Adam looked at her sharply, and for the first time she saw a mounting impatience in him.

She continued to gaze at him, her own face a bit pale, the defiant lift of her chin back again. She saw a man who stood more than six feet in his high-heeled boots. He was young, perhaps in his late twenties, and the hair under his dusty black Stetson was a reddish brown. He had dark gray eyes and there was a hint of humor in the firm mouth under the dark *caballero* mustache he wore. She sensed quiet efficiency in every inch of him.

She said, puzzled, "It is only your hair that is like his. He's tall, too, but his face is mean, vicious, and his eyes are a muddy brown and can look so wicked." She smiled faintly. "He wears a scar on his lip instead of a mustache."

Adam was staring at her, his face a bleak mask.

She continued nervously: "I'm talking about the other Adam Marshall. You have the look of him—at a distance."

"What do you know about him?"

"He's John Marshall's grandson," Linda

replied. "He's not really a bit like you. It's only his hair—his build. I was frightened for a moment when I saw you in the street." Her voice broke. "It is so—so confusing and terrible."

"Do you know John Marshall?"

"I've only met him once—" Linda hesitated. "I was at the ranch when he was taken ill."

Adam looked away. He did not want her to see the dread in his eyes. "Is he—*dead?*"

"I—I don't know—" Linda spoke slowly. "It was terrible. He was told his grandson had been drowned in the Rio Grande. He had a stroke. I don't know what has happened since. They wouldn't let me see him when I went back." She gestured tragically. "I can't bear to think of it."

"It was a lie," Adam said. "His grandson wasn't drowned."

"I wish he *had* been drowned." Linda spoke fiercely. "He's a beast—a murderer. It's hard to believe that such a fiend can be that fine old man's grandson."

"He's not," Adam said quietly.

Linda gazed at him, puzzled, bewildered, and then of a sudden she glimpsed the truth. "You mean—" Excitement took her breath.

"That's right—" Adam's smile was stern. "You've guessed it."

"I should have known—" Linda hesitated. "I had such a strange feeling about you—back there in the hotel, and now I understand. It's

101

because you are really and truly John Marshall's grandson. I should have known at once when you told me your name. There is something in you that is so like him." Color waved into her cheeks, and she added softly, "He was wonderful to me that day . . . promised to be my friend."

They stood there, looking at each other, and after a long moment Adam said quietly, "I don't know what has happened at the JM, but I'm keeping that promise for him."

"It is all very mysterious and terrifying," Linda said unhappily. "I was warned that sheep are not wanted in the Dos Ríos and was afraid of trouble. That is why I went to see your grandfather. He told me the JM would stand by me . . . that he and all his men would be my friends." Her voice broke. "It was the same day, on my way home from the JM, that I found my father lying dead in the chaparral. We thought it was an accident at the time, but now I'm not so sure that it wasn't murder."

"Why do you accuse JM of the raid?" questioned Adam. "You must have some good reason."

"This man rode over to see me a couple of weeks ago. He told me he was Adam Marshall and that he had come home and found his grandfather helplessly paralyzed. How was I to know it was a hideous lie? I believed him."

Adam nodded. "You wouldn't know he was lying—"

"He told me he was in charge of the JM," Linda continued. "He called me a nester, warned me to get out of the country or be burned out." Her cheeks flamed. "He acted like a beast—" She clenched her hands. "It was lucky I was wearing my gun. I don't know what might have happened. He rode away, laughing like a fiend and threatening dreadful things."

Adam said bleakly, "I'll be asking him about it."

Linda repressed a shudder. "It was horrible . . . last night. I hid in the chaparral when they came to the house, a lot of riders. I think they were drunk."

"You can't be certain they were JM men," Adam said.

"Yes, they were," declared Linda. "That terrible man was with them. I recognized him. The burning house made a big glare and I could see them plainly."

"JM men don't burn and murder." Adam was pale. "You've met my grandfather, Miss Seton. You know he wouldn't stand for such horrors."

"No," she said simply, and her eyes were full of pity for him. "Of course he wouldn't. I've been thinking it was John Marshall's grandson who was responsible for what happened. I know different, now, because here you are, the *real* Adam Marshall, which means that the other man is a wicked impostor."

Adam's eyes were on her. He was thinking, *Here is a brave girl. . . . We're in this thing together and we'll fight it out together—to the finish. She's lovely. I wonder what her first name is.* He said to her soberly, "I'm glad you are trusting me, Miss Seton. It's good for us to be friends. We've got a job of work to do."

She was suddenly smiling at him, a hint of mischief in her eyes. "Your grandfather said you were a born cowman and had no use for sheep. He said I would have to teach you to like sheep. Can you be friends with a sheepman, Mr. Marshall?"

He grinned. "I'll maybe teach you to like cows better than sheep. Anyway, sheep or no sheep, I want to be your friend. And my friends call me Adam," he added with another grin.

"Mine call me Linda," she smiled, and then, soberly, "Your grandfather said something that sticks in my mind. He said you've got to fight and keep on fighting when trouble is in the saddle."

Adam nodded. "I've heard him say that more times than I can remember." He was suddenly silent, and studying her with concerned eyes. "We shouldn't be standing here. You're needing that coffee—food and rest."

"This talk has done me more good than anything else in the world, right now," Linda assured him. Bright eyes and freshened color bore witness to her assertion. "You see, I have an ally, now."

"Yes," Adam said. His smile was warm on her. "We're allies—Linda." He gestured at the *cantina* half hidden in the cottonwoods. "Let's see about that coffee—"

Neither of them noticed the vague shape lurking behind a great shadowed buttress of the ancient church. A sharp-faced youth with ferret eyes and unkempt straw-colored hair. Linda would have recognized him as the clerk who worked in Berren's store.

He continued to watch until they disappeared inside the *cantina*, then hurried across the little plaza and turned into the street.

8
AT THE CANTINA

The *cantina* was an ancient adobe building with small latticed windows that kept out the morning sunlight. Linda was vaguely aware of a low ceiling supported by *vigas* roughly axed from juniper logs, and there were small round tables and home-made chairs with rawhide seats.

A man was leisurely mopping wine stains from one of the tables and the quick frown on his dark, unshaved face indicated that he was not pleased to have customers at this early morning hour.

He said gruffly, "Thees place no open—"

Adam grinned amiably. "Tell Severino Moraga an old friend is here." He spoke in Spanish.

The man's eyes widened, and then evidently impressed by the tall gringo's air of authority he hastened to improve his manners, drew out chairs from the table, gestured for them to sit down. "I will take your message to Señor Moraga." Curiosity was in his eyes as he looked at Linda, took in her brush-torn clothes and scratches, her obvious fatigue. "A little brandy—while you wait?" He gestured at the array of bottles behind the short bar.

Linda shook her head, and Adam said, "It is coffee and food and rest she needs. Hurry, hombre—tell Señor Moraga he is needed."

"*Sí*, señor—" The Mexican went swiftly across the room and disappeared through a door.

Linda sat down in one of the chairs. She had never been so completely tired, and she was painfully conscious of an overlooked *cholla* thorn somewhere in her leg. She would have to wait until she was alone before she could roll up her jeans and get at the thing.

She said, wistfully, "What I'd like right now is hot water—lots of hot water and soap."

"Severino will fix you up," Adam assured her. "Severino is about the only man in this town I can trust, an old friend of my grandfather's."

Linda saw the sudden pain in his eyes, the crushing dread, and knew what was in his mind. She wanted to comfort him, but could find no words. It did not seem possible that old John Marshall could still be alive.

Adam, looking at her, read her thoughts, felt the warmth of her compassion. He said, gently, "Don't worry about me, Linda."

"I *do* worry." Linda tried unsuccessfully to keep her voice steady. "I—I liked him so much—" She broke off at his gesture, and she saw a man framed in the doorway, a motionless vague shape in that dim light.

Adam called out softly, "*Buenas días, amigo.*"

The man muttered a startled ejaculation, approached swiftly now, and the excitement in him put a bright gleam in his eyes. He had a heavy shock of coarse white hair, and a ragged white mustache drooped over a wide, thin-lipped mouth. Despite his evident great age, there was a hard, durable look to him.

"*Válgame Dios!*" Emotion put a throb in the old man's deep voice. "You are one back from the dead, Adamito. *Madre de Dios!*"

The two men gripped hands, and Adam said, "It's a long story, Severino. I was almost dead, more times than I like to remember."

The old Mexican was silent for a long moment, his expression thoughtful, as if he was turning a question over in his mind, then his look went curiously to the girl, took her in from head to foot, noted the torn clothes, the ugly red scratches.

Adam said, "Miss Seton is in a lot of trouble, Severino. That's one reason why we came to you."

"Ah!" The Mexican's harsh face softened into a warming smile. "You 'ave come right place, señorita," he told her in his halting English. "Adamito's frien' all time my frien'." He bowed, hand on his heart. "Thees 'ouse yours, señorita."

The sincerity in him touched her. She got out of the chair and held out her hand. "You are very kind—" Her voice trailed away, and suddenly Adam's arm was around her. She was glad to let her weight relax against him. Her legs felt like rubber.

Adam threw the Mexican a worried look. "She

needs food—some safe place where she can rest—"

"*Sí.*" Severino turned hastily back to the door. For all his bulk and years he was like a cat on his feet. "I have just the place—where she can rest in safety."

"You think fast," grinned Adam. "Safety is the word right now. She's been through hell."

Severino led them down a narrow hall that opened on a patio. There were flowers, and a tiny spring that bubbled into a pool under a huge chinaberry tree. The dog pressed close to Linda as if fearful of losing her. The Mexican glanced at the animal doubtfully.

"Thees your dog?" he asked.

Linda hesitated. "I'm keeping him for—for a man," she answered.

It was plain that the innkeeper was puzzled. He shook his head and said rapidly in Spanish to Adam, "That dog looks like Gaspar Mendota's sheep dog. I do not understand this."

Adam recalled what Linda had told him about the dog's picking her up. He said laconically, "Looks like Gaspar's in jail—if you're right about the dog."

"*Por Dios!*" ejaculated Severino. "This is bad news. Gaspar is a good man—and my friend." He came to an abrupt standstill, inquiring gaze on the girl. "You know Gaspar Mendota, señorita, that you keep thees dog for heem?"

Linda shook her head. "I only know that the man who owns him is in jail. That is what Mr. Berren told me." She gave the dog a pitying look. "He's starving for food."

The old Mexican nodded gloomily. It was plain that he was worried and angry. He said nothing more, continued along the *galena* to a door which he opened with a key he drew from a pocket.

The room was large and comfortable-looking. Navajo rugs covered a flagstone floor and there were deep chairs upholstered in leather, ancient Spanish pieces that were obviously old Moraga's pride. He gave the girl a sharp look, showed pleasure in the appreciation he read in her eyes.

A door opened into a bedroom in which was a massive old Spanish bed and more rugs. The bed was made up and covered with a great Spanish shawl. Severino removed it, gestured at the bed.

"The señorita can rest until the coffee and food come," he said in Spanish to Adam. "I will send hot water—fresh clothes."

Adam translated for her. Linda's smile thanked the old man. "A hot sponge will do me more good than food," she said. She fingered her dust-streaked face ruefully.

"Breeng 'ot water pronto," promised Severino. He vanished into the other room and they heard the door close, the soft pad of his feet fading up the *galena*.

Linda looked curiously at the great bed and at the exquisite shawl flung on a chair.

Adam smiled at the wonder in her eyes. "These rooms are something of a shrine to old Severino. His paternal ancestor, Don Severino José Epifanio Moraga, came over with Cortez, or so he claims. His grandfather brought this stuff from Mexico City more than a hundred years ago when he built this place for a ranch house."

"He's a bit frightening, at first," Linda commented. "His fierce eyes—"

"Severino has Yaqui blood in him," Adam explained. "He's a good friend, and a bad enemy." He glanced significantly at the dog. "He doesn't like what they've done to his friend, Gaspar Mendota. Somebody is due for a lot of trouble."

"I like him." Linda sat down on a chair, closed her eyes wearily.

Adam stood looking at her. He still had only the haziest idea about her. He knew that her name was Seton and that she had known his grandfather. And he knew that a gang of night riders had raided her sheep camp, murdered and burned. JM men had done it, she had said. Something was indeed dreadfully wrong. He hated all this delay, was in a fever of impatience to continue his journey to the ranch. He would leave just as soon as he was sure this girl was in safe hands. She would be safe enough with

Severino Moraga. Nobody would know where to look for her. He would tell Severino to keep her hidden, deny any knowledge of her if questions were asked. His own experience had warned him of the ruthlessness of the man who now posed as Adam Marshall. The girl's life was in danger. It was lucky he had run into her. Lucky for her— and perhaps something more wonderful for him. The thought quickened his heart. He had never known a girl who could so deeply stir him.

Her eyes suddenly opened on him. "He calls you *Adamito*." Her tone was faintly quizzical.

"Severino's colloquialism for little Adam. He's known me from infant days."

Sounds drew up the *galena* and the innkeeper padded into the room. An elderly woman followed him. She carried a steaming bucket of water, towels and soap. She beamed at Linda.

"Maria feex you nize," Severino said.

"*Sí*," smiled the woman. She gave Linda a swift, appraising look, added in Spanish to Severino, "Carmela's clothes will fit her. They are the same size."

Severino nodded satisfaction. "My gran'baby, Carmela, weel lend you clothes," he told Linda. "Carmela same beeg as you."

"I will tell Carmela." Maria gave the girl another smile and hurried from the room.

"You are very kind." Linda's eyes glistened as she glanced at the steaming bucket.

Adam followed Severino Moraga out to the *galería*. The Mexican pulled the door shut, turned his head in a searching look at his tall companion.

"Is it known you are in Dos Ríos?" His tone betrayed anxiety.

"Sam Doan knows," Adam said. "I got in late last night. Sam let me bunk down in the hayloft."

"Sam did not tell you anything?"

Adam shook his head. "He acted scared to death at the sight of me." Adam's face darkened. "I couldn't figure Sam out. He used to be a good friend. I'm not so certain about him—now."

Severino nodded. "He is not to be trusted, Adamito." He spoke gloomily. "This is bad business. It is very dangerous for you in this town."

Adam gave him a thin-lipped smile. "It seems that my presence here makes one too many Adam Marshalls in the Dos Ríos country. What do *you* know about it, Severino?"

"Only that there is bad trouble at the ranch," muttered the old Mexican. His face was a mask of grief. "There is a devil at work."

Adam was silent for a moment, his face pale, a great dread in his eyes. He brought the question out with an effort. "Severino—my grandfather? Is—is he—?"

The innkeeper lifted a hand. "No, *amigo* . . . the old señor is not dead, but he is like one dead, ever since the news came that you had died in the quicksands of the Rio Grande."

Relief showed in Adam's eyes. "I heard about it from Miss Seton. She was there when he had the stroke. That was months ago. She couldn't tell me anything more. I've been awfully afraid that he was dead by now."

"He is like one dead," repeated the Mexican sadly. "He cannot speak, say that this wicked man is not his grandson. A few of us know the truth, but can do nothing."

"Bill Clemm, Celestino—are they dead?"

"Nobody knows," answered Severino. "We do not see them any more."

"You mean the old outfit is gone?"

"*Sí.*" Severino spoke unhappily. "The men who now ride for JM are all strangers, *amigo.*" His haggard eyes questioned the younger man. "I do not understand." He gestured despairingly. "I only know that the devil is at work."

"The thing began months back," Adam said. "I can't make sense of it myself. Somebody did his best to have me killed on that Presidio trip." He gave Severino a brief account of the affair up to the point where he had followed Linda Seton from Sam Doan's livery barn.

Severino Moraga listened attentively, his seamed brown face a somber mask. He asked worriedly, "Were you recognized on the street when you followed the girl from the barn?"

"I think Miguel Estrada spotted me," Adam said. "He looked at me as if I were a ghost."

"Anybody else see you?"

"The hotel clerk, but he wouldn't know me, and there was another man. Linda Seton said his name is Berren."

"*Sí.*" Severino nodded thoughtfully. "Señor Berren is a newcomer. He bought Pete Cline's store several months ago, when old Pete died. He is well liked."

His shrug drew a sharp look from Adam. It was his shrewd guess that Severino did not include himself among those who had a liking for the bearded storekeeper.

A slim girl with a madonna face under smooth black hair came quickly along the *galena*. She carried feminine garments, and there was wonder in her dark eyes as she saw Severino Moraga's companion.

She said, breathless, excited, "It is a blessed miracle, to see you, Adamito!"

Adam's face softened. "Hello, Carmela."

Her grandfather opened the door, motioned her inside. "Look after the señorita. She is in bad trouble."

Carmela nodded. "She will know me. We have talked at the post office, and one day I met her in Sombrio Canyon. She was very sad. Her father had just been killed in an accident. His horse ran away, dragged him to death."

Adam narrowed his eyes at her. "When did this happen, Carmela?"

She hesitated, brows puckered in an effort to remember. "Oh, just a little while ago . . . about a month." She half closed the door, peered back at her grandfather. "Miguel Estrada wants to see you. He is in the barroom and says it is important." She closed the door slowly, her dark eyes lingering with bright interest on her grandfather's friend.

Her news about Miguel Estrada disturbed Severino. He gave Adam a dismayed look.

"Miguel has followed you," he said uneasily. "I do not like this—"

"Miguel is all right," Adam assured him. "He's an old JM man."

"*Sí.* He is a good man—" Worry deepened the lines in the old Mexican's face. "It is that I fear he brings bad news." He gestured. "Come, *amigo*, we will soon know."

They found Miguel sitting at one of the small, round tables. His brown face under tall steeple hat was grooved with anxious lines.

"Señor—" Excitement took his breath, he puffed and blew, gesticulated wildly.

Severino seized him with big hands. "What is it?" he demanded.

Miguel regained control of his voice. He wagged a finger at Adam. "Death already seeks for him," he gasped. His eyes rolled an apprehensive look at the street door.

"*Por Dios!*" Severino's face was gray with fear. "What is this talk?"

"It is known that Adamito is here at the *cantina*," explained Miguel. "Al Deen comes to arrest him."

"*Por Dios!*" repeated the innkeeper. He gave Adam an aghast look. "You must get away—quick!"

"I'm not going to run," protested Adam.

"You do not understand." Severino spoke frantically. "Al Deen is a bad hombre, a hired gunman. He will throw you in jail—or kill you on sight." His eyes gleamed fiercely in the harsh brown mask of his face.

"I'm not afraid of the town marshal," Adam said stubbornly.

Severino gestured despairingly. "You cannot do much—in jail, *amigo*, and to be dead is the finish."

Adam stared at him, his expression thoughtful. He was grimly aware that Severino spoke true words. He had a job to do, a mystery to untangle. He had only the haziest idea of what it was all about. One thing was a stark fact. His grandfather was ill, a helpless victim of treachery and intrigue. Also it was apparent that the same dangerous conspiracy threatened Linda Seton.

He said soberly, "You're right, Severino. I can't chance jail, or a bullet in my back." He glanced doubtfully at the street door. "They'll be watching the plaza—"

"*Sí.*" Severino went swiftly to the door, peered cautiously into the plaza. Alarm spread over his face. "Quick," he whispered. "Get out!" He motioned at the hall door. "Men come now. . . . Deen is with them!"

Adam slid into the hall. Severino paused long enough to speak to Miguel Estrada and the startled barman. "You have not seen Adamito," he told them. "He has not been here . . . you know nothing of him. That is your answer to questions."

The door into the hall shut behind him. They heard the click of the bolt, the whispered beat of his sandals as he hurried to overtake Adam.

They heard too, the heavy tramp of approaching booted feet on the century-old stones outside the *cantina*. The barman snatched up a wine bottle, placed it on a tray with a glass, and sped over to Miguel's table. He was pouring wine into the glass when the door slammed open. He turned his head and looked, the bottle still in his hand. An ingratiating smile wreathed his face. "*Buenos días, señores,*" he greeted.

No response came from the newcomers. They stood there, just inside the doorway, hard-eyed, watchful men who plainly were not making this early-morning call for pleasure.

The town marshal, a lean little man, took in the long, dim room with one swift look that slid over

Miguel, sitting at the table with his glass of wine. "Seen a red-headed jasper in here, Tomás?" he asked the still-grinning barman.

"I jus' come," evaded Tomás. "No hombre in *cantina* w'en I come." He gestured at Miguel. "Only Miguel Estrada come for dreenk." The town marshal's eyes stabbed at Miguel. "You didn't see the feller when you come in?" Miguel gestured indifferently, shook his head. "No hombre in *cantina* w'en I come." He picked up his glass, took a leisurely sip.

"Looks like he ain't here," one of the men said. He grinned at Tomás. "How about settin' up the drinks, feller?" He holstered his gun. "Could do with an eye-opener."

"Sure t'ing," smiled Tomás. He slid to his place behind the bar and reached for a bottle of whiskey.

"Right smart idee," chuckled another man.

There was the slap and scrape of leather as guns slid into holsters, a quick surge of booted feet. Only the town marshal stood motionless, suspicion, discontent, in his cold eyes.

"Was a gal with him," he said, staring hard at Tomás. "The Seton gal that runs a sheep outfit up on the mesa."

Tomás shrugged, shook his head, his smile polite, regretful. His conscience was quite at rest on this point. He had not seen Linda when she passed through the barroom. "Too bad, señor," he sympathized. He lifted his bottle suggestively. "You 'ave leetle dreenk, no?"

Al Deen nodded gloomily. "Sure, Tomás." He lined up with the others and picked up the glass Tomás deftly slid into his fingers. "Where's Severino?"

Tomás gestured vaguely, shook his head. Deen glowered, drained his glass and moved purposefully to the door that led into the hall. It resisted his push.

The town marshal muttered imprecations. "Somebody's throwed the bolt—"

Smoldering suspicions flared. "Hell! It's a trick to hold us here while he gets away." He reached for his gun. "Bust her open, fellers."

It was a stout timbered door, reinforced with straps of iron, and the adobe wall was more than three feet thick. The cursing men soon realized they were wasting time.

"No sense stickin' here," yelled Deen. "He'll have sneaked out some back door by now. Let's scatter, fellers. We'll nab him!"

They went pounding into the sunlit plaza, hands clawing guns from leather as they ran.

Tomás wiped cold sweat from his face with the back of a trembling hand, stared dazedly at old Miguel, limp in his chair.

"It is the finish," he groaned.

"*Sí*," muttered Miguel. "Death rides him close."

9
DARK CANYON

It was plain that Severino Moraga was reluctant to reveal the secret of the little room so cunningly concealed in the massive buttress of the adobe wall at the lower end of the garden.

"Swear you will never tell." The old man showed an odd embarrassment. "It is for your life—I do this."

Adam gave him a reassuring grin. He was not interested in the innkeeper's private affairs just then. The seconds were precious. Any moment might bring the town marshal hot-foot into the garden.

Severino fumbled at an iron ring and a great square stone slab slid aside, revealed a crude ladder made of poles, the crosspieces lashed secure with strips of rawhide. Cool air touched Adam's face as he peered down into the blackness.

He heard the strike of a match, looked up, saw that Severino had lit a torch of pitch-pine.

"Quick," whispered the old man. "They must not find you here."

Adam took the torch, stood listening for a

moment to the sudden uproar that came faintly from the *cantina*. He said worriedly, "I hate running like this . . . leaving the girl—"

"You cannot help her if you are dead." Severino scowled.

"You'll look out for her?"

"*Sí, sí*—" The old Mexican gestured impatiently at the ladder. "You waste time—"

"Tell her she'll soon hear from me," Adam said. He went cautiously down the ladder. The torch sent dancing shapes into the darkness.

The passage descended steeply, and the flare in his hand showed it varied in height and width. In places it was more than twice the height of a tall man and wide enough to walk three abreast. Once the roof dipped until he was forced to bend almost double, and occasionally the tunnel narrowed until his shoulders scraped granite-hard rock worn smooth by countless centuries of running water. He guessed the channel was the former subterranean outlet of the spring now trapped in the patio garden and bubbling under the big chinaberry tree.

A pinpoint of light suddenly appeared in front of him. He lowered the torch, dimmed its flare behind a huge boulder that partially blocked the passage. The pinpoint of light took on size in the deeper blackness beyond.

He pushed on, the way not so steep now, the coarse gravel under his feet deeper and softer;

and soon the tunnel widened into a great cave faintly touched with sunlight.

He bent down, snuffed the torch in the soft sand, and tossed it aside. The flare continued to smoulder and he moved after it, crushed the ember into the sand with the toe of his boot. Bits of similar half-buried and blackened stubs drew his attention, and it came to him that his little business with the torch had been done many times before by others who had passed that way.

He understood now why Severino Moraga had begged him never to divulge the existence of the underground entrance to the *cantina*. It was apparent that his old friend did a little smuggling when a chance for profit offered. It was more than probable that his father and his grandfather had done the same. Severino merely carried on an old family tradition and saw no wrong in it. With the border less than twenty miles away the setup would be irresistible to these descendants of old-time *Comancheros*.

It required several minutes and the use of his knife to force his way through the dense tangle of brush that blocked the entrance to the cave. He took a certain satisfaction in this. The heavy undergrowth was proof that the cave had not been used in years and that Severino Moraga no longer dealt in contraband from below the border.

Heavy cloud masses laid shadows on the mesa beyond the vast sprawl of the canyon. Adam could see the leaden glint of the river, low at this season of the year, hardly more than a trickle in the sandy waste. There were times when the stream was a roaring white-maned torrent and must have been so when the pioneering padres had made camp on the bluffs.

They had a way of putting names to things, and the river became *El Rio Blanco*, and the stream that flowed down the dark gorge lying west of the camp became known as *El Rio Sombrio*. It was natural that the place where they had rested on their arduous journey through the unknown wilderness be given their blessing and the name of *El Pueblo de Dos Ríos*.

Adam paused long enough to get his bearings. His first objective was Sam Doan's livery barn where he had left his horse. He was not sure of Sam Doan, but the horse was a necessity and he would have to take the risk.

He pushed on cautiously, followed the bend of the canyon which he knew angled within a few yards of the big corral in the rear of the barn. There was no trail here and the heavy underbrush made progress slow. It would take him a good half-hour to cover the quarter of a mile or more.

The uproar from his balked pursuers had subsided. He surmised that Al Deen would be making a quiet but thorough search in the Mexican quarter, which would mean a combing of most of the town. The population of Dos Ríos was perhaps less than three hundred, of which a good eighty percent were Mexicans. Severino Moraga would pass the word to keep their mouths shut if any of them chanced to see him. He could count on these simple, honest people not to betray him to Al Deen.

He thought of Catalina Ortiz, her staunch loyalty and belief in him, her simple faith that her prayers had brought him back to the Ortiz *ranchito.* She had shown no surprise. For her it was only one more Blessed Miracle that had rescued him from the San Carlos jail, guided him unscathed to her. He had rested there during the day, taken the opportunity to rid himself of the beard, and let Catalina trim his shaggy hair. Juan had been hard to persuade, but he was finally convinced of his innocence. Nightfall had seen him again pushing north for El Paso, a good horse under him and an enormous gratitude in him for Catalina and her husband. He owed them a debt he would someday repay with more than the few gold pieces he had persuaded them to take for the horse.

He had been nearly three weeks making his way to Dos Ríos, after wasting several days in Phoenix trying to get in touch with the deputy marshal, an old friend whose help he realized he was going to need. The deputy marshal was out of the Territory he finally learned and all he could do was leave a message.

Now that Monte Cline was dead, obviously murdered, there was no law in Dos Ríos. He would have to carry on the best he could. Monte would have been a world of help, one of the few honest men in this nest of border desperados. Someday there would be law in the Dos Ríos, but for the present a man's only protection was his gun—and his ability to use it.

There was the problem of Sam Doan, his thinly veiled hostility. Adam's face hardened as he reflected on the liveryman's odd behavior. Sam was a former JM top hand. John Marshall had set him up in business after the accident that had cost him his arm. Sam had got entangled in barbed wire and the arm had been amputated above the elbow. His own fault, really, but John Marshall had been generous with him, made him an outright gift of ten thousand dollars for Sam to go into the livery and feed business. JM had always given him their trade, and that meant a lot, considering there were usually more than thirty riders in the outfit. If there was one man in Dos Ríos he could have depended on it should have been Sam Doan, and Sam apparently regarded him with unfriendly eyes, had shown all the terrified emotions of a man guilty of treachery.

He recalled Severino Moraga's warning. *He is not to be trusted. It is very dangerous for you in this town.* Too bad there had been no time to question Severino about Sam. Al Deen's promptness in picking up the trail had rushed matters. One thing was certain about Sam Doan. He would have to be on his guard against the man.

Harassed with gloomy speculations that seemed to get him nowhere, Adam finally reached a deep gully that broke down from the bluffs just below the corral. Erosion had choked the place with boulders, and the steep slope was treacherous with slides and loose shale.

He went up stealthily, hands clinging to stunted shrubs, and after a few minutes came to a clump of buckthorn that grew on the edge of the bluff. The thorny bush made good cover, and he crouched there, studying his surroundings and deciding on his next move.

Several horses were in the corral, nosing at a pile of straw thrown down from the long stack outside the fence, and as Adam continued to watch, two men appeared from the rear door. They carried ropes which they built into loops as they approached the horses. A third man watched idly from the door, a pitchfork in his hand. Adam recognized the stable hand who had helped him put up his horse.

He waited impatiently while the pair of cowboys got their ropes on the horses they eased out of the bunch. The men were strangers, but the horses were not. They were JM stock. To see them led into the barn by these men made rage rise in him. The fingers of his gun-hand itched. He was forced to use all his self-control to keep from an act of folly that could only prove fatal to his plans.

For long minutes he lay motionless, and there was cold, deadly purpose in him now, a fierce resolve to smash the sinister mind responsible for the monstrous evil that threatened to destroy all that he held dear. For some reason he thought of Linda Seton, was aware of an odd thrill. She was in it, too, was one of the reasons why he must keep his brain cool. More than his grandfather's life was at stake now, and more than the ranch. He had Linda Seton to think of. Adam realized with some amazement that Linda was irrevocably included in all that he held dear.

Hoofs pounded in the street beyond the long barn and he caught a glimpse of the two cowboys as they rode east out of town.

He waited a few more moments, heard sounds from the barn that told him the stableman was forking manure from the stalls. He heard other sounds, the jingle of bells that warned him of an approaching freight wagon. It was more than likely the muleskinner would pull into the feed yard.

Adam moved swiftly now, reached the open door of the barn. A cautious look inside gave him a glimpse of the hostler, busy with his fork, his back turned. Adam drew his gun, slid into the gloom of the stable. Despite his caution, the man heard the whispering of straw underfoot. He turned his head for a look, dropped the fork with a startled oath, and reached for his holstered gun. Perhaps the threat of instant death in Adam's eyes warned him it was useless to resist. His hand fell away from the gun. He stood rigid, sullen, waited for Adam to speak.

Adam's decision about him was already made. He could not waste time with this man. The moments were too precious. The simplest way was brutal, but he was at war with brutes who gave no mercy. There could be no mercy for this hard-faced thug who stood between him and the horse he must have without delay.

He said in a whisper, "Turn around—"

It was plain the man guessed his intention. Fear made a mask of his ashen face, held him rigid, unable to move. Adam saw this, stepped swiftly behind him, swung up his gun for the crushing blow and suddenly found he could not do the thing he planned. It was too much like murder.

He lowered the forty-five, reached for the gun in the man's belt, and thrust it into his own holster. He rasped a command, and the man obeyed now, shuffled into the empty stall he had been cleaning, stood there, facing the manger. Snatching a coil of rope from the peg near his shoulder, Adam followed. He spoke again, and the hostler obediently lay face down on the straw.

In less than a minute he had his victim securely trussed and gagged. He lifted him bodily, lowered him into the manger, and covered him with straw. It would take considerable searching before Sam Doan located his missing hostler.

Satisfied he had done his best, Adam found his saddle gear and hurried to his horse, a rangy red bay he had purchased in Willcox. Swiftly, making each motion count, he saddled and bridled the animal, aware now of voices in the feed yard. The freighter had pulled in, was exchanging profane comments with his swamper.

"Where the hell's that damn hostler? . . . Figgered to git feed for the team . . . Hell of a way to treat customers—"

Another voice broke into the conversation. Sam Doan's voice. "Hello, hombre! . . . Sure we got feed, plenty feed. I'll go chase that damn hostler out to you. Looks like he's layin' round some place snorin' his head off."

Adam took a quick look at the rear door. No chance to get out that way with the horse. Already he could hear the hasty tread of boot heels, and Sam's voice, loud, angry, calling for the missing stableman.

Discovery was imminent. Adam slid into an adjoining stall, waited, gun in hand. His one chance was to take Sam by surprise.

The liveryman's shouts faded. It was plain that he was puzzled. Adam heard him muttering.

"Layin' drunk some place, the damn loafer. I'd sure like to fire him with a kick in the pants. . . . Newt wouldn't stand for it. . . . Dassent buck Newt. . . . He's a devil—"

Adam's subconscious took note of the name. *Somebody named Newt . . . and Sam Doan feared him.*

The whispering sounds of feet on straw came closer, and suddenly the two men were face to face. Adam had the advantage of surprise, and there was no compunction in him now. His ready gun-barrel cracked with a sickening impact against Sam Doan's skull.

He caught the limp body, lowered it to the straw, and hastily reached for another rope. He hated the loss of time, but he could not leave Sam lying for the impatient teamster to find. And his quick look told him the liveryman was not seriously hurt, would soon recover consciousness.

In a few moments he had Sam tucked away in the manger and covered with straw. He felt oddly guilty, ashamed of himself as he did this. It was no way to treat a one-armed man, a cripple. And Sam had once been a loyal member of the old outfit.

Adam was aware of a quick anger at himself. He had done the only thing he could do. Sam was a traitor, was hand-in-glove with ruthless murderers. This was no time to be soft-hearted. He had to think of old John Marshall—of Linda

Seton. For their sakes it was up to him to use every trick in the bag—kill, if necessary.

He led the horse boldly into the front yard and stepped into his saddle. The teamster hailed him, a lean, dusty-faced man.

"Whar in hell did Sam git to?" fumed the man.

"Went out back some place, looking for the hostler," Adam told him.

"Plumb out of grain for the mules," grumbled the teamster. He spat disgustedly.

"Sam said to help yourself. You know where the granary is."

The teamster's face brightened. "Reckon that's a idee." He beckoned to his swamper. "Come on, Pete—" He slouched off in the direction of the granary, a small adobe building.

Adam swung his horse and rode into the street. He was in a hurry to get away from there. It was quite possible the muleskinner would find the granary door locked, in which case he would soon be storming back to the stable in search of Sam Doan.

He resisted the impulse to send the bay into a fast run. He must do nothing to attract attention. The street was livening up, but nobody took any notice of him. He was just another cowboy making an early-morning departure for the home ranch.

This country was as familiar as the palm of his

hand. He knew every turn in the dusty, winding road, every short cut, and presently he found the trail he was looking for. Despite his impatience, Adam kept the bay to the same steady running-walk. A spent horse was useless. Only a fool ran his horse to death. He recalled a saying of his grandfather's, *a fool and his horse soon part.* The old man had a lot of wisdom stored in him and he was never shy about passing it on. He had no use for a man who abused his horse.

Fear's dark hand laid hold of him again as the horse rocked along. He had as yet no definite plan. He wished there had been more time to question Severino Moraga. One thing seemed almost a certainty. Bill Clemm was dead, and Celestino Baca. Those two old-timers would never have deserted their boss.

The affair was as baffling as it was terrible. If Severino Moraga was right about it, John Marshall was still alive. The thing made no sense. These ruthless men who had seized the ranch would want the old cattleman dead.

There was one possible explanation. They planned to use John Marshall, get his signature on a document—a deed to the ranch. It meant his recovery was expected, or at least hoped for.

Adam knew with deadly certainty that any such scheme was doomed to failure. They could never force John Marshall to sign away the great ranch he had wrested from the wilderness. He would tell them to go to hell—and they would kill him.

A gunshot shattered the stillness. Adam swung his horse from the trail and took cover behind a gnarled old juniper, sat tense in his saddle, listening to the echoes reverberating down in the canyon.

Whoever it was down there could not be gunning for him. He was too far back on the rimrock to have been seen. Puzzled, he finally slid from his saddle, and leaving the horse tied behind the juniper he crawled cautiously to the edge of the cliff.

The floor of the canyon was a good five hundred feet below. He could see the river, a silver thread between the towering black walls that had given this great gorge the name of *El Cañon Sombrio*. A pair of buzzards drifted up, dark shapes that swung in ever widening circles that carried them higher and higher.

Adam watched them distastefully. He did not like buzzards. They fed on dead things—dead men. He had once found a JM rider lying dead in the chaparral, his eyes pecked out. The picture had remained with him and he had never lost his horror of the carrion birds. They had their usefulness as scavengers and range men left them alone as a rule, never shot them unless outraged by some experience similar to his own.

The same thing must have happened down in

the canyon. A dead man, and somewhere near, a live man whose shot had driven away the feasting buzzards.

The minutes dragged past. Adam continued to lie there, waited for some stir that would draw his eyes; and suddenly he saw the man, a dark moving shape hardly visible under the trees.

Adam returned thoughtfully to his horse. A dead man lay down there. He was interested in dead men. Bill Clemm and Celestino Baca were dead men. Their disappearance was proof they were no longer alive. He swung up to his saddle and sent the bay across the rimrock, and found the trail that looped down into the gloom of the canyon. He was determined to have a look at the thing from which the gunshot had driven the buzzards.

He risked discovery, perhaps recognition, if he encountered the man he had espied from the rimrock. The thought did not lessen his resolve. He could think only of Bill Clemm and Celestino Baca, both of them dead. Perhaps it was here he would find their bodies.

It took him nearly fifteen minutes to reach the spot where he had glimpsed the stranger. He halted the bay, waited, ears and eyes alert. No sound broke the stillness, but he had the feeling that eyes were on him, watching his movements.

Adam reached for papers and tobacco sack, coolly shaped a cigarette. If the watcher were friendly, he would speak, if not he could only continue to wait for some movement that would betray where the man was concealed.

He finished making the cigarette, put a match to it, and suddenly the silence was broken.

"Waal, son, wasn't figgerin' I'd ever lay eyes on you ag'in."

The sound of that familiar drawling voice almost jolted Adam from his saddle. The cigarette fell from his fingers. He said huskily, "My God, Bill! I—I thought you were—dead." He stared with unbelieving eyes at the lean-faced man limping toward him.

"I ain't as dead as some hombres I know of is goin' to be when I get done with 'em," Bill Clemm said bleakly. He glanced at the burning cigarette, snubbed it with the toe of his boot.

Adam got down from the horse. "I heard that shot—saw the buzzards—"

Bill nodded, his expression grim. "You guessed right, son." He seemed reluctant to explain further.

"A dead man, you mean?" Adam felt sick. He knew from the expression on the old foreman's face that the dead man was Celestino Baca.

"I figgered he was lyin' some place in the canyon," Bill Clemm said slowly. "Found him a few minutes ago—and them damn buzzards goin' for him." He paused, added sorrowfully, "I reckon you savvy what I mean, son?"

Adam nodded. "That's why I headed this way—"

The foreman gave him a mirthless smile. "Figgered it might be me or him—or both of us, huh?"

A silence fell between them, broken by Bill Clemm. "I figgered to cover what's left of him with stones . . . find a hole some place and pile stone on him."

Adam nodded. He had vastly more important things on his mind. His grandfather's life hung by a hair and the minutes were precious. But Bill was right. It was only decent to find a hole some place . . . pile stones.

He said desperately, "You do it, Bill. I've got to keep moving—get out to the ranch—"

"You'll ride smack into hot lead," Bill Clemm told him. "You wait until I get this little job done for old Celestino. I kind of hanker to hit the trail with you."

"Got a horse?"

Bill shook his head. "Been on the dodge for a lot of weeks. Took some lead in my hip same time my bronc was killed. Crippled me some."

Adam looked at him attentively. It was plain that Bill Clemm was in bad shape, a starved and ill man. He said quietly, "You need a doctor, Bill."

The foreman's iron composure seemed to crack. His leathery face twisted and for a horrified moment Adam thought he would break down and cry.

"Ain't carin' nothin' for myself no more, son. Was wantin' to last long enough to send that damn hombre to hell on a shutter for what's done to the boss."

"We'll do it, Bill."

"It's a hell of a mess," groaned the half-crazed foreman. "I don't even savvy what it's about."

"I was hoping you could tell me things." Adam spoke dejectedly. "I hardly know which way to turn. I'm like a blindfolded man." He gestured savagely. "I've got to get to the ranch before it's too late."

Bill Clemm made no comment. He looked sick, stood there, shoulders hunched forward, hands clenched on the two guns in his holsters.

"Can you hold out here for a day or two?" Adam asked.

Clemm nodded. "Reckon I can." He gave the younger man his mirthless smile.

Adam turned to his horse, climbed into the saddle. He was doing a hard thing, leaving this sick man. There was nothing else he could do, himself a fugitive from evil men.

He said quietly, "I had to run for it from Dos Ríos, Bill. Right now we're in the same fix."

"I savvy, son." Bill's tone was gentle. "The boss comes first. You know me."

"I'll be back," Adam said.

The old foreman limped close to the horse, reached out a hard, thorn-scratched hand. "I'm bettin' all my chips on you, son. Sure you'll be back, and then you and me will make heap big medicine. We'll show them killin' wolves there's plenty fight left in the old JM, huh?"

"That's right, old-timer." Adam threw him an affectionate grin, swung his horse back to the trail. He was thinking grimly that he was not so sure he would be back. It was quite possible that this trail he followed might well be a trail of no return.

10

MR. BERREN

Linda came out of her sleep with a violent start. She was trembling, still fighting terror. She had never been so frightened by a dream. Red flames in the night, shouting, cursing demons on plunging horses—herself, running, stumbling, falling—the rending claws and fangs of the chaparral, the dark canyon with its ghostly shapes—the wolves.

She sat up in the great bed, fingers clutching the covers. That fearsome sound was still in her ears, and she was wide awake now—not dreaming.

Horror held her rigid, and then suddenly she understood. The sheep dog, somewhere outside, lonesome, miserable. His wolfish howls had awakened her.

She slid from the bed, dismayed to realize it was late afternoon. She must have slept for hours. Adam Marshall would be wanting to see her. There were so many things to talk over.

The thought of Adam Marshall sent a chill of apprehension through her. There had been a dreadful uproar, and Severino Moraga had come in, told her that Adam had gone away, but would be back when it was safe for him to return. In the meantime she was not to worry.

Linda went slowly to the washbasin. It was hard not to worry, wonder what had happened to Adam Marshall. It was evident that his enemies were already aware of his presence in Dos Ríos. He was one against so many. It was hardly possible he could escape.

Somebody had been in while she slept, refilled the bucket and the basin with fresh water, no longer hot, but still warm. She took a hasty sponge and got into the clothes Carmela had left on a chair, a full yellow skirt of some soft material, and a white, tight-fitting bodice. There were stockings, and soft leather *huaraches*. She put them on. Her own clothes had vanished. They were beyond repair and Carmela must have carried them off with her.

Linda studied her reflection in the mirror. With her warm coloring and chestnut hair the Mexican girl's clothes gave her quite the look of a *señorita*.

The long hours of sleep had refreshed her enormously. She was hungry, despite the anxiety that gnawed at her. She wanted food and coffee and above all she desperately wanted news of Adam Marshall.

She heard footsteps and hurried into the front room. Severino Moraga greeted her with a smile from the doorway. He came in, followed by Carmela who carried a bright-colored Mexican tray.

"*Buenos días, señorita—*" Severino broke into his halting English: "You sleep mooch nize, no?"

"Too long." Linda's tone was rueful.

Carmela placed the tray on a table. "You will like this," she smiled: "*arroz con pollo.* Maria made it for you."

"Thank you. It looks—delicious." Linda hesitated, inquiring eyes on Moraga. "Is—is Mr. Marshall back?"

Severino lost his smile. "Adamito no come back, señorita."

Panic surged through her. "They—they caught him?"

The old Mexican shook his head. "No, señorita. I 'ave keep watch—" He smiled grimly. "My frien's all time keep eyes sharp, ears wide. No news 'ave come. Adamito too smar-rt for those *malo hombres.*"

"I'm frightened for him," Linda said. "They want to kill him." She repressed a shiver. "That poor dog!"

They stood silent, listening to the long wolfish howl.

"He's lonesome," Linda said. "I want him with me—"

Severino's slight frown indicated some doubt in his mind. She guessed he was not in sympathy with the request. He did not like the idea of a dog in the sacred room.

She said quietly, "He's in trouble, too—"

The Mexican's expression softened. "*Sí—*" He gestured. "I breeng thees dog now. Thees dog 'ave beeg like for you, no?"

He hurried outside, and Carmela said coaxingly, "You must eat the *arroz con pollo* while it is hot, señorita."

Linda smiled at her, sat down. "Linda," she said, "call me Linda. We're friends."

The Mexican girl dimpled. "I like you. Yes, we are friends."

"You speak very good English."

"I am American," smiled Carmela. "I'm going to be a schoolteacher."

"I was a schoolteacher," Linda said.

Carmela stifled a delighted shriek. "This is too wonderful. Now I know we are friends. It is very exciting!"

Severino came in with the tawny-maned dog. The animal whimpered, ran to Linda, licked at her hand. She said affectionately, "You're another friend. I'm going to call you *Amigo*." The dog's tail wagged violently and content now, he lay down close to her side.

Severino smiled, nodded his approval of the arrangement, and disappeared into the patio. Carmela followed him, paused at the door to say she would be back soon and then they could have a good talk about school teaching.

Linda finished her coffee, her mind busy with a plan that slowly was taking shape. She was thinking of Mr. Berren, his kindness. He had told her she would need clothes, said she could select anything she wanted and no charge. It was generous of him, but of course she would pay for anything she needed. There was still a little money left, almost a thousand dollars in the Willcox bank. It was nice of him, though, to make the offer.

Linda put the empty coffee cup down and went into the bedroom and took another look at herself in the mirror. The dog followed, sat down and watched her intently.

The dress would do for the street, she decided. Very few of the Mexican girls wore hats, and she really did look quite Mexican. Nobody would notice her, except in the way men noticed any girl. In fact she doubted whether anybody would recognize her as Linda Seton. It would be safe enough for her to run over to the store and make a quick selection of the things she needed. Another pair of overalls, a flannel shirt, stockings—a hat. Her boots were still in good shape, brush-scarred, but wearable.

Another reason strengthened her resolve. She wanted to urge Berren to send word to the jailed Mexican sheepherder that his dog was being cared for. Sheepherders valued their dogs and it was a shame to let the poor man worry.

Back in Linda's mind was another thought, a vague hope that she might hear some news of

Adam Marshall. Of course she would not mention his name to the storekeeper. She wouldn't want Berren to know that she was aware of Adam's true identity. But the storekeeper might be in the mood for gossip and any scrap of information would be valuable. If anything had happened to Adam, it was more than likely that Berren would have heard.

She hurried into the sunlit patio, stood for a moment trying to recall just where she had noticed the little gate in the high adobe wall. Somewhere near the fountain. She crossed over, found the gate, which was fastened with a wooden bar that slid into a socket. She glanced around, saw that she was unobserved, and in another moment she was outside and holding the gate for the dog to follow.

Amigo's behavior puzzled her. He seemed reluctant to leave the garden, and there was an odd uneasiness in him. She wondered if he feared the street where he had met with kicks and curses and suffered starvation. His reluctance to leave the patio would be natural.

Linda opened the gate, motioned for the animal to go back. Amigo's response was to sit down on his haunches and gaze up at her solemnly.

She saw it was no use, closed the gate, and went swiftly up the alley formed by the high patio wall on one side and the ancient church on the other. Amigo kept close to her heels.

She reached the plaza, crossed over and turned into the dusty street. Several horses stood at the long hitch-rail in front of the hotel. A man sat there on the veranda steps. He wore batwing leather chaps, and two guns in the holsters that flanked lean hips. His head lifted as he caught sight of the girl on the opposite sidewalk and he kept his gaze on her until she disappeared inside the store.

Berren was talking to a rancher who was examining a set of work harness. He gave her a casual glance and spoke to the yellow-haired clerk who was stacking bolts of cloth on the long counter. Linda realized that the storekeeper had not recognized her, took her for a Mexican girl.

The clerk was under the same misapprehension. His mean, shifty eyes leered at her unpleasantly as he approached. Linda loathed him. She said sharply, "I want to buy a few things, Fred. I'm in a hurry."

He gaped, stuttered confusedly, "Wasn't knowin' you in them Mex clothes, Miss Seton."

Linda brushed past him and went to the dry-goods counter. Amigo, close at her heels, lifted a snarling lip.

The clerk's pale eyes took on an ugly glint. He went to Berren, whispered something. The storekeeper's head swung in a look at the girl. Her back was turned, or she would have been

146

startled by the exulting gleam in the man's deep-set eyes.

He returned his attention to the rancher, said in his husky, whispering voice, "Drop in next week, Jensen and I'll have the loan papers ready. You can take the harness along with you."

"Thanks, Newt." The rancher was grateful. "You sure treat a man white." He slung the harness over an arm and disappeared into the street.

Berren's gaze shifted to Linda, absorbed with a pile of blue overalls stacked on the counter. He said to the clerk, "I'll take care of Miss Linda, Fred," and he moved behind the counter, gave the girl his slow, benevolent smile.

"Should be your size in that lot," he told her. "You're a bit slim, but I always carry a full line. Lots of the cowhands are kind of lean-waisted."

"I want some shirts, and stockings," Linda said. She pulled a pair of overalls from the pile. "These will fit, if the label is correct."

"Got a room back there if you want to try them on," Berren said. He looked past her at Fred, made a covert gesture at the dog.

"I'm sure they'll fit," Linda assured him. "I'd like to look at some shirts, Mr. Berren." She gave him her size, and he turned his broad back on her, fumbled in the shelves.

"How about these?" He placed the garments on the counter. "Pure wool—the best I carry, and we won't talk price. I told you this is all on me, Miss Linda."

"Oh, no!" Linda protested. "You're awfully kind, but I much prefer to pay for them. I still have some money." She examined the shirts critically. "These will do. I'll take them—and half a dozen pairs of stockings."

"I'd like to help you," insisted the storekeeper. "You sure had a rough deal." He shook his head worriedly. "Too bad you won't take my advice and get out of this lawless country."

"Why don't you and other decent citizens do something about it?" she asked. "Why do you allow murderers to roam around and kill people?"

"That's a fair question." His eyes were intent on her. "Shouldn't be surprised but what we'll do a bit of hanging right soon."

Linda looked at him doubtfully. "You mean the men who raided my camp?" Her voice hardened. "You can find them easy enough—at the JM."

"Now, Miss Linda—" Berren's whispering voice was gently chiding. "You've got it in your head it was JM that done it. You're awfully wrong. I've an idea that the man who pulled off that job will soon have a rope on his neck." He was staring at her intently. "I'm puzzled about you, Miss Linda."

"Puzzled?" Linda frowned. "I don't understand you, Mr. Berren."

"This man was seen in town this morning. You

seem to know him, went with him to Moraga's *cantina*."

Linda looked at him uneasily. Something in that square, bearded face frightened her, and for the first time she was conscious of a doubt in her against this big and seemingly kind man. The smile was still on his face, but it had oddly changed, taken on a cold malevolence. And the warmth had left his eyes. They were like dull glass, without expression in their shadowed sockets.

He leaned toward her, big hands on the counter. "Don't pretend, Miss Seton. You know too much, I'm thinking."

Instinct warned her to dissemble, hide her rising terror. She only wanted to get out of the store now, get back to the high-walled garden she had so foolishly left.

She shook her head, forced a smile. "I—I don't understand—" She indicated the purchased garments. "If you will please wrap them up—"

His attention was not on her, and completely frightened now, she turned around, saw the clerk suddenly drop a noose over the dog's head. Amigo snarled, leaped at him. The clerk backed away, jerked furiously on the rope, and the dog sprawled on his back, strangling and helpless.

Linda cried out, sprang at the youth, felt a great hand fasten on her arm. Another big hand closed over her mouth, shut off her scream.

Berren said in a rasping whisper, "Take the dog out to the yard, Fred. Shoot him, or knock him on the head."

"I'll try out my new Colt on him," grinned the clerk. He dragged the struggling dog through a rear door.

Linda's eyes closed, and she was suddenly a dead weight in the iron grip of the hands that reached over the counter. Berren released his hold and she crumpled to the floor.

Approaching footsteps drew an annoyed grunt from the storekeeper. He faced around, saw a man framed in the wide entrance. He said in a relieved voice, "Hello, Bert," and came without haste from behind the counter, stood looking down at the unconscious girl.

The newcomer hurriedly joined him. He was the same man Linda had noticed sitting on the hotel steps. He said curiously, "She's the Mex girl I seen come into the store. What the hell's happened to her, Newt?"

"Got took with a fainting spell." Berren's gaze lifted in a speculative look at the cowboy who was staring avidly at a slim leg under disarrayed yellow skirt. "She's not Mexican, Bert. I'm advising you to forget you saw her in this store."

The undisguised menace in the whispering voice seemed to affect the cowboy unpleasantly. He took a hasty backward step. "Sure, Newt. Wasn't figgerin' to butt into *your* game."

"See that you don't." Berren bent over the girl. "Help me take her into the office. Don't want folks to see her laying here."

Outside in the yard, Fred stood jerking at the rope until the dog got to his feet.

"I'm filling you with lead," he told Amigo. He licked loose wet lips.

The big sheep dog stared back at him with watchful yellow eyes. He showed no fear, only bristling rage, and contempt for the cowardly human who faced him so gloatingly.

The clerk grinned, the lust to kill in his eyes now. He liked to kill. It gave him a feeling of power to kill. This time it was only a dog, but he had once killed a man, shot him out of his saddle. Newt Berren had been pleased, given him the new Colt forty-five now in his belt.

Fred reached for the gun and his fingers were closing over the butt when the dog leaped, a tawny, snarling shape. The horrified man jerked frantically at the forty-five, screamed as Amigo's wolf fangs slashed his arm from elbow to wrist. The gun exploded, dropped from his nerveless fingers. The big dog whirled, leaped over the fence, and disappeared.

11

WILD HORSE PASS

The horse moved along at a fast shuffling gait. Adam liked this big red bay. He was easy on a man, willing—liked to have his head and keep going. He was almost as good as the buckskin, which was saying a lot. Anger smoldered in Adam's eyes as he thought of his slain horse. Old Buck was a horse hard to beat. Losing him was losing a dear and loyal friend.

The trail dipped across a sandy dry wash, climbed a slope, and now cliffs closed in, towering sheer walls with a ribbon of blue sky above.

Adam rode with the tireless ease of his kind, shadowed eyes wary. This was Wild Horse Pass, his own JM range where death now lurked behind every bush. He must be on the alert for any sign that would flash a warning of peril ahead.

The gorge widened and the cliffs drew back, allowed gentle slopes to break down from the hills. Great boulders as big as houses lay on the slopes, and there were trees and grass and scattered clumps of brush.

Dust lifted, made a golden haze above the hills. Adam heard the bawling of cattle. He drew the horse to a standstill, squinted thoughtfully at the distant haze that told of an approaching trail-herd, a big one by all the signs.

There was only one answer that could explain the presence of a trail-herd in Wild Horse Pass. It was the easiest and shortest route to the border less than twenty miles west of the Rio Sombrio. It meant that the looting of the ranch was already under way, perhaps hastened by news of his escape from the Mexican jail.

Anxiety grew in Adam. Anything could happen once these men took the alarm. They would not want old John Marshall to live long enough to tell what he knew.

The pass was choked with cattle. He would have to turn back, find another trail—or wait for the herd to go through. He decided to wait. The only other trail meant a steep mountain climb and was miles longer. He could wait and still save time. Also he had a burning desire to get a look at the men in charge of the herd.

The rattle of wheels and the clatter of shod hoofs warned him that the chuckwagon was coming. Adam rode up the slope and cached his horse behind a dense thicket of buckthorn. He hurried now, crawled hastily up to a great boulder on the edge of a bluff, and stretched out behind a clump of brush that had taken root there.

The chuckwagon lurched around the bend, came banging up the rough road. The four-mule team was on the trot, the cook hunched over in his seat, foot on squealing brakes, lines bunched in his hands. The man's lurid comments indicated he was in a hurry. Adam guessed some delay had put him behind his schedule and he was annoyed to have the herd so close on his heels.

A lone rider swung around the bend, his horse on the jump, and at his hail the driver of the chuckwagon jammed on brakes, glared irately at the newcomer.

"What the hell's wrong *now,* Farg? I'd shore like to git camp set up afore she's plumb dark on me."

"We ain't pushin' on to the river tonight," the rider told him. "Tod figgers to hold the herd down on the flats a couple a miles west of the pass. Thar's plenty feed there, and good water in the crik."

"Why in hell didn't Tod tell me?" howled the cook. He was in a quarrelsome mood. "Like to have busted a axle, tryin' to git to the river afore she's dark." He kicked off the brakes. "Git movin', you wall-eyed sons of jackasses!" The chuckwagon lurched on its way.

The grinning rider eased himself in the saddle and leisurely fished the makings of a cigarette from a shirt pocket. Adam had never seen him before, but he recognized the roan horse under him.

The sight of the outlaw on Roany put a

momentary wildness in him and his fingers closed hard over the gun-butt. The senseless rage as quickly passed. To shoot the man would gain him nothing, and a gunshot would give the alarm. They would smell him out like blood-lusting wolves.

He lay there, seething, fuming at his helplessness, and of a sudden he remembered something about the roan horse that brought a thin smile to his lips. Roany was temperamental, subject to frenzied outbursts. The touch of a fluttering leaf, an unexpected slap, anything that took him by surprise would often send him into a wild orgy of bucking.

Adam reached for a small flinty stone, his gaze on the man lolling at his ease in the saddle, leg dangling free of stirrup, his hands busy with the cigarette.

Hardly daring to breathe, Adam measured the distance, sent the sharp-edged stone whizzing at the roan's rump. It was a good throw, and Roany's reaction was instantaneous. He went into the air with a startled snort, hit the ground stiff-legged, and then really exploded. The second jump sent the man flying from the saddle, and the outraged horse went bucking and pitching on his way up the gorge in the direction taken by the chuckwagon.

The outlaw staggered to his feet and screaming curses went limping in pursuit, unaware of

Adam's grinning face peering down from behind the bush.

Another rider whirled around the lower bend and overtook the unhorsed one. "What the hell's goin' on, Farg?" The newcomer drew to a plunging halt.

"That damn bronc went loco, got to pitchin' when I wasn't lookin'," grumbled the man. He rubbed a bruised knee. "Go git yore rope on him, Tod. I shore ain't chasin' him afoot the way my laig hurts."

The other man nodded curtly. "Climb up," he said. "Them dogies is comin' fast." He loosened his rope. "Hell of a time to lose your bronc," he added disgustedly.

"I'll bust him proper," fumed Farg. He climbed awkwardly up behind Tod. "Feel like my laig is broke," he complained. "I shore crave to take the hell out of that bronc."

"Got to catch him, first," reminded Tod, a hint of a sneer in his quiet voice. He was a long, lean man, dark and tight-lipped and his eyes had the watchful quality of a predatory hawk.

"I ain't losin' that saddle," Farg said angrily. "I *got* to catch him."

Adam watched them go with some misgivings. He was too soft. He should have killed them while he had the chance. They were a dangerous pair of renegades, especially the soft-spoken trail boss. He knew men, recognized the qualities that made Tod a tough and ruthless enemy. Had the position been reversed, Tod would not have hesitated to squeeze the trigger, shoot him down in cold blood.

The cattle were coming up with a rush. Adam lay there on the bluff, watched the bawling herd pass.

He raged at his helplessness. These were JM cattle, more than two thousand of them, and he could do nothing, only lie there tortured almost beyond endurance at this wholesale rustling under his very nose. Any attempt to interfere meant certain disaster. He had to think of his grandfather—of Linda Seton. He was their one hope.

The men riding swing had fallen back when the herd entered the pass, and now came up with the drag. Adam checked them as they rode by. Seventeen men in the outfit, counting the cook. A formidable crew, all of them strangers, and riding JM horses.

Adam wondered gloomily about the fate of the old JM men. Celestino Baca was dead, old Bill Clemm in hiding, recovering from his wounds. Others of the outfit were probably dead, murdered, certain old-timers it would be impossible to hoodwink. The weeding would have been skillfully done. Cowboys were not too curious. A man was fired from the payroll and that was the end of it. One thing was certain, the old crew was gone, scattered, and no man of them would know the truth.

Adam lit a cigarette, sat there in the deepening twilight. An idea was shaping in his mind, and he wanted to think it out. Something to do with the conversation between Farg and the cook. Farg had said that Tod planned to hold the herd on the flats two miles west of the pass.

Excitement began to stir in Adam. Perhaps he was crazy, but there was just a chance he could cause Tod a lot of trouble during the darkness, after the big herd was bedded down. Crazy or not, the scheme was worth a try.

He went hastily back to his horse and swung into the saddle. He would have time to get out to the ranch and have a cautious look at things there, perhaps get in touch with his grandfather, or at the least find out if old John Marshall was still alive. It was impossible to make definite plans until he knew more of the situation. In the meantime he had some eight or nine hours.

He kept the bay moving at a fast clip through the pass, eyes alert, gun eased in its holster. It was possible he might run into somebody, a delayed member of the outfit riding to overtake the trail-herd.

Darkness came down, and he rode under the hard glitter of the stars. Adam was glad for the darkness. It was a help, rather than a hindrance.

Here on the old home ranch he could find his way around blindfolded.

The glimpse of the tall trees looming out of the blackness sent a lump into his throat. His grandfather had planted them, seen them achieve their stateliness. John Marshall had made this ranch, wrested it from the untouched wilderness, fought red men and white to preserve it, stood indomitably under crushing blows of drought and storm and financial stress.

Adam sat rigid in his saddle, fierce resolve in his eyes. Not while life was in him would he give up the fight. He too, was a Marshall.

He swung to the left and rode toward the corrals until he came to a deep gully in the rear of the barn. There was a small spring there and he was anxious to water the horse. The place would be easy to reach if he had to get away in a hurry.

Something moved, down there in the little gully, a dark shape, hardly visible in the blanketing night. The bay's head went up, ears pricked forward, and suddenly Adam knew that what he saw was another horse, come to the spring to drink.

He pulled quickly into the shadows of a bush, got down from his saddle, and crawled stealthily along the gully for a closer look. The horse turned away from the spring, began to nibble at the grass, and Adam made out a saddle on him. He grinned. Roany had lost no time heading back for the home ranch.

He moved nearer, spoke the roan's name. The horse nickered softly, made no attempt to run as Adam took hold of his bridle. It was plain that he had not forgotten Adam during the long months of absence. Adam tied him to a sapling alder that grew near the spring. He was thinking of Bill Clemm. Here was a horse for Bill. He had planned to try and get a horse for the sick foreman, and the roan was Bill's own favorite. For some mysterious reason, Bill was the one man in the outfit Roany never got temperamental with.

Adam watered his own horse, tied him in the alder thicket near the roan, and went stealthily up the slope to the network of corrals. He noticed several horses in the small horse corral, was tempted to turn them loose, but abandoned the idea as dangerous. For his grandfather's sake he must not let these men know he had been prowling around. Turning the horses loose would be sure to arouse their suspicions.

Lamplight glimmered from the bunkhouse windows, otherwise there was no sign of life in the big ranch yard. Adam slipped into the darkness under the tall trees and made his way to the house, a low, rambling structure inside a high-walled garden.

Adam halted, gaze on the glow of lamplight in the kitchen windows. He heard noises that told him the cook was washing the supper dishes. The other windows on this side of the house were dark. The dining room, the big living room, and the ranch office. The bedrooms were on the other side, five of them in a long wing that opened on a veranda his grandfather always called the gallery.

The rattle of dishes ceased and the cook suddenly appeared in the open doorway of the kitchen. Adam, inside the gate now, ducked behind a bush.

The cook was evidently finished with his work. He stood there, a dark bulky shape against the yellow lamplight, and the flare of a match as he lit a cigarette briefly showed a fat face and untidy drooping mustache.

He jerked at apron strings, threw the apron aside, and came out on the porch. The movement allowed the lamplight to flow from the doorway and touch his face. Adam guessed from his speculative frown that the man was debating some plan of considerable interest to himself.

A shadow crossed the doorway behind the deliberating cook. He turned his head. "Figger I'll set in at that game over to the bunkhouse, Rosa. Shore crave to git back some of that *dinero* Pete took off of me last night."

"*Sí*—you go—"

Adam felt his heart turn over. Rosa Baca's voice. Rosa was there—in the house. He could hardly believe his ears.

"I've set my potato yeast to rise. Was figgerin', you'd mebbe keep a eye on it," the cook said.

"*Sí*—I watch for you," assented the woman's voice.

"Shore white of you, Rosa—" The cook descended the porch steps and pushed through the gate into the yard. Adam was thankful for the blanketing darkness. He could have reached out and touched the man as he passed.

He waited until he heard the slam of the bunkhouse door, the brief chorus of men's voices greeting the newcomer, and then swiftly went up the steps and into the big kitchen.

Rosa was moving toward the hall door, her back to him, and not even her keen ears had heard his soundless entrance. He spoke her name, softly.

The woman halted abruptly. She seemed hardly to breathe, and slowly, almost fearfully she turned, looked at him.

Adam's quick gesture stopped the scream that trembled on her lips. He said in Spanish, his voice hardly above a whisper. "Rosa—quick—into the hall. I must not be seen—"

She gazed at him with dilated eyes, and the fright in them was suddenly replaced with an incredulous joy. Her face began to work, and she said in a hushed, dazed whisper, "*Adamito! Ave María Purísima!*" Her hand went to her breast. "But you are not a ghost, Adamito?"

He was on her swiftly, his arms around her in a tight hug. "Not a ghost, Rosa—but quick—

before somebody comes!" He pushed her into the dark hall, pulled the door shut.

The feel of him pressed close to her side reassured her. She held his hand tight. "It is a miracle, Adamito. We have thought you dead these long months."

He squeezed her hand. "No. Not dead—" His head was lowered so he could look into her face. Her eyes, wet with tears, were luminous in that darkness. "Rosa—my grandfather—"

"He still lives, Adamito—"

Adam spoke again, his voice puzzled. "Why are you still here in this house, Rosa? You are the only one who has stayed, been allowed to stay."

"I told them they would have to kill me," answered the Mexican woman. "Not while I live will I leave the old señor alone in their wicked hands." Her voice choked. "My Celestino—I do not know where he is gone. He does not return."

Adam had not the heart to tell her that Celestino was dead. Perhaps she divined the truth from his silence. She said simply, "If he is dead, it is because he was brave."

"He was brave," Adam said very gently.

Rosa understood, was silent for a moment, and then, "Come—I will take you to the old señor." She paused, her hand tightening over his. "They do not want him to die—yet, and because they do not want him to die they let me stay with him, look after him. It is all very strange, Adamito. I do not understand why they don't want him to die."

"You say *they*, Rosa. Who are these people you call *they*?"

Rosa shook her head. "I know nothing, Adamito. Only that they are very wicked. There is one who comes who does not want me to see his face. They lock me up in my room, your old room, which I use to be near the señor. I have listened with my ears to the wall, and you know my ears. They hear the fall of a pin. This one who comes and hides his face from me has a strange voice, a low, whispering voice that makes me think of the Evil One who reigns in hell. My flesh creeps and I hold the Blessed Cross to my heart to drive this terrible fear from me." Rosa spoke rapidly, in a tone so low that Adam could hardly hear her. Also his mind was already in the room on the other side of the door.

He said, urgently, "Yes, yes, but open the door." His heart was pounding, and he snatched the key from her fingers, inserted it shakily in the lock.

12
MARSHALL MEN

Adam paused in the doorway, and his look went swiftly to the great bed between the tall windows. He was suddenly moving, and on his knees, hand groping across the covers until they touched and closed over the hand of the man lying there.

He felt the hand tighten over his, and John Marshall opened his eyes, said quietly, *"Adam!"*

Adam could hardly believe his senses. Words refused to come.

John Marshall seemed to guess his amazement. He said, grim amusement in his voice. "Yes, boy, I've got my speech back, and I can use my hands. I'm keeping that gang of killers fooled. I don't want 'em to know."

"Can you walk?" Adam tried to keep his voice steady. "I'll get you out of this tonight—"

The soft glow from the low-turned lamp showed the old cattleman's face, lined, haggard—his suddenly grim expression.

"No, boy. Not tonight or any night. These scoundrels are not going to drive me from my own home. They'll get this ranch only over my dead body."

"I've only got a few minutes," Adam said. "I hate to leave you here."

"They'll not kill me—yet." The old cowman spoke calmly. "They're waiting for me to get the use of my hands . . . got a deed all fixed up for me to sign." He paused. "Got an extra gun on you, boy?"

Adam remembered the gun he had confiscated from the stableman. He produced it, laid it in Marshall's hand.

"Feels mighty good," the old man said. "Stick it under the pillow for me, Adam. I'll maybe find use for it." His hand again tightened in an iron grip on Adam's. "I was told you were dead, but I kept on hoping. We Marshalls are mighty tough, and when trouble's in the saddle we sure go to war. You're a Marshall, boy. You'll be dead too, before those scoundrels get our ranch away from us." He added softly, "Knew the feel of your hand the moment you touched me. It felt good—*good*."

"I've been too long getting here," Adam said bitterly. "I don't know yet what is back of all this hell."

"Tell me your end of it," rumbled his grandfather.

"I want to get you away from here," insisted Adam. "Rosa and I can carry you across the front garden to the avenue. Or can you walk?"

"No, I can't use my legs—yet, and if I could I wouldn't use 'em to run away. Forget it, boy."

"I'll catch up a team. We can use the buckboard," urged Adam. A desperate plan was shaping in his mind. He would get the jump on the card-players in the bunkhouse, shoot them down before they could reach for their guns. The advantage of surprise would be his.

"I told you I'm not running away," growled the old cowman. Impatience was in his voice. "I'm waiting to hear about this Rio Grande mixup."

"I wrote you three letters," Adam told him.

"Letters don't reach this ranch any more," John Marshall said grimly. "JM is cut off from the outside world, and has been from the time I got word you were drowned in the river."

"I sent a messenger from San Carlos," Adam went on. "He came back with a story of a man who claimed he was Adam Marshall."

"I wasn't told about any messenger," growled the old cattleman.

"Have you ever heard of an outlaw known as Brazos Jack?"

The old cowman nodded, his face stern.

"He's the man who claims he is Adam Marshall. Looks like me at first glance."

"He's kin to you, Adam. Not very close. There was a fool Marshall girl ran off with a no-'count half-breed renegade. This hombre is her grandson, and he's hang-tree fruit."

"I can't make head nor tail of this thing," Adam muttered. "It's incredible!"

"This stroke I had left things wide open," explained his grandfather. "I've a notion the gang is sitting pretty in Dos Ríos—run that damn cowtown to suit themselves."

"You think Monte Cline was murdered?"

"Sure, Monte was murdered. This ranch is isolated, Adam. They were smart, let folks see me those first few weeks when I was so paralyzed I couldn't speak. Jim Oland of the JO came, and half a dozen other old-timers. They could look at me and that was all. I couldn't speak, tell 'em I was a prisoner in my own house. They always took care to keep Rosa locked away out of sight."

"Anybody who knows me wouldn't be fooled by Brazos Jack, or whatever his real name is," argued Adam.

"His name is Adam right enough." The cattleman grimaced. "The half-breed scoundrel that sired him was hung for horse-stealing before the worthless pup was born. His fool mother was never properly married and so the kid took her name of Marshall. Calls himself Ad Marshall down here."

"He's Brazos Jack, and he's a killer," Adam said angrily.

"Sure he's Brazos Jack. I knew him the minute I laid eyes on him. Wasn't easy, lying here, listening to him talk about being my grandson. I couldn't let anybody know he was a damn liar. When Jim Oland and the others came to see me he kept out of sight. All they know is you weren't drowned after all and that you're back on the ranch taking good care of your dying grandpa."

"You're damn right I'm back!" Adam's voice was husky, "and you're not a dying grandpa, either!"

"Not this time," smiled the old cowman. "We'll show these wolves, huh, boy?"

Rosa's hand was light on Adam's shoulder and she said softly, "You are very tired, Adamito, and very hungry. I can tell by your voice."

"Haven't eaten in twenty-four hours," he admitted. "Things have kept me on the jump."

"I will bring food—" Rosa hesitated, pressed her hand warningly on him. "Be careful lest men come and find you here."

The admonition seemed to amuse John Marshall. "Don't need to tell him that, Rosa," he chuckled.

They waited until the door closed quietly behind her. Marshall broke the brief silence. "Was afraid to ask in front of her," he said in a troubled voice. "I'm awfully worried about Bill—and Celestino. Not a word from them since the day those scoundrels showed up."

Adam told him briefly of his encounter with Bill Clemm in Sombrio Canyon, the foreman's discovery of Rosa's slain husband.

"I was sure those two wouldn't run off and

leave me," muttered the old cattleman. "Poor old Celestino. I hate to tell Rosa."

"She's guessed it," Adam said. He continued, told of the trail-herd in Wild Horse Pass, the recovery of the roan horse from the rustlers.

"I'm heading back to the canyon as soon as I leave here," he said. "If Bill can sit a saddle I'll have him fork Roany and hightail it for Jim Oland's place with the real news of what's going on here at JM."

"Jim won't be home," Marshall said doubtfully. "He'll be in Willcox by now. The Cattlemen's Association meets there this week. Most of the old-timers will be on hand."

"Johnny Wilson will be on the job. Johnny and Bill are old friends, and Johnny used to be a JM man before Jim Oland took him on as foreman."

"It's an idea, boy," agreed Marshall.

"We'll have a hundred fighting men headed for the JM, once the news spreads." Adam spoke confidently. "It's only a matter of time, and I'm scared. This gang knows I'm loose, and I get scared about you, what they might do to you. They won't want to leave you alive—to tell what you know."

His grandfather's face hardened, took on stubborn lines. "I'm staying here, boy."

"What do they want out of you? Forcing you to sign a deed to the ranch won't do them any good."

Marshall shook his head. "If you happen to die, and they'll do their best to kill you, a deed will give them undisputed ownership to the ranch and everything on it. They've got to have the deed because Brazos Jack can't hope to pass himself off as my grandson forever. Once the deed is signed he'll disappear, and you'll again be reported dead. They'll stop at nothing to get you, Adam. The plot calls for both of us to die."

"Sounds crazy," muttered Adam. "It's the truth, though, and the thing began months ago, when I went to Presidio on that cattle deal."

"Goes back further than that," John Marshall said. "But go on, boy. Tell me about it."

Adam gave him the highlights. His grandfather listened without comment until he came to the meeting with Linda Seton in Dos Ríos.

"I've been worrying about that girl," he said somberly. "Thought it was JM that burned her out, huh?"

"She took Brazos Jack's word for it that he was Adam Marshall. She had no reason to think different."

"She's not thinking that way now, boy?"

"No," answered Adam. "She knows the truth, knows that I'm your grandson."

"Stand by her, Adam."

"Don't think that I won't," Adam said in a low voice.

John Marshall looked at him sharply, and content came to his eyes as he studied the younger man. He said softly, "She's a good girl, Adam. She's what I'd want for you. Knew it the minute I laid eyes on her. She's got what it takes for this country. I told her so."

Adam was silent, but it was not a silence that disturbed his grandfather. He smiled to himself, there in the darkness, and his next words returned them to Brazos Jack. "He's not the brains of this business. He's only the hands—a hireling killer, and so damn like you that the brains found him useful."

Adam recalled Rosa's words. *This one who comes and hides his face . . . a low whispering voice that makes me think of the Evil One who reigns in hell.*

He said grimly, "The man with the whispering voice. He's the brains. Is that right?"

"How did you guess?" Marshall's voice showed surprise.

"Rosa told me about him. She's never seen him, only heard his whispering voice. Makes her flesh creep, she says."

"He's a devil, and the son of a cow thief I dangled from a tree years ago." The cowman spoke slowly, his voice a hoarse whisper. "It was years before you were born. He swore to even the score, saw his chance when he met up with Brazos Jack. A cunning and dangerous man who cloaks his black heart under a mask of kindly benevolence you'd look for in a parson."

"I don't know any such man," fumed Adam.

"You wouldn't, having been away from Dos Ríos these many months. He bought Pete Cline's store in Dos Ríos. I didn't know, until it was too late. He came out to the ranch after my stroke, gloated over me, told me his plans. He was so sure of himself, then."

Adam's face was a mask of horror, and peering at him, his grandfather sensed the dreadful dismay in him.

"You've run into him already, boy?"

Adam shook his head, forced himself to speak. "Linda—Linda Seton trusts him. She told me he was good to her . . . her friend."

A long sigh came from the old man on the bed. He closed his eyes, and after a moment, said quietly, "Get her away from Dos Ríos, Adam. Don't you waste time with me. You ride like hell and take that girl over to the JO. Jim will keep her safe, and she won't be safe in Dos Ríos."

Adam was recalling those last moments at the *cantina*. Al Deen had picked up the trail. He would know that Linda Seton was there. His grandfather was right. He must get the girl away—take her to Jim Oland's ranch.

"I'm on my way," he said hoarsely. He stood up, was suddenly aware of Rosa standing by his side. In his distraction he had not heard her entrance.

"Here are sandwiches, Adamito, good beef and bread, and a pot of hot coffee."

"I can't wait," he protested frantically.

"Don't be a fool!" rasped John Marshall. "A man can't fight on an empty belly. You eat that food. You'll need it for mind and body."

"*Sí*," whispered the Mexican woman. "The señor knows best, Adamito. He is wise."

Adam stood silent, crammed a sandwich into his mouth, chewed it down, obediently drained the cup of coffee Rosa gave him. The food and hot drink steadied him, and he thought of Bill Clemm, loyal old Bill, wounded, living like a hunted wild animal, a cave his shelter, his food what the wilderness provided.

He said to Rosa, "Throw some provisions in a sack for me. Bread, bacon, coffee." He met her questioning look, added gently, "I found Bill Clemm. He's in bad shape—been shot."

The faint hope in her eyes faded and she went swiftly from the room.

Adam bit into a second sandwich. There was a brightness in his face, a cold purpose in his eyes. The momentary panic was gone and his mind was functioning with the precision of a perfectly balanced machine. He knew just what he was going to do and the details were fast taking shape, falling into their proper places, a clearly outlined blueprint of action.

His grandfather watched him, sensed the decisions forming in him. He said quietly, "It's the mind, now, boy, and courage to back the mind. You're a Marshall and you have mind and courage."

Adam grinned. "You doggone old longhorn!" He tried to throw lightness into his voice, could not conceal his deep affection, the admiration he felt.

John Marshall grinned back at him. "No moss on my horns, young feller."

"You keep 'em too sharp," smiled Adam.

"I'm not asking questions," continued the cattleman. "I'm leaving your end of it to you. I reckon you know which end of the rope to pick up."

"I'd have liked to get you out of here," Adam told him. "You know best about what *you* want to do." He paused, eyes narrowed thoughtfully. "What you've told me about the storekeeper fits a lot of pieces into the puzzle. Linda Seton calls him Mr. Berren. I'm wondering if he's the man I heard Sam Doan speak of as Newt."

Old Marshall nodded. "That's him. Newt Berren."

"Sam Doan is scared to death of him," Adam said. He added purposefully, "Sam is going to be more scared of me."

"I wouldn't have thought Sam would turn crooked," muttered his grandfather.

"He's yellow," Adam said contemptuously.

"Don't be too quick to judge him, boy." The old man's voice was oddly gentle. "We don't know about Sam—yet. Looks mighty bad for him, but we don't know all that's back of it. I've known Sam a lot of years."

Rosa was suddenly in the room, a partly filled flour sack in her hand. She thrust it at Adam. "Somebody comes," she whispered. "I think it is the cook. Quick, Adamito." She gestured at a window. "Sometimes he comes in here and looks at the señor. He watches us both like a hawk."

Adam nodded, moved quietly to the window, which was open, the shade drawn. He glanced back at the Mexican woman. "Rosa—you are brave, too—"

She gave him a smile, eyes suddenly bright with tears, and her hand went inside her dress, drew out a thin-bladed dagger. "It is his—my Celestino's," she whispered. "I will use it if they try to harm the señor." She gestured again for him to go, bent quickly to the lamp, and blew out its dim light.

Adam cautiously raised the shade, and Rosa saw his tall shape vanish through the window into the starlit night. She crossed herself, and her lips moved. "*Vaya con Dios, Adamito mio.*" She crossed herself again, bent down to relight the lamp.

13
ACTION BY NIGHT

The moon was well up, and Adam could make out the dark blur of the massed herd, the chuckwagon beyond, and the slow-moving shapes of the circling night men.

He halted under a shadowing bluff and gazed for long moments at the scene. He had a job to do here. A single mistake might easily prove fatal. There would be no opportunity for a second try. He would be dead.

The little mesa lay between the two low ridges and sloped down to the willow brakes of the creek on the west. The country reaching to the east was a bewildering maze of canyons and gullies, a cowman's nightmare. It was plain that the rustlers were unfamiliar with the terrain or Tod would not have risked holding the cattle on the mesa.

Adam's lips twisted in a mirthless grin. He had the advantage of knowledge gained from a lifetime in this rugged country. If he worked the thing right it would take days and weeks to comb the cattle out of that labyrinth of canyons and there would be no drive to the Mexican border.

Keeping well in to the bluffs that covered him

from the moonlight, Adam reached the brakes and forded the shallow stream. The roan horse, with the sack of food tied to the saddle, followed freely on his lead-rope.

He found the place he wanted, a small clearing behind a fallen mass of boulders and within a hundred yards of the trail that plunged down the steep slope of Sombrio Canyon.

In a few minutes he was back in the brakes on the other side of the creek and cautiously crawling through the chaparral toward the sleeping herd.

A rider drifted up through the moonlight. Adam recognized Farg, the man Roany had pitched from his saddle. The rustler was singing dolefully to the cattle, telling them about some cowboy who would *never see Texas no more, for his bones now lay white on the Grande's bleak shore.*

Adam flattened behind a greasewood. He would have liked to make certain that the singer never saw Texas or any other place again. A senseless, childish impulse that annoyed him. Killing from ambush was not in his code, and he was here for more important business. Also it was essential for these rustlers not to suspect he had been in the vicinity of the camp. He must not do anything that might increase his grandfather's peril. It was imperative for them to believe the stampede was just one of those things that happen to a trail-herd.

Farg halted his horse, and now Adam made out the shape of another rider circling in from the opposite direction.

Farg addressed him grumblingly as he drew alongside. "Shore wish the relief men would show up. I crave to git me some shut-eye."

"Ain't time, yet," answered the newcomer. A match flared between his fingers, showed a lean, unshaven face as he lit a cigarette. "Got any likker left in that flask you got hid in yore shirt?"

"Reckon so." Farg spoke grumpily. "A couple of swallers, mebbe." He reluctantly drew the flask from the inside of his shirt. "Go easy on it, feller," he begged. "I'm cravin' *some* of that likker my own self."

"I ain't no hawg," indignantly retorted the man. He tipped the flask to his lips, handed it back with a contented grunt. "Shore got a kick, that stuff."

Farg took a long swallow, returned the flask to its secret place inside his shirt, and leisurely shaped a cigarette. "Listen, Slim, me and you is plain dumb," he said thickly.

"How come we're plain dumb?" Slim was inclined to be resentful. "You leave me out of this dumb stuff."

"I'm claimin' we're dumb," insisted Farg. "Me and you both. Ain't no sense for the two of us to be ridin' circle, the way this herd lays so quiet."

"You just let Tod hear you say that," jeered

Slim. "He'd shore tie a can to you." He grinned. "You're hittin' that flask too frequent."

"Tod's snorin' his head off, and what he don't see he don't know," argued Farg. "I figger to git even with that skunk, bawlin' me out like he done." The rustler loosed an oath. "Don't savvy yet how come that damn bronc got to pitchin' so crazy."

"Git back to yore big idee," rasped Slim impatiently.

Farg leered at him. "I figger to git me some shut-eye while you make a round. When you git back, I'll do the same for you."

Slim considered the proposition, eyes narrowed at his companion. He said slowly, "Hand over that flask, Farg, and it's a deal."

"You shore like a bargain," sneered Farg. He handed over the flask and got down from his horse, stood watching until Slim became a phantom shape in the moonlight. A grin slowly creased his hard face, and his hand dipped again inside his shirt, drew out another flask.

"Shore lucky Slim didn't know I had two of 'em," he exulted aloud. "He'd have tried to skin both of 'em off me, the damn skunk."

He took several long pulls at the flask, returned it to his shirt, and stretched out full length under a boulder. He was snoring almost instantly, and Adam got cautiously to his feet, gaze fixed on the horse, a short ten yards away, motionless, head drooping, reins dangling on the ground.

What to do had been something of a puzzle, and up to this moment Adam had been letting things ride, waiting for his opportunity. Thanks to the snoring, half-drunk Farg, the opportunity was ready for him to seize. He couldn't have asked for a better chance. Also there was an angle reminiscent of his earlier encounter with Farg that made Adam grin as he moved stealthily to the renegade's horse.

The smile faded when he got close enough to read the brand. He was familiar with every horse in the JM remuda, and this was a JM. For a fleeting instant the purpose in Adam faltered. The affair was going to be painful for this unsuspecting horse, and quite different from the trick that had sent Roany into a fit of bucking hysterics.

It was no time to give way to compunction, and with two quick motions he slid the vicious cactus spikes under the saddle blanket, gave the horse a gentle, apologetic pat, and stole quietly away.

He reached a small knoll covered with greasewood and decided he had gone far enough. He could stand there, screened from observation, and wait for Slim to rejoin his fellow nighthawk.

Faint sounds came from the vicinity of the chuckwagon where the rustlers made cocoon shapes in their rolled blankets. The relief men were reluctantly bestirring themselves. Matches flared as cigarettes were lit and he could see the men now, vague shadows moving toward the horse cavvy inside the makeshift rope corral. It was apparent that the night-wrangler had brought the cavvy in soon after midnight, which indicated that Tod planned to have the herd moving at the first crack of dawn, if not sooner.

More sounds drifted over from the camp, the glow of a lantern sprang up and Adam saw the cook staring dejectedly at the cold ashes of his fire, heard his gruff voice angrily demanding that somebody go drag up some wood. The signs were plain now. The rustler foreman was not waiting for daylight. He was in a hurry to point the stolen herd for the border.

Adam began to yearn for Slim's return. He wanted action now, fast and furious and demoralizing. A few minutes delay could spoil everything for him. As it stood, the setup was perfect, the camp between the herd and the *malpais*. The fuse was laid and hell was due to explode in the faces of that rustlers' outfit.

To his vast relief he spied Slim cutting across to his sleeping companion. He was too far away to hear the man's words, but it was plain that he was annoyed. He slid from his saddle and prodded Farg with the toe of his boot, gesticulating vehemently toward the camp.

Farg got to his feet and climbed hurriedly into his saddle. The horse moved off, stiff-legged, ears laid back. Slim, idly watching, reached for his flask.

Adam began to worry, then suddenly, as Farg's weight drove in the stabbing thorns, the horse exploded under him.

Farg let out a surprised yell as the horse went bucking wildly into the herd. The third jump sent the rustler hurtling from the saddle.

Adam held his breath. In an instant the thing was done, the cattle up in one billowing motion and surging frenziedly toward the *malpais*. A massive, deep-roaring tidal wave swept over the rustlers' camp, scattering men and horses like spray. Tails up, four thousand hooves pounding the hard earth, the big herd thundered into the distance.

Slim's horse was in full flight, following Farg's still wildly bucking animal. Farg was on his feet, staggering around like a man bereft of his senses. Slim, after a frantic dash to catch his horse, had abruptly halted, stood there, flask tilted to his lips.

The damage at the camp was complete, the chuckwagon overturned and lying on its side, the demoralized rustlers shouting curses as their dazed eyes saw the horse cavvy vanish into the night.

A tall shape came limping toward the half-crazed Farg. Adam recognized the foreman, obviously in a towering rage.

"What in hell's got into you, Farg?" Tod was screaming like a maniac. "Cain't you stick on a bronc no more? Look what you done!"

Farg stared around stupidly, saw a boulder and sat on it, put his head between his hands.

"The whole damn cavvy lit out!" stormed the rustler foreman. "We're left afoot!"

Farg leaped to his feet, fists clenched to the sky. "I'm quittin'!" he yelled. "These here JM broncs is spooked or somethin'. Been forking broncs since I was weaned and never got throwed thisaways before. Somethin' doggone funny goin' on and I ain't standin' for you to lay it on me."

Adam left them shouting curses at each other. He had done a good job, struck a devastating blow. The scoundrels were thoroughly demoralized. They were in for a lot of trouble catching up their horses. In the meantime the stampeded cattle were lost for weeks to come in a vast and bewildering maze of gorges. Few men knew their way about in this rugged and remote country. He did, and Bill Clemm and perhaps a scant half-dozen of the old JM outfit, including Sam Doan. He would have to do something about Sam, make certain he did not help the rustlers comb those canyons for the lost herd.

He was relieved to find Bill Clemm on the watch for him. The JM foreman grinned appreciatively when he saw the sack of food.

"I figgered you'd mebbe head back this way,"

he said. He peered hungrily into the sack. "Cawfee, huh, and bacon. Mighty fine of you to think of me, son. Tobacco, too. Was sure cravin' a smoke."

He listened with grim attention to Adam's brief account of his activities. "You're smart, son. Couldn't have done better my own self. I reckon them rustlin' wolves is a mighty sick bunch and wonderin' what in hell happened to 'em."

Adam told him about the plan for him to ride to the Oland ranch. "How about it, Bill? Can you make it? It's a long ride."

"Sure I can make it," Bill assured him. "I'm tough, son. Just kind of weak for some decent grub right now." He looked longingly at the sack. "Just as quick as I've fixed me a pot of cawfee and a bacon sandwich I'll fork Roany and be on my way."

"It's a hard ride," worried Adam. "You're in bad shape, Bill. I wouldn't ask you, only I can't go myself. I've got to get to Dos Ríos in a hurry. No telling what's happened to that girl."

The old foreman eyed him shrewdly. "You get movin', son. I ain't so stove-up but what I can set a saddle. Should make the JO come next sundown." He chuckled. "She's a right nice gal if she and her pa *did* run a sheep outfit."

Adam grinned. "You old sheep-hating range hog!"

The cowman's eyes twinkled. "You hightail it

away from here, son." His weathered face sobered and he added gently, "I reckon she's a mighty good argument for sheep at that. Your grandpa sure took to her." He nodded emphatically. "Me, too, son, me, too—"

Adam said in a low voice, "I'm thinking the same way, Bill. *Me, too*—" He gave his old friend an affectionate grin and swung his tired horse back to the trail.

As dawn flowed over the eastern hills, he came again into the canyon of the Rio Blanco and close to the brush-covered entrance to the ancient smuggler's cave. He found a small clearing with plenty of nourishing grass, and a seepage of water, probably from Moraga's spring, enough for the horse to quench his thirst.

Adam stripped off the saddle gear, put the leg-weary bay on a rope, and left him to do the best he could for himself. The horse deserved better treatment after the long, grueling ride to the ranch and back. He would have to turn him over to Severino Moraga's care. Severino could arrange for one of his Mexican friends to stable the animal. One thing was certain, he was going to need a fresh horse, and a horse for Linda. He would ask Severino to arrange for them, have them waiting in the canyon.

Adam hurried now, and soon he was in the cave and climbing up the dark and narrow passage. He would bring Linda down through the same passage. It offered the only safe way of escape from the town. It was going to be very necessary for Severino to arrange to have the horses waiting near the cave.

He came to the short, steep ladder under the trap door and felt a momentary panic. He was going to be out of luck if Severino kept the thing locked. The thought sent chills down his spine.

He went up the ladder and pushed lightly on the trap. It was either stuck, or locked.

Adam pushed harder, felt the trap move. He tried again, and the heavy stone slab slowly tilted. He got one hand on the edge of the floor, kept on pushing with his other hand until suddenly the massive block of stone shifted to one side.

He scrambled into the little room, stood for a moment to get his breath, his gaze on the door that he knew opened on the patio. There were no windows, only a small grating that let in a glimmer of the gray dawn. He was remembering something about that small, heavy door. Severino had used a key. This place was the closely guarded secret entrance to the underground runway once used by the old Mexican's smuggling ancestors. Severino was not likely to leave that door unlocked.

His attempt to open the door proved his guess correct, and impatient now, Adam drew his gun and rapped the steel barrel sharply against the planking.

Somebody was sure to hear the noise. He hoped it would be Severino. He was reluctant to betray Severino's secret by attracting the attention of anyone not in the Mexican's confidence, although it was more than probable the place was known to all the members of his household. The tunnel was a secret to be kept only from *Americanos*.

Adam rapped again, harder this time, and now his alert ears heard the soft stirring of approaching feet, and suddenly a low, cautious voice.

"*Quien es?*"

"Let me out," whispered Adam. "Quick—Severino."

He heard an astonished "*Por Dios*," the lock clicked, and the door opened, framing the innkeeper's amazed face. "*Por Dios!*" he repeated. "It is *you,* Adamito!"

Even as he stepped outside, Adam sensed tragedy in the old Mexican's seamed brown face. He waited until Severino closed and relocked the door.

"What's wrong, *amigo?*" He asked the question quietly, hopelessly, like one who already knew the answer.

"She is gone, Adamito." Severino gestured expressively. "I can tell you nothing more—only that the señorita has vanished. I have looked for her, our friends have looked for her. We cannot find her."

"Gone?" Adam's voice was a whispered groan.

"*Sí—*" Severino Moraga gestured again. "Through that little gate—and she did not come back."

14

TERROR

Linda opened her eyes. Something had happened. . . . She couldn't quite remember, and now somebody was holding a glass to her lips. It was all she could see for the moment, the glass, and the fingers holding it, big-knuckled fingers covered with coarse black hairs. It was whiskey in the glass and some of it was in her mouth. She shuddered, choked, pushed the glass away and it slipped from the hairy fingers and splintered on the floor.

She heard a muttered exclamation, a raspy whispering voice, and now she sat bolt upright in the chair. The man standing in front of her was Mr. Berren, and his eyes in their deep sockets were not human. They were cold, malignant, the eyes of a snake, and were things apart from the gentle, benevolent smile on his bearded face.

"You fainted, Miss Linda. We carried you into my sitting room back of the store." Berren's eyes shifted for a moment, fastened on somebody standing just out of her view. She turned her head, saw that he was the cowboy she had noticed on the hotel steps. At least he was dressed like a cowboy, and the face under the wide-brimmed hat was darkly sunburned. A hard face, with watchful, callous eyes.

The storekeeper spoke to him in his husky, whispering voice. "Get hold of Sam Doan, will you, Bert. Tell him I want him over here right away."

Linda, her eyes again closed, heard the quick rap of the man's high-heeled boots as he hurried away. She was feeling sick and her head was spinning. It seemed she had fainted, which was silly of her. She had never fainted before in her life. She was not that kind of girl. The dreadful night—those frightening hours in the chaparral, the darkness, must have broken down her nervous system more than she realized. And then the shock of the hideous truth about Mr. Berren. It had been too much. She had a right to faint.

Berren was speaking again, and she saw that he was holding another glass to her lips. "It will do you good, Miss Linda. You look awful white in the face—"

The real concern in his voice was shocking to her unbelieving ears. This monster pretending pity for her. She began to feel a ghastly horror of that low whispering voice. It did not belong to the wide, red-lipped mouth, the white teeth that gleamed behind the beard as he coaxingly smiled. That mouth with its array of teeth was made for wolfish snarls. She must have been blind not to have noticed it before, realized these oddities about the man. His benevolence was a pretense, a mask behind which crouched a black and loathsome *thing*. It came to her vaguely that here was the source of the evil that had engulfed her, thrown its dark shadow over the Marshall ranch. This man was responsible, and she had counted him a friend, walked like a little fool into his deadly clutches.

She brushed feebly at the glass. "You—you told him to kill the dog."

"It was to save you, Miss Linda—" His tone was gentle, forbearing. "The dog was mad, preparing to attack you. Fred got the rope on him just in time." The square, bearded face nodded. "Only one thing to do with a mad dog. That's why I told Fred to shoot him."

"You—you hypocrite," Linda said contemptuously. With returning strength anger grew in her, put a clear, hard ring in her voice. "I'm not deceived any more, Mr. Berren. It was the shock of finding you out that made me faint."

Her outburst left him unperturbed. "Now, Miss Linda. You're too upset to think right about me. I'm your friend and you've no need to be frightened. I have fine plans for you." He nodded again. "We'll get along awful well together. I like you, Miss Linda. Took a liking to you the first time you came into the store."

She regarded him with growing horror. His meaning was all too plain. He was telling her that she was in his hands, to do with as he pleased.

He read her thoughts, said with what was an attempt at reassurance. "I can make you very happy, give you everything a girl likes, silks, diamonds—a carriage and pair. You will be the first lady of Dos Ríos." His whispering voice deepened. "I will be the next thing to a king in this country, Miss Linda." He knotted a great hairy fist. "Power," he said softly, "power over men—the power of life and—*death*."

Linda stared at him, fascinated, unutterably shocked. The man was mad, and because of his madness, all the more dangerous. Fear constricted her heart. She heard her own voice, thin, shaky.

"You—you murdered my father—"

He shook his head, smiled reproachfully. "I leave such things to others. I command and they obey. No man's death can be laid to me."

Linda wanted to scream, but no sound came from her parted lips. She tried to struggle up from the chair, cringed under the weight of his hand.

"You'll find things a lot easier if you mind me," he said, not unkindly. "I wouldn't want to *hurt* you."

Slow, hesitant footsteps approaching from the hall that led to the store swung his head in a look. Linda's sick eyes saw the ferret-faced clerk in the doorway. He wore a white rag wrapped around his forearm. There were dark blotches on the rag. Bloodstains, Linda recognized, and she was conscious of a thrill. Amigo's teeth. Amigo had turned on his killer, marked him with his fangs.

Berren's face darkened as he saw the blood-stained rag. He said slowly, almost menacingly, "Let the dog grab you, huh?"

Fred nodded, an uneasy look in his pale eyes. "Went for me like a wolf. Wasn't expectin' for him to get mean with that rope on him."

"You killed him," Berren said. "I heard the shot."

"Had my gun on him when he grabbed me—" Fred lifted his bandaged arm. "Ripped me clean to the wrist—"

Berren repeated his question. "You killed him?"

"He was too quick for me . . . knocked the gun from my hand. Was gone over the fence before I could get in another shot." The clerk's eyes wavered in a brief glance at the girl. "I figgered to have the doc fix me up."

"Come here—" Berren beckoned with a huge forefinger. "I'll take a look—"

Fred approached him, held up the bandaged arm. Berren stared at it. He said quietly, without lifting that look, "I reckon this is the medicine you need." His open hand smashed the youth savagely across the face. Fred staggered, sprawled on the floor. He squealed like a frightened rabbit under the closing jaws of a hound, hid his face under his arms.

"Get up," Berren said in the same toneless

voice. "You go find that dog and kill him."

Fred got to his feet. He was breathing hard, half sobbing gulps that made Linda shudder. The terror she saw in his ashen face disgusted her. She felt no pity for him, only a deep shame to know that such cowardice could exist in a human being.

As the clerk's dragging footsteps faded down the hall, Linda heard different footsteps, the heavy tramp of booted feet. More than one man coming. Several men, and all of them entering the hall that led from the store. She felt Berren's look on her, and from his expression guessed he was wondering whether or not he should remove her to another room.

A man's voice spoke from the doorway. "You wanted me, Newt?"

Linda recognized Sam Doan, the one-armed liveryman. He wore a bandage under his battered Stetson, and a curious concern sprang to his eyes as he saw her slumped dejectedly in the chair.

Another man pushed arrogantly past the liveryman. He was tall, with dark red hair and there was a scar on the lip drawn back in a grin at her.

Linda almost stopped breathing. This was the man who had told her he was Adam Marshall, the man who had come to the sheep camp with his terrible threats. Yes, the same man who had come in the dead of night, burned her out, murdered poor old Martinez, and harried her sheep to destruction over the cliffs. She shrank in the chair, fear and rage growing in her as she met his insolent stare.

Berren was speaking, his whispering voice mildly casual. "Sure, Sam. I'm using the buckboard after dark—" He paused, looked at Bert who had halted in the doorway. "Lock the store door, Bert. Put up a sign the store's closed all day tomorrow, and then tell the rest of the boys I'll be needin' 'em."

Bert vanished and Berren's attention returned to the liveryman. "Deen get back yet?" he asked.

Sam Doan shook his head. He seemed fascinated by the girl in the chair. "Ain't seed him if he has." He dragged his look from Linda, narrowed his eyes at the storekeeper. "What's she doin' here?" He gestured at Linda.

"You know Miss Seton, Sam. She's a friend of mine, a very good friend." His smile was warmly benign, his eyes cold, like pieces of slate.

"Sure I know her," Sam said hoarsely. "I was just askin' what for she's here."

Linda wanted to scream then, tell why she was in this loathsome room. Caution held her wordless, a wild hope in her that perhaps here was a friend.

Sam's next words shocked the hope from her. His expression had oddly changed, and he said harshly, "Was askin' because Deen said Marshall took her over to Moraga's *cantina.* Don't savvy how she got away from Moraga's place. He's Marshall's friend."

The tall red-haired man with the scarred lip grinned at him. "Marshall sure broke your head for you, Sam. I'm right proud to be wearin' his name. He's sure some fightin' hombre."

The liveryman looked at him with expressionless eyes. "I got a long mem'ry, Ad. I figger to let Marshall know I don't forget things easy."

Berren was watching the other man, and Linda sensed a growing annoyance in him. His voice was casual enough when he spoke.

"You should be out at the ranch, Ad. You know I told you I'd take care of things at this end." He paused, added significantly, "No tellin' when somebody might turn up in Dos Ríos, somebody who knows Brazos Jack."

"Figgered I needed a little ree-laxation," sniggered the renegade. His eyes hardened as he looked at the storekeeper. "I ain't takin' orders from you nor nobody, Berren. I got as big a say in this business as you, and don't you go gettin' queer notions I ain't."

Berren smiled at him. "Sure, sure, Jack. I'm just thinking about the ranch—those cattle—"

"All fixed," boasted Brazos Jack. "Tod's got that trail-herd halfway to the border by now. More'n two thousand head. Soon as he gets back we'll gather a couple thousand more."

"That's fine, Jack," congratulated Berren. There was a gleam in his cold eyes as he gazed at the rustler. "Don't forget, though, that we have more important business. We can't risk any mischance—like you being recognized."

"You make me sick," grumbled the red-haired man. He grinned at Linda. "Mighty sorry to hear about what happened to your sheep outfit, Miss Seton. I warned you the boys was gettin' up on their hind laigs. The smell of sheep makes a cowman sick at his stummick." He laughed raucously.

The disdain in her eyes seemed to annoy him. Ugly lines creased his face. "Wildcat, huh . . . like to get your claws on me." The scarred lip lifted, showed a gap where a tooth was missing. "Tamin' wild she-cats like you is what I do best."

Linda had no words for him. She could hardly believe this was real. These men were so sure of themselves, so confident of success now that they were willing to discuss their crimes openly in her presence. She wondered miserably about Adam Marshall. It was evident they believed that Adam would soon be in their hands. They would make a quick finish of him. Adam was the one remaining barrier that stood in the way of these callous and bloody-minded wretches. Every trail would be watched and sooner or later they would have him. She could not bear it. Adam Marshall

... Adam—her Adam. She knew it now. Adam's life was more to her than her own.

Berren was speaking, and there was an odd change in his voice, a clear edge to it that drew her eyes to him. He was staring at Brazos Jack. "I am not pleased with your way of talking to Miss Seton. Keep your mind and hands away from her, my young friend. I tell you for your own good."

The desperado's hand went swiftly to the gun in his holster, and he stood there, tense, watchful, teeth bared in a wicked grin. "I ain't takin' talk from you, Berren. You got the big head. I've a notion to fix you here and now."

Berren looked at him steadily, and the sudden ominous stillness made Linda hold her breath. She could not see the storekeeper's eyes, but something in them had a startling effect on the other man. The fingers curled over the gun-butt relaxed and slowly his hand fell limp to his side, and she saw unmistakable fear spread like a gray mask over the outlaw's hard face.

His uneasy laugh broke the silence. "Wasn't knowin' you was *that* way about the gal, Berren. Hell—I ain't cravin' to horn in on your range."

"See that you don't," whispered Berren. His urbane smile was back. "I'm advising you to return to the ranch immediately, and from now on you must keep away from Dos Ríos."

"Sure," grunted the outlaw. He reached into a pocket for tobacco sack and papers. "I'm heading to the Panhandle quick as this deal is finished and I get my split." He shook tobacco into a paper, began shaping his cigarette. "I'll have enough to get me a good spread down in the Panhandle. Plenty mavericks runnin' loose that's goin' to feel my iron on their hides. I figger to settle down."

"A commendable ambition," smiled Berren. He added significantly, "When I'm finished with your services, Jack."

"Sure," quickly agreed the desperado. "Ain't leavin' until I get my split." He lit his cigarette, gave the storekeeper a hard, mirthless grin. "I'm watchin' my step awful close from now on, Berren, and watchin' any hombres that figger to lay for me in the chaparral. I'm tough, and don't you think I ain't."

Without another glance at Linda he swung on his heel and went clattering down the hall.

Berren smiled at the girl. "An unpleasant man, Miss Linda, but useful, very useful. You need have no more fear about him. I know what to do with men when they are no longer of use to me."

Linda closed her eyes. She felt she could not bear to meet his look. She heard his unclean whispering voice speaking to Sam Doan:

"You will have the buckboard waiting at the back gate after dark, Sam. You will drive us."

Sam Doan said in an alarmed voice, "I'd ruther not go out to the ranch, Newt. I'd kind of like to keep away from *that* place."

"Afraid of old Marshall, Sam?" The storekeeper seemed amused.

"It ain't that," muttered the liveryman. Linda, opening her eyes, met his sidewise glance, and again hope stirred in her, and as quickly faded as Sam continued vehemently, "I hate his guts like poison. I'd likely want to use my gun on him, and that would spoil things for you, Newt."

"You don't need to see him, Sam," assured Berren gently. "At least not until the funeral, and then we will want all his good friends on hand, to gather around the grave, mourn the passing of an old pioneer." His whispering voice hardened. "You see, Sam, it is very necessary to have a proper funeral. I will be among the chief mourners." His low laugh made Linda shrivel in her chair.

"Brazos Jack dassent show his face," Sam muttered in a frightened voice. "Too many folks would know he ain't the real Adam Marshall."

"Jack will be too prostrated with grief," smiled Berren. "He will not be among those present. Don't be a fool, Sam. I do not make mistakes, and nothing can now alter the course of events to come."

"There's Adam Marshall," reminded the liveryman in a stifled voice. "You ain't settled with *him*—yet."

"He's as good as dead," Berren said sharply. "He's the least of my worries." He smiled, added with a smirk at Linda. "And I have no worries—not any more."

"You ain't knowin' him the way I do," muttered Sam Doan. "He's a Marshall, the spittin' image of his grandad. Look how he busted out of that Mex jail, got back to Dos Ríos come hell or high water."

Berren's expression showed annoyance. He said sourly, "Look what I've done to his grandad. Don't be a fool, Sam. Nothing can stop me now and I don't want any more of your talk."

Sam got out of his chair, and he said, not looking at Linda, "You're takin' the gal, huh?"

"The ranch is the best place for her," smiled Berren. "Yes, she'll go with us, Sam."

Sam turned to the door. "I'll have the rig out at the back," he said, and he went slowly from the room.

Berren got out of his chair, moved to the door. "Tell Bert I want him," he called to the livery-man.

Linda heard Sam's "Sure, I'll tell him," heard his footsteps fading into the store.

Berren returned to Linda, stared down at her thoughtfully. "You'll need some clothes," he said. "Not those pants you selected. A woman looks indecent in pants. Pants are for men, skirts for women."

"You are a strange man," Linda said wonderingly. "You with blood on your hands and worrying about what is decent for a woman to wear."

He ignored the comment, continued his minute inspection. "That yellow skirt becomes you, and the white waist, but I do not care for you to wear Carmela Moraga's old clothes."

She flared up, resentful of the thrust at the Moragas' kindly generosity. "They're not old clothes, and if they were rags I'd prefer them to anything from you."

Her outburst left him unmoved. He might have been deaf, and she sat there, helpless, growing fright squeezing her heart while he calmly went on enumerating the various articles she would need.

"We can get along with what I have on the shelves," he said. "We'll take a trip to Kansas City soon and you can engage the best sewing woman. I want you in the finest silks and satins. You are too beautiful for common things."

Linda said faintly, "You unbelievable monster."

He seemed not to hear, turned and spoke to Bert who was looking questioningly from the doorway. "You will stay here and care for Miss Seton. I am going over to the hotel and won't be back for an hour at least."

Bert nodded, said laconically, "Al Deen got back. He's over to the hotel now, eatin'."

"He has news?" Berren's eyes gleamed.

Bert glanced at Linda, shook his head. "Reckon not, boss."

The disappointment in Berren's face put a glow in the girl's heart. Adam was still free of the town marshal's clutches.

Berren moved to the door. He had an oddly light step for so big a man. He said over his shoulder, "I'll bring you a dress and things when I come back, Miss Linda. I'll want you to change into them." He moved on, halted again. "No conversation with the young lady, Bert. Your only duty here is to see that she does not leave this room."

"I savvy," grinned the man. He closed the door behind the storekeeper and stood for a moment, gaze idling around the room.

"Reckon this here chair with the leather paddin' looks easy to set in," he said aloud. He pulled the chair close to the wall, near the door, and sat down, eyes on the girl.

Linda averted her face. She was hopelessly trapped, a prisoner. It was hard to hope. This was the end. She did not want to keep on living. There would be nothing to live for, not with Adam Marshall dead. She had had one short hour of life with him. She wondered if he would be thinking of that hour with her. Something in her told her he was. Life had brought them together at a crucial moment, brought them very close to each other. It was too cruel for it all to end so soon. She must not let go of hope. The faint little spark in the cold ashes of her heart must be kept alive. The fact that Adam Marshall still lived was reason to hope. *She must hold on to her courage—be ready.*

She forced herself to meet the man's gaze, smiled at him. He was young, despite his hard face. Perhaps she could manage to lull his vigilance.

"You're from Texas, aren't you?" she asked. "Your voice has the Texas drawl."

His face softened. "Yes, ma'am, I was bo'n down in Texas. Yes, ma'am, I reckon I'm a Texan." He frowned uneasily. "The boss said for no talk, ma'am."

"He can't hear us," smiled Linda.

He stared at her suspiciously. "I ain't talkin', ma'am." He spoke sullenly, lowered his gaze and began shaping a cigarette.

"I'd like a drink of water," Linda said.

He shook his head, not lifting his eyes. "Cain't leave this room."

"You seem awfully scared of Mr. Berren," she taunted.

Bert kept silent, and looking at him, Linda realized it was no use. This man was her jailer and nothing she could do would tempt him to relax his guard of her.

She lay wearily back in the chair, tried to keep sickening fears from clouding her mind, tried to keep alive that tiny spark of hope, and suddenly she was aware of footsteps approaching along the hall. Not Mr. Berren's footsteps. Some other man, and he had paused outside the closed door.

Bert got out of his chair, eyes alert, hand on the gun in his holster. The door opened and Linda saw Sam Doan's face peering in.

Bert spoke sharply. "What you want, Sam?"

Sam came into the room. He made no attempt to look at Linda, fixed his attention on the frowning guard. "Newt wants you down at the barn. Said for me to stay with the gal."

"He ain't at the barn." Bert's face darkened with quick suspicion. "He went over to the hotel."

"He's down at the barn talkin' to Al Deen," Sam said. "Al's got Marshall located and Newt figgers you to go along with Al and nab him."

The young renegade hesitated, his eyes hard on the older man. "The boss told me to stick here close," he grumbled.

"Afraid to go after Marshall, huh?" gibed the liveryman.

"Like hell I'm scared!" Bert glowered. "I'd a lot sooner go out and kill the skunk than stay here."

Linda felt it was more than she could bear, this callous talk of killing Adam. They were planning murder, and she could not stop them. She looked longingly at the guns dangling in their holsters.

She would like to do some killing herself—kill these beasts.

Sam Doan said indifferently, "Suit yourself, young feller. I'm only tellin' you that Newt sent for you." He was standing close to Bert's elbow now, and of a sudden Linda sensed some deep purpose in him. She held her breath.

"I ain't leavin' here," Bert declared. "Not on your say-so. The boss told me to stick here until he come back, and what he says goes with me."

"Suit yourself," Sam said again. He turned as if to make for the door, and his hand came up with the striking speed of a snake, fingers wrapped over gun-butt. The heavy steel barrel of the forty-five smashed with a sickening thud against the other man's temple.

Bert's knees buckled and Sam caught him as he fell, eased the dead weight to the floor. Without so much as a glance at the inert body, Sam ran to the door, closed it and turned the key.

Linda was on her feet when he faced around and looked at her. She said shakily, "I'd given up hope—almost."

Sam nodded. "Took some figgerin'—" He went quickly to the man lying on the floor, studied him attentively, and the girl saw a curious expression flit over his face.

She said softly, "He's—*dead?*"

"I reckon so," answered the liveryman laconically. He bent down, hastily stripped off the dead behind him, the gray mare running easily, head up, ears pricked forward.

They came to a fork in the trail. Sam slowed to a walk, swung off into the chaparral, and drew to a halt in a dense thicket of tall sagebrush. He gave the girl a contented grin as she drew alongside.

"We'll give 'em a chance to blow," he said. "Don't do to run a bronc off his legs, not when there's distance to make." He slid from his saddle. "I'll take a look back on the trail. Seems like I noticed fresh tracks where we hit the fork." He disappeared, and Linda let herself go limp in the saddle.

Her skirt had pulled up above her knees. She rearranged the yellow folds, lip curled disdainfully as she recalled Berren's remark about pants being indecent for women. She wished she had pants now. Even her old brush-torn jeans were better than the skirt she was wearing. Darkness was coming, though, and she wouldn't have to worry about her knees. And Sam Doan hadn't seemed to notice, had kept his eyes carefully averted. She had completely misjudged the old liveryman. He was not the murderous scoundrel she had thought. She was confused about him. His earlier talk indicated that he was a member of Berren's gang of cutthroats, and yet he was risking his own life to get her away from Berren's clutches.

The thing had happened with such appalling

swiftness, herself crushed under the news that Adam Marshall's capture was imminent, the last flickering spark of hope in her turning to cold ash. And then suddenly, a man lying dead, and Sam Doan hurrying her through the window, his quiet voice calming, reassuring. Sam Doan was a mystery—his outspoken hatred of Adam Marshall a pretense.

Linda's heart turned over as she thought of Adam. Perhaps it was true that the wolves were closing in on him. Perhaps Sam had not lied to Bert. And here she was, running away, leaving Adam, one man against many, and she had said they were *allies*. A fine ally she was, Linda told herself bitterly, deserting Adam. She would have to go back, tell Sam Doan he must take her back.

Her listening ears caught the faint rustle in the brush, and she saw Sam approaching. He looked worried, preoccupied.

He said slowly, "Fresh tracks all right. Come in from Dos Ríos along the west fork. Whoever it is ain't much more'n a mile or two down the trail."

"You mean he's in front of us?"

"That's right." Sam fished a plug of tobacco from his pocket, gnawed off a piece, and chewed reflectively. "I figger we'd best set here for a spell."

"Where does this trail go?" Linda asked.

"Forks ag'in 'bout five miles down. East fork heads for the Marshall ranch, west fork makes for Jim Oland's JO, and that's where I figgered to take you. Jim's an old-timer, a good friend of the Marshalls."

"We're close to the Rio Blanco, now," Linda puzzled. "I thought we had to cross Sombrio Canyon to get to the Marshall ranch."

"The east fork follows down the Rio Blanco and then heads across the mesa to the Sombrio. Some longer and ain't used much." He nodded. "We'll give the feller time enough to make the forks. If he turns east we'll know he's headed for the JM. Won't need to worry no more 'bout him, 'cause we're headin' *west*—to the JO."

"Whoever it is that heads east to the JM won't be a friend of ours," Linda said. "Unless—" Excitement widened her eyes. "Unless it could be Adam Marshall—"

Sam shook his head. "Wouldn't be Adam—"

Panic seized her. "It was true, then, what you told that man—about Al Deen having him cornered?"

He gave her a bleak smile. "Don't you get skeered, ma'am. I cooked up *that* story to fool Bert, get him off guard. No, they ain't got Adam located far as I know."

Linda studied him with puzzled eyes. "I can't make you out," she said. "Are you Adam's friend?"

An oddly abashed look spread over his face. "He don't think I'm his friend, ma'am. I ain't blamin' him none. He's got plenty reason to think I'm a low-down skunk."

"Why do you say that?"

" 'Cause it's the truth." Sam's voice was a despairing groan. "I throwed in with Berren, got so deep he had his jaws on me afore I knowed what was happenin'."

Linda said gently, "I don't understand yet, Sam, but you got free of his jaws this afternoon."

"Mebbe so," muttered the former JM rider. "It don't make up for what I done to the old boss, to Adam. Newt Berren told me Adam was dead, drowned in the Rio Grande, and then Al Deen came along with a warrant he said had been sworn out by the old boss for my arrest, claimin' I was a cow thief. I went hawg-wild and it weren't hard for Newt to get me roped and workin' with him."

Despite her debt to this man Linda could not help feeling disgusted. No wonder the burden of guilt was too much for him.

Her momentary repulsion was not lost on Sam. "Ain't blamin' you none," he said somberly. "Berren got me to thinkin' that the old boss was due to pass in his checks most any minute, and with Adam dead, I figgered I'd be a fool not to cut in with Berren on the loot. Of course I knowed Brazos Jack weren't Adam, but figgered it was all part of Berren's scheme. Like I said, thinkin' Adam was dead and his grandpa dyin' I figgered I'd be a fool not to ride along with 'em."

"You didn't try very hard to do anything about it," Linda said coldly.

"Never had a chance to talk with Bill Clemm, or any of the boys." Sam shook his head despondently. "Berren said they'd cleared out, left the country, and by the time I knowed different I was hawg-tied. Couldn't do nothin' if I wanted to, not with Berren in the saddle and Dos Ríos full of his killers."

Linda looked at him curiously. "What made you want to help me?"

"Adam showed up at the barn last night," Sam muttered. "I couldn't believe my eyes, thought he was a ghost, but it weren't a ghost . . . it was Adam, shaking my hand, firin' questions at me 'bout his grandpa. I was ready to drop in my tracks and all I could tell him was to get away from Dos Ríos pronto . . . told him he was due to die awful quick if it got known he was alive and back in town."

Forgetting her resentment, Linda felt compassion growing in her. "It was terrible for you," she said, "terrible for both of you."

"I reckon Adam thought I acted awful queer. I got away from him quick as I could, hid out to think things over, and then, this mornin', he jumped me in the stable, knocked me cold with his gun." Sam fingered his bandaged head. "Hawg-tied me and rolled me into a manger.

Seems like he got suspicious and weren't takin' chances with me no more."

Linda heard him only vaguely. *This morning! It was this morning that she had stumbled into Sam Doan's feed yard, talked to the kindly freighter. . . . It was this morning she had encountered Berren on the porch of his store. He had been so sympathetic, so outraged . . . he had urged her to leave the country . . . of course he would never have let her escape. He had planned for months to possess her. He was responsible for the murder of her father, the murder of poor Martinez, the destruction of the sheep. Yes, she had learned so much since the dawn of this morning, and dreadful things had happened since this same dawn. She had seen a man die, and for a brief hour had known the wonder of another man. Only this morning—since a gray dawn she would never forget, and the day not yet done, the sunset glow just now fading.*

Linda was suddenly aware of a voice that was not Sam Doan's voice. The shock of it held her rigid, drained her face of color. *She was losing her mind—hearing things.*

"Take it easy, Sam. Wouldn't want to kill a old hombre like you, Sam."

Linda forced herself to turn her head and look, saw Brazos Jack, his smile insolent, his eyes wary, his gun leveled at Sam Doan.

"Seen you way back on the trail," the outlaw

drawled. "Figgered from that yeller skirt it was you." He flashed her a gleeful look, returned his gaze to the dazed liveryman. "Sure mighty kind of you to fetch her out here to me, Sam."

Linda began to tug at the heavy forty-five Sam had buckled around her waist, the gun taken from the dead man they had left on the floor of Berren's sitting room. It caught in the folds of her skirt.

She heard Sam's furious voice: "You damn snake!" His gun flashed up, belched smoke and flame, and the gun in the outlaw's hand belched smoke and flame. The crashing reports that stunned her ears were like one.

Her shocked eyes saw Sam stagger, fall, and again the gun in his hand spat death at the other man. Brazos Jack, the grin frozen on his face, stood for a moment, gun dangling in limp hand, then suddenly he was flat on the ground, long body shuddering and twitching.

Linda came to her senses, scrambled from the saddle and bent over Sam. His eyes fixed on her and he smiled, said gaspingly, "Took both his bullets, but I scotched him, gal. He ain't botherin' you no more—"

She gazed down at him frantically. "Sam—"

"I ain't mindin' for myself," Sam said. "Reckon it's a good way for me to go." His voice grew faint. "You tell Adam I—I done my best to—to fix it right—"

"I'll tell him," Linda promised. She wondered wildly if she would ever see Adam again.

"You head for the JO," Sam continued. "Turn west when you hit the fork. . . . Close on fifty miles to the JO but you can make it."

"Yes," she said. "Don't you worry, Sam."

He gazed up at her. "Couldn't stand it when I seen what Berren was up to with you—" His voice faded.

Linda slowly stood up. Sam was dead, had given his life for her. She felt sorrow for him, but knew he was right when he said it was a good way for him to go. He had died better than he had lived, gallantly, for decency and justice. These last hours had proved the man, lifted him from a black mire of shame.

Her look went to the dead outlaw, and her eyes hardened. She could feel no pity there. Only sadness that one could be so base. The man was far better dead. He had traveled a bloodstained trail, fouled the air he breathed. Not a man, but lower than the beast, a ruthless killer.

She stood there in the fading sunset. *So much had happened since the dawn of this day, and this same disappearing sun had seen two more men die in front of her eyes. When would it end?*

Reaction set in, and she stumbled on shaky legs to a boulder and sat down. She thought she was going to be sick, but after a moment the dizziness left her, and she resolutely fought off the fit of trembling. It was no time to collapse, give way to nerves.

The wind was stirring in the sagebrush, made soft, rustling sounds, and the lavender hills were darkening now. Soon it would be completely dark.

Linda recalled Sam's words: *"You head for the JO . . . turn west when you hit the fork . . . close on fifty miles to the JO . . . but you can make it."* He wanted her to go to the Oland ranch. Jim Oland was Adam's old-time friend. She must do her best to find this friendly ranch that was somewhere fifty miles away. It was her only way to help Adam, carry the news of his peril to Jim Oland. She hoped that Sam was right about Jim Oland and that he was *indeed* a friend.

She recalled something else Sam had said. She was still miles from this fork in the trail that led to the Oland ranch. About five miles down, Sam had said, and already the dark night was throwing its mantle over this vast and remote country.

Panic rose in her. More than fifty miles to go, and night closing down—an unknown trail to locate. Easy enough for an old-timer like Sam Doan, but a frightening task for her. She knew from experience the difficulties of following one of these trails in the dark. So easy to make a wrong turn, follow some cowpath that led to nowhere. She was going to need a lot of luck to find this fork that was somewhere five miles down.

She got up from the boulder, forced herself to go to where the slain liveryman lay. She hated to leave him like this. Pictures of prowling creatures came to her, made her shudder. Creatures of the night that ate dead flesh. She couldn't bear the thought, and now, despite her haste to be gone she went to the dead man's horse, stripped off the saddle, and shaking out the blanket spread it over the lifeless body. She found rocks and weighted the blanket down against the wind. It was all she could do for this man, except untie and set free the horse to make his way back to the barn in Dos Ríos.

Calmer now, Linda got into her saddle and turned the mare into the trail, careful to keep her eyes averted from the dead outlaw. She sent the mare into a lope and found to her surprise that Sam's horse, a rangy sorrel, was following. She made no attempt to turn the animal back. The mare was his stablemate, she realized.

They were some hundred yards along the trail when she heard a sound that made her rein the mare abruptly. The outlaw's horse, nickering to them, left tied to a sagebrush. Linda hesitated, then pulled off the trail. She hadn't the heart to leave the animal tied up, unable to look after himself. The least she could do was to turn him loose, let him wander back to his home ranch.

She had no quarrel with the horse and it was possible he was a JM animal—the property of old John Marshall.

She found the horse concealed in a clump of sagebrush, and was about to turn him loose when a sudden thought stopped her. It was more than likely the animal would lose no time getting back to his home barn. His appearance would arouse immediate speculation about his missing rider. It would be known by Brazos Jack's fellow desperados that he had ridden the horse to Dos Ríos.

It came to Linda that here was a chance to draw a veil of mystery over the outlaw's disappearance. She recalled the scene between him and Berren, their mutual animosity. If she could take this horse to the Oland ranch there would be no clue to explain what had become of the missing Brazos Jack. Berren would think the man had taken fright and secretly left the country. And anything she could do to puzzle and worry the storekeeper was a blow struck for Adam, for the old man lying sick and helpless at the JM—for herself.

She got back into her saddle and sent the mare into a lope, the dead outlaw's horse following freely on the lead-rope. The riderless sorrel had wandered a bit, nibbling at the grass. Now he whinnied, set after them at a gallop. Linda was unable to refrain from a smile. There was something coltish about Sam Doan's big horse. She wondered if the gray mare was his mother.

The dark blanket of the night covered the landscape now. Only the stars, and these too soon vanished under clouds that drew across the heavens, adding to the blackness and peril of this unknown trail.

The loss of the starlight dismayed her. She could not tell when she was on the trail or off and was forced to trust herself to the gray mare. She knew that a horse would not willingly leave a trail. She was in dread, though, of some intersecting trail enticing the mare into the wrong direction. She had nothing to guide her, not even a star from which she might pick a westward course. So fear rode with her, mounted with the passing hours to sheer panic. She was lost in this impenetrable black wilderness, must have long ago reached the west fork that led to the Oland ranch. She was either on the west fork now, or the mare had turned east and every mile was taking her closer and closer to the Marshall ranch.

It was a shocking possibility. Linda found herself pulling desperately on the reins. She dared not go on like this. She must stop, think the thing out, decide what to do.

She got down from her saddle, stood by the mare's head, and stared about her miserably. Nothing but darkness wherever she looked. She knew, though, that the trail had been winding steeply down and guessed she was on the floor of a big canyon. There were dark shapes that she knew were trees, and her ears caught the sound of running water. A creek, not far distant.

Another sound touched her ears as she stood there, listening, eyes trying to penetrate that darkness. The rustle of leaves, a stealthy, slithering sound that sent a chill waving over her. A man, stalking her—or an animal—a cougar—bear.

Linda's cold fingers closed over the butt of the gun in the belt strapped to her waist. The sound was close now, and the mare's head went up, ears twitching, and suddenly Linda glimpsed a shape, low to the ground. She lifted the gun.

She heard the low whimper just in time to keep her from pulling the trigger. She cried out joyfully, *"Amigo!"*

The big sheep dog whimpered again, was at her side in a moment. Linda could hardly believe her senses. She thrust the gun into its holster, stooped and put an arm around the thick-maned neck, felt his warm, moist tongue on her hand. His coming was like the coming of an old friend, and for a moment she forgot her despair. She hugged him, babbled to him, and little answering whines and growls came from his throat.

She stood up at last, comforted by the press of him against her legs, and marveling at the instinct that had led him to her. How he had managed it was beyond her comprehension. If only the same blessed power could be Adam's so that he too could find her in the black desolation of this remote canyon.

Linda's heart quickened. Her thoughts of him and for him were unvoiced prayers. Amigo, a sign, bidding her to hold on to her courage through these dark hours of terror and despair. There must be no weakness in her, for weakness paved the way to disaster. She must go on and the way through the darkness would bring her at last to safety, bring her to Adam.

16
DAWN IN DOS RÍOS

Adam knew there was only one answer that could explain Linda's disappearance from the *cantina*. Newt Berren was the answer.

They were in the room where he had last seen the girl, and Carmela had brought in coffee and a plate of ham and eggs. He resented wasting time to eat, but Severino Moraga was insistent.

"For the señorita's sake you must replenish your strength, Adamito. Your eye must be sure, your gun-hand steady. Eat now, while you can. This will be a long trail."

Adam realized that Severino spoke true words. He was famished, and as his friend pointed out it might be a long time before he saw food again.

He flung questions at them, learned there was nothing they could tell him, only that Linda must have left in the late afternoon.

"She was asleep when I went into her room," Carmela told him. "I took her some hot water. She was asleep and it seemed useless to awaken her. It was then past three o'clock."

"She went out through the side gate," Severino said. "We found the bar drawn on the inside. The dog was with her," he added thoughtfully.

"His tracks showed in the dust of the little alley that runs past the church. The girl was wearing *huaraches*. It was easy to follow the trail as far as the plaza."

"Go on," Adam said, "I want every scrap of information you can think of."

"She was wearing my yellow *fiesta* skirt," the Mexican girl told him. "A white waist with little black ribbons on it, and a pair of my stockings." Carmela paused, her large dark eyes thoughtful. "She said she would need new pants because the old ones were ruined, and also said she hoped she could find her size at the store."

"That's where she went," Adam said somberly. "She wouldn't know Berren was dangerous. We hadn't warned her."

"I sent Carmela to the store. She was to pretend there were things she wanted to buy, and perhaps learn if the señorita had been there." Severino scowled. "The store was closed."

Carmela's nod confirmed his story. "A sign was on the door. It said, 'Closed all day.'"

"That was yesterday," Adam said quickly.

"It is still closed," Carmela told him.

"The post office used to be in the store when Pete Cline ran the place," Adam frowned. "I suppose it's still there, and if it is, the place has got to be open for the mail."

"Today is Sunday," reminded Carmela with a faint smile. "And tomorrow is the birthday of

George Washington. Mr. Berren does not need to open the post office."

"I'd forgotten," muttered Adam. He drained the coffee cup and got out of the big Spanish chair. "You'll send for that horse of mine, down in the canyon, Severino?"

"*Sí*," promised the Mexican. "I will care for the horse, *amigo*." Worry clouded his eyes. "Al Deen is in town. It is dangerous for you to be seen."

"I'm not dodging danger," Adam said with a bleak smile. "I've got to find out what's happened to that girl, and I'm beginning with Al Deen and Sam Doan. If I can find Berren I'll find Miss Seton. I'm going to get the truth out of those men if I have to choke it out of them with my bare hands."

"They will kill you on sight," worried Severino.

"I'll kill the first man who tries to stop me going where I please or taking what I need. I'm going to show Berren and his thugs that their day in Dos Ríos is finished." Adam spoke with grim finality.

"God ride with you," muttered the innkeeper. A hard gleam was in his sunken eyes. "You have friends here who will not fail you, *amigo*. Without a leader we are helpless against these *gringo* wolves. Your name means much to my people, Adamito. With a Marshall they find their courage."

"I'll remember," Adam said. He gave Carmela a

smile, thanked her for the breakfast, and stepped into the gray dawn. Severino let him out by the side gate and he went swiftly along the alley under the gray adobe wall of the church.

The plaza was empty of life, except for an old Mexican woman under her *ramada*, plucking red peppers from a string that dangled from a rafter. She gave him a brief glance as he crossed the plaza, and when he reached the street she looked again, stood watching until he crossed and disappeared into the hotel. She went hastily to her doorway, spilling red peppers from her apron in her hurry, and almost instantly an elderly Mexican came quickly out and ran toward the *cantina* on the other side of the plaza.

Adam was aware of a curious sensation as he halted inside the dingy lobby. Time had stood still, it seemed to him. The lifeless town, the same gray dawn, the same dissolute old man with the ragged mustache behind the desk hurriedly replacing his whiskey flask in the top drawer. It was just the same twenty-four hours earlier. Only Linda was missing in the picture.

He saw startled recognition leap into the clerk's red-rimmed eyes, and he moved closer, hand on gun-butt, fastened a cold, menacing look on the man.

"Where's Deen?" Adam kept his voice low, but there was a steel-hardness in it that made the clerk jump as if he had been struck.

"Up in his room, sleepin', I reckon." The man forced a grin. "Wasn't you in yesterday—'bout same time? Seems like you was."

"I was," Adam said. He was watching the clerk carefully. "Put your hands on the desk . . . keep them in plain sight."

The clerk slowly withdrew a hand he was lowering to a drawer, dropped his other hand from the untidy mustache, and rested them both on the desk. "I was reachin' for my flask," he explained with a grin. "Was thinkin' you'd take a snort with me."

"The flask isn't in *that* drawer," Adam said with chilly emphasis. "You were reaching for your gun, mister." He moved swiftly, jerked the drawer open, and took out a long-barreled Colt. He thrust the gun into his belt, drew his own forty-five and gestured for the clerk to get out of his chair. "You're taking me up to Al Deen's room," he said gently. "No argument about it, mister."

The clerk's face was ashen. He said feebly, "Al won't stand for it, stranger. Al is awful mean if you wake him up sudden. He won't stop to ask what for you crave to see him. He'll go for his gun—and he's lightnin'-fast."

"I said no argument," rasped Adam.

Something he read in the younger man's cold, watchful eyes warned the clerk that here was a danger more to be feared than the town marshal's wrath. He got out of his chair, went stumbling toward the stairway.

Adam nudged his back with gun muzzle. "No noise," he warned. "Just take me to Deen's door, and mind you do exactly what I say after we get there. Savvy?"

"Sure," mumbled the now thoroughly frightened man. "I savvy, stranger." He started up the stairs, Adam close on his heels.

They reached the landing and the clerk led the way along a narrow hall. He walked softly, cautioned by another prod from the gun.

Snores that came rhythmically from behind the various doors told Adam the hotel's guests were sleeping soundly. He doubted if footsteps in the hall would arouse curiosity. Guests came and went at all hours and cowmen were often up early for the long ride back to some distant ranch.

His unwilling guide paused at a door at the end of the hall. It was apparent from the loud snores that the town marshal was not awake.

Adam said in a whisper, "Open the door—"

The clerk turned the knob, found the door was not locked. He pushed it open, and obeying Adam's gesture went into the room. Adam followed him.

He said in another low whisper, "Get around the other side of the bed . . . wake him—"

The man obeyed, got around the bed and leaned over the snoring town marshal who lay on his side, and faced him. "Al," muttered the clerk, "wake up, feller—"

Deen grunted, opened his eyes in a sleepy look at the man bending over him. He said in a surly voice, "What the hell you want?"

"There's a feller askin' for you," mumbled the clerk. His eyes lifted in a furtive look across the bed at the silently waiting man there.

Guessing he was trying to think of some way of warning the town marshal, Adam lifted the gun menacingly.

The clerk's manner had already aroused Deen's suspicion that something was wrong. Muttering an oath he rolled over and met Adam's hard gaze. He said stupidly, "I'll be damned!" and his hand slid under the pillow.

"Don't try it, Deen." Adam's gun was covering both men. "Keep your hands where I can see them." He leaned over the bed, reached under the pillow, and secured the marshal's gun.

Deen glared up at him with furious eyes. He said in a tight voice, "What the hell do you want, feller, bustin' into my room?"

Adam saw that this man was no coward. There was both courage and cunning in him, and the ferocity of a cornered wildcat in his small, wiry frame. He was dangerous.

A gun in each hand now, he spoke to the hotel clerk cowering opposite him. "Get that rope lying on the chair under the window."

The town marshal was wide awake now. He started to sit up, and Adam said sharply, "Keep as you are, or I'm killing you this instant."

Deen sank back on the pillow, leathery face convulsed with rage. He was brave enough, but the hard gleam in the other man's eyes warned him that death was very close.

Adam spoke again, "Keep your mouth shut, Deen. No talk from you—yet. When I'm ready I'll make you talk plenty."

Deen cursed him softly, and Adam, in a mood not to take anything, leaned over and tapped him across the head with the barrel of his gun. Deen winced, but his curses stopped. He lay there, breathing hard, hands clenched into fists. Adam gave him a mirthless smile. "Nothing soft about me, Deen. I'm fed up with you skunks."

The hotel man brought the rope to him. Adam shook his head. "I'm letting *you* tie him up," he said.

"He—he'll kill me," muttered the man.

"He's done his last killing," Adam said grimly. "Roll over on your belly, Deen, or do you want another crack on the head?"

The town marshal squirmed over, lay flat on his stomach, and at Adam's direction the clerk pulled his hands back and tied them at the wrists with a piece of the rope he fumblingly cut with his knife.

Adam tested the knots and, satisfied, told

the hotel man to tear a strip from the sheet.

"We'll have to tie his mouth up," he said with a thin smile.

In a few moments the gag was adjusted. Adam inspected the knots and then ordered his victim to slide off the bed.

Deen obeyed, got sullenly to his feet, stood there in undershirt and long drawers, but far from ridiculous with his venomous eyes fairly spitting hate at the man who was so outraging his pride.

"No time to waste getting you into your pants and boots," Adam said. "You'll walk softer without your boots." He motioned for the hotel man to unlock the door. "You go in front, mister, and be very careful—if you want to keep on living."

The snorers were still undisturbed as they moved quietly along the hall and down the stairs. As they came opposite his deserted desk, the clerk halted.

Adam shook his head, gestured for him to keep on going. "I'm needing you too, mister," he said.

"I cain't leave the desk," protested the man. "Berren will git my scalp."

Adam looked at him sharply. "You mean Berren is in town?"

The clerk shook his head sullenly. "He ain't in town . . . went off some place last night." He shuffled past the desk. The carpet slippers he wore were too big and he walked with a scraping motion to hold them on his feet.

Adam prodded the town marshal with his gun. He was in a hurry to get his prisoners away from the hotel. He had risked a lot, daring to show himself in this town, dragging Deen from his bed. It was worth the risk. The man's disappearance would frighten his fellow ruffians. Without a leader they would be helpless, unable to think for themselves.

They were out on the porch now, and something he saw brought him to an abrupt standstill. Mexicans, some score of them, were grouped on the opposite sidewalk, and all of them were heavily armed. They stood there, silent, intent; and looking at them, Adam was aware of excitement surging in him. These men were friends. Severino Moraga was with them, and Miguel Estrada.

He prodded his prisoners down the steps, drove them across the street and into the plaza, beyond observation from the hotel windows.

The Mexicans crowded up. Deen rolled nervous eyes at them. It was plain he feared this was a hanging party.

Severino gave Adam a wry smile. "*Por Dios!* You work fast." Amusement gleamed in his eyes as he looked at the town marshal. "He is a gamecock plucked of his feathers, this one."

He stared at Deen's bootless feet. "A poor thing without his spurs."

"A rope around his neck would make him prettier to my eyes," muttered Miguel Estrada. "He keeps Gaspar Mendota in his jail to rot until they take him out to hang."

Adam eyed them thoughtfully. He sensed a dangerous mood in these men. Many of them had received rough treatment from Al Deen.

He said gravely, in Spanish, "This is only the beginning. We'll make Dos Ríos a decent place for decent people, and that means the Law is back."

"*Sí!*" Severino nodded vigorously. "You have come back, and you bring the Law, and you bring the courage to make our hearts strong. We are men again, and fight by your side like men."

"*Bueno!*" Adam grinned at them. "The Law is back in the saddle, *amigos*, and our first job is to put these men in the jail, and the Law will judge and punish them."

"*Sí, sí!*" Teeth flashed in answering grins, and Adam's uneasiness left him. There would be no explosion, no quick rope for his prisoners. He wanted them alive, at least long enough to make them do some talking. Al Deen would know where Newt Berren was to be found. The most important thing at this moment was to locate the missing storekeeper—rescue Linda from his clutches.

His mind fastened on the problem of the jail. "We must do this business quietly," he said. "Severino will go with me to the jail, and I'm leaving Miguel Estrada in charge of these men. Some of you keep a watch on the hotel, but don't start any trouble."

"*Si*," grinned Miguel, "we do as you say, Señor Adamito."

The jail stood on a low hill between the town and the river, an old building with massive adobe walls pierced with loopholes. The padres had built it in earlier days when defense was needed against marauding Indians.

Adam and Severino approached cautiously, with the stealth of those same stalking Apaches of the long ago, vague slinking shapes in that gray dawn.

They guessed from the stillness there that the jailer was asleep. The walls were thick and the windows stoutly barred. He had no cause to suspect danger.

They reached the door and Adam stood close to the wall, motioning for the old Mexican to do his part. Severino pulled his shirt loose from his trousers, let it fall over his cartridge belt and gun. He tousled his hair, put on the distracted look of a man suddenly aroused from his sleep by some tragedy.

Adam grinned, said softly, "Fine—"

Severino made an amused grimace, leaned

against the door, beat loudly with both fists. "Señor, señor . . . queek . . . bad trouble, señor!"

Silence, then the thud of feet, a gruff inquiring voice, "What the hell's wrong, Moraga?"

"Al Deen—'e mooch seek," babbled the innkeeper. He rolled ecstatic eyes at his companion. "Make beeg 'urry, señor."

They heard a grumbling response, the quick pad of bootless feet, and the door jerked open, framed the jailer's startled, unshaved face. He repeated his question, "What the hell's wrong, feller?"

Severino retreated a few steps, gesticulated wildly, "You come queek—"

The man stepped outside. He was in his undershirt and trousers, and still dazed with sleep. Adam slid along the wall, jabbed a gun-barrel hard against his ribs.

The jailer froze in his tracks, and his head turned slowly in a stupefied look at the man with the gun. Adam said curtly, "Inside, mister—" He waggled the gun. Severino had his own gun from under his shirt. He said with mock politeness, "Move queek, señor. We beeg 'urry—"

The jailer turned and stepped inside the office. He stumbled against a chair and the sharp blow on his kneecap seemed to bring him out of his trance. He halted abruptly and his eyes took on a maniacal glare. Adam couldn't blame him if he felt quite as crazy as he looked. This thing was enough to drive any jailer crazy.

On the table lay a bunch of keys, a couple of pairs of handcuffs, and a long-barreled Colt, a forty-four Frontier Model. Several rifles and a sawed-off shotgun leaned against the wall, and there were more handcuffs and several coils of rope. From the looks of the office it was apparent that the jailer was a man of untidy ways.

"We're taking over for you," Adam told him. "You're out of a job, mister, but we're giving you free room and board for a few days."

The jailer was disposed to be truculent. "Like hell you're takin' over," he sneered. "Al Deen will sure nail your hide to the door."

"You can select your own room," smiled Adam. He picked up the bunch of keys and motioned the man to precede him into the corridor.

The ancient blockhouse had been made into a fairly commodious jail. Some half-score iron-barred doors lined the long corridor, and at the far end was another door opening into the rear wing of the building. A quick look showed only two prisoners occupying the smaller cells on the corridor. One of them was a Mexican who stared with frightened eyes at the newcomers.

Severino Moraga made clucking, sympathetic sounds. "Gaspar Mendota! My poor friend—at last we come for you!"

Gaspar could only stare, his mouth slack, his eyes unbelieving.

The door of the opposite cell was open and in another moment they had the jailer inside.

Adam locked the door. "We'll bring Al Deen to keep you company," he told the scowling man. "We're going to fill up these empty cells for you."

Severino reached for the bunch of keys and quickly opened the door of Mendota's cell. He dragged the dazed Mexican into the corridor. "*Por Dios!*" he spluttered. "Do you not understand? You are free. They cannot hang you now."

A sobbing breath came from the Mexican. His dark face had a pinched, haggard look. He said dully, "I am hungry—"

Severino flung an enraged look at the jailer watching from his cell, and then to Mendota, "I will take you to the *cantina, amigo.* Food, *sí,* all you can eat and drink."

Adam had moved to the next cell, and amazement grew in him as he looked at the man who sat there on a pile of dirty straw.

He exclaimed incredulously, *"Monte!"*

A slow grin spread over the man's thin, drawn face. He said laconically, "Hello, Adam. Sure mighty glad to see you, feller."

"They said you were dead, murdered." Adam was working furiously at the lock. He jerked the barred door open, ran inside, and bent over the other man.

"Come close to bein' murdered," Monte Cline

said with a thin-lipped smile. "I reckon it would have come to that in the end."

"No savvy," puzzled Adam.

"Newt Berren can mebbe tell you," grinned the former town marshal. He touched his leg gingerly. "Took a bullet, but I reckon I can hobble some with a stick." He gave his friend a keen, questioning look. "What's goin' on?"

"Doing some house cleaning," Adam told him with a grim smile.

"This town sure needs plenty cleanin'," Monte said. "You're the hombre to do it, feller."

He got carefully to his feet and hobbled into the corridor, gave Severino Moraga a cheerful grin. "You old sonofagun! I'm headin' pronto for your *cantina* for some eats. They keep a feller awful hungry in this jail."

Adam said, "I'll take a look at that back room." He went swiftly down the corridor. Monte leaned against the wall, eased his leg, and grinned happily at Severino. He was a lean, durable-looking man, a few years older than Adam and he had blue eyes that could be merry but that just now were very tired. "Never figured you'd be lookin' like a angel," he chuckled. "Right now I can sure see a halo floatin' 'round your haid."

"Our young señor is God's Hand," the old Mexican said very solemnly.

"Huh?" Monte looked thoughtful.

Adam hurriedly rejoined them and they followed him to the office where Miguel Estrada and several Mexicans were waiting with the prisoners, now increased to four.

"These two come from the hotel," Miguel said with a pleased grin. "They no suspect . . . we grab 'em queek."

"Good work," Adam told him. "We don't want a man of this outfit to get away. Pick 'em up as fast as they show themselves. We can have 'em all in jail before they know what's going on."

"*Sí.*" Miguel grinned. "They fall into our hats like ripe plums from the tree."

"Watch the saloon, and post some men at Doan's barn. Grab every man that shows up there for his horse."

Miguel hurried away with his grinning aides. Adam turned his attention to the deposed town marshal. "I'm wanting some talk out of you." He gave Severino a look and the Mexican removed the gag from the man's mouth.

Deen spat, licked his lips. "Never was much on talkin'," he said laconically.

Adam ignored him for the moment. He said to Monte Cline, "You're town marshal again. These men are your prisoners. I'm leaving it to you—"

"Sure." Monte stared with bleak eyes at Deen. "You low-down skunk!" He reached for one of the gun-belts on the table, buckled it to lean hips. "I'm on the job right now, Adam."

Adam's hard look fastened again on Deen. "I

want all the information you can give me about Berren. Where is he?"

Deen spat again, and his eyes took on a stubborn glint. "I told you I ain't talkin'," he answered. "Go chase yourself, feller."

Adam saw he was up against it with this man. Time was precious. Every moment's delay added to Linda Seton's peril.

His questioning look went to the hotel clerk, sullen and frightened. The man shook his head.

"Ain't knowing a thing about Newt Berren," he mumbled huskily. "I just work at the hotel. Berren don't tell me nothin'."

Adam turned to the door. "I'm leaving things to you, Monte," he said. "I've got to pick up Berren's trail, and I don't know where I'll be for the next day or two."

"Sure." Monte was troubled by the anguish in his friend's eyes. As yet he knew nothing about Linda Seton's part in the affair. "You go ahead. I'll take care of this end of it." He watched with frowning eyes until Adam disappeared in the cottonwood scrub.

17

BLIND TRAIL

Sunlight lay like prairie fire on the mountain ridges, flowed down the dusty street in a golden flood, and threw a long shadow in front of Adam as he made his way swiftly toward Sam Doan's livery barn.

He saw with bitter eyes the dark shape dancing ahead of him. Not his own shadow, there in front of him, drawing away with each stride he took. It was Newt Berren's shadow, a black and evil thing he must overtake and trample to death.

The screech of a saw abruptly halted him. The sound came from a tumble-down frame building set back some score yards from the plank sidewalk. He knew the place, old Pop Sidler's carpenter shop. Adam's eyes narrowed thoughtfully. Pop was a tough-minded old-timer, which perhaps explained why he was one of the few Americans not frightened away from the town by the influx of border desperados. He was also a long-time friend.

The old man saw him approaching through the jungle of weeds. Excitement flickered across his sun-dried face. He carefully placed the saw on the bench and fished a plug of tobacco from his pocket.

Adam said, "Hello, Pop." His gaze went curiously to the long box that rested on trestles. "Looks like a coffin—"

"It is," Pop answered. He gnawed off a chew from the plug. "Kind of reckless, showin' yourself in this town."

Adam continued to stare at the crude coffin. "Who's needing it?" he asked.

"I'll be makin' one for you if you ain't awful careful," Pop said dryly. "This town ain't no place for decent folks, young feller."

"You are still here," Adam retorted.

"Too old to git up and hunt me another place," returned the old man. His leathery face creased in a grin. "I manage to git by, a job here and a job there, and a coffin to make now and ag'in."

"You do work for Berren?"

Pop eyed him cautiously. "What for you want to know?"

"I'm looking for him."

"He's lookin' for you," Pop said a bit grimly. "He'll be orderin' another of these pine boxes if he sees you first, or if Al Deen lays eyes on you."

"Berren order this coffin?" asked Adam.

"Friend of his got kicked by a bronc," Pop told him with a dry cackle. "The feller's layin' back thar on that table yonder."

"I'll take a look," Adam said.

Pop offered no objection, watched in silence

while Adam drew back the piece of canvas from the body lying on the table.

The dead man's face was unfamiliar. Adam replaced the covering and went back to where Pop leaned against his bench. He said quietly, "Wasn't a kick from a horse that killed him."

Pop gave him a sly look. "I ain't sayin' you're wrong." He spat a dark brown stream into the sawdust. "I was just givin' you Newt Berren's story."

"A gun did that," Adam said. "Somebody cracked his skull with a gun-barrel."

"I git by, keepin' my nose out of other folks' business," the old man told him dryly. Worry crept into his eyes. "You should be makin' tracks away from here, young feller. Al Deen's bad poison."

"Al Deen's in jail." Adam grinned. "You don't need to be afraid of talking, Pop. We're house cleaning, and Monte Cline is back on the job as town marshal."

Pop's gray-whiskered jaw stopped its rhythmic movement, his eyes widened, and after a moment he said huskily, "No foolin', Adam?"

"No fooling."

"I knowed Monte wasn't really dead," Pop said. "I do the undertakin' in this town. They fotched Monte in here for me to fix him up in a box, and I found he wasn't dead. Shot up bad, but not dead." The old man's voice hardened. "Newt

Berren was new in town then, had just bought out the store after Monte's pa died. Wasn't knowin' Berren for the devil he is and I went and told him about Monte not bein' dead. Fust think I knowed Monte just vanished from where he was laid out on the table yonder and when I asked Newt Berren how come, he told me I'd git along fine with him if I kept my nose out of business that didn't consarn me."

"They had him in jail," explained Adam.

"Mighty queer business," puzzled the old man. "What for would they want to keep him alive?"

Adam said slowly, "I've an idea Berren planned to use him, pin a murder on him, and then have a legal killing, a hanging for the murder of my grandfather. A lot of things are clearing up in my mind, Pop."

The carpenter nodded, jaw moving reflectively. "Been some things goin' on that had me puzzled," he said. "This dead feller was brung in here soon after sundown. Berren claimed a horse had kicked him over at Sam Doan's barn. I knowed he was lyin' soon as I took a look, and I happened to know they fotched him over from the store and not from the barn. Seed 'em come from the yard back of the store. I reckon that's where the feller was killed. Wasn't long after when Berren went off in a buckboard."

"See anybody with him?" asked Adam, his voice not quite steady. "A girl?"

"Was a feller with him," Pop answered. "Didn't see no gal." He paused, added quietly, "Berren was askin' about a gal when he was in with the dead feller. Asked me if I'd seen a gal in a yeller skirt."

Adam stared at him, and sensing his surprise, Pop Sidler gave him a sly grin. "I could mebbe have told Berren somethin' that might have put him on the gal's trail—"

"What do you mean?" Adam flung the question fiercely.

"Waal—" Pop was suddenly cautious again. "I'm only tellin' you what I seen about an hour before sundown. Didn't think nothin' of it at the time. Used to see Sam Doan head over to the yard back of the store lots of times. Him and Berren is thick as thieves." He chuckled softly. "Thieves is right, I reckon, thieves and worse—"

"All right, go on," urged Adam. "I want to know about Sam Doan."

"Waal, he had a couple of broncs along with him, kind of kept to the cover of the cottonwood scrub yonder. Like I said, I didn't think nothin' much about it at the time, but got to wonderin' afterwards about the way he worked through the scrub with the horses and left 'em there hid out of sight."

"Where did he go after he left the horses hid in the scrub?" Adam asked. His heart was pounding.

"Waal, he come back over to the street and I

reckon he went into the store the front way. Didn't see him ag'in."

Adam thought it over for a long moment. "I'm taking a look at that back yard," he said.

Pop hesitated. "I should git this doggone box fixed, or I'd go along with you."

"I savvy—" Adam was making for the side door. "Thanks, Pop."

He reached the high fence that enclosed the big yard in the rear of the store. Somebody had been in a hurry and left the gate open. Adam moved on toward the high platform that ran the width of the building. There were steps leading up to the big double doors, now closed. The silence indicated that nobody was inside the store.

He stood there, somber gaze on the building. Pop Sidler's story baffled him. Apparently Berren had not taken Linda with him when he left town. Also it was apparent that she had in some way managed to escape, or Berren would not have questioned Pop about her. The answer seemed to be mixed up with Sam Doan and the horses he had concealed in the cottonwood scrub. It was an answer that did not make sense. It meant that Sam had helped the girl in her time of peril. It did not fit into the picture he had of the former JM man.

He recalled something his grandfather had said only a few hours earlier. *Don't be too quick to judge him . . . we don't know about Sam yet . . .*

looks mighty bad . . . but we don't know all that's back of it.

A vague hope began to stir in Adam. Perhaps—perhaps—

Something his restless eyes saw suddenly broke into his thoughts. He bent low to the ground, stared intently at a reddish-brown stain there.

He straightened up and his gaze moved slowly to the steps, followed the faint trail of blood incrusted in the dust. There were other marks, the imprints of a dog's paws, a man's high-heeled boots.

Adam's gaze came back to the first smear of blood. Something had happened here. The imprints indicated a tussle, a leaping dog, a man staggering back under the dog's savage charge.

He paid close attention to the dog's tracks now, followed the tracks to the fence, saw where the dog must have leaped over. Gaspar Mendota's sheep dog—Linda's dog. Severino had said the dog had followed Linda from the *cantina.*

Adam's pulse quickened. He hurried back to the open yard gate and began a careful scrutiny of the hard ground; and now he saw something he had missed, the faint imprints of sandaled feet. Severino had said Linda was wearing *huaraches* when she left the *cantina.* There were other imprints, the larger traces of a man's boots.

He hesitated, decided against following the trail back to the store. The important thing was to follow where they led, and from what Pop Sidler had said about Sam and the horses, the trail would lead to some place in the cottonwood scrub.

In less than five minutes he found where Sam had tied the horses, saw the firm imprint of a sandal when the girl had pressed down for her spring into the saddle.

Adam wasted no more time and went on the run back to Pop Sidler's shop. The old man gave him a grin from behind the pine box he was nailing together.

"Pick up sign?" He tossed his hammer down and reached again for his plug of tobacco. "Somethin' else was kind of queer," he continued. "Fred come in short time before I seen Sam sneakin' his broncs into the scrub. Wanted me to loan him my old Winchester . . . said he was goin' after a mad dog that had chewed him some."

"Who's Fred?" Adam asked. "I'm in a rush, Pop. I think I've picked up a trail."

"He's a mean little skunk as works for Berren." Pop nodded. "Pizen mean. . . . Waal, he grabs my Winchester down from the peg and hightails it away on that paint horse he rides." The old carpenter gnawed savagely on his plug of tobacco. "I sure don't like that beady-eyed sidewinder."

Adam stood very still, his eyes cold, remote. Mendota's big sheep dog had taken a liking for

Linda. If this Fred had not already found and killed him he would probably pick up the girl's trail and follow her. Dogs could do amazing things.

Pop was speaking again, his eyes sharp now, and intent on the younger man. "Fred had his arm tied up with a rag. Looks like the dog bit him bad. He'll sure kill that dog if he catches up with him. Figgers to comb the range 'til he does catch up with him, from the way he talked."

Adam wondered if the old man knew of the dog's connection with the girl and was trying to warn him of a danger he might not suspect.

He asked bluntly, "Does this man you call Fred know the dog has taken up with Miss Seton? She's the girl in the yellow skirt," he added.

"Sure, I know the gal." Pop nodded. "I knowed all the time she was the one Berren was askin' about." He paused, averted his gaze as if something on his mind made him ashamed to meet Adam's look. "Seen her when she come up the street yesterday before sunup. Seen the dog take up with her. Seen you, too. You mebbe figger I'm a low-down skunk, keepin' out of it the way I done."

"I haven't thought anything about it," reassured Adam. "I'm not blaming you for not wanting to mix in."

"Wasn't knowin' how to figger it out," Pop went on. "I'm talking this way 'cause I seen

Berren send Fred trailin' you when you and the girl went over to Moraga's *cantina*." He spat disgustedly into his sawdust pile. "Was scairt to death for you, but couldn't figger out no way to warn you, the way Berren was watchin' things."

"I savvy." Adam waited for him to continue, sensing there was more to come.

"Figgered you should know about Fred chasin' the dog," Pop said. "He'll stick to that dog's trail like a tick huntin' blood. Which means he'll likely run into the gal."

"Thanks, Pop." Adam was moving fast. "If Fred shows up, have Monte Cline grab him—"

He was in a fever of impatience to get to the barn and throw a saddle on a horse. All the more need for haste now that he knew about Fred. It was plain that Pop Sidler regarded him as dangerous.

He hit the plank sidewalk on the run, became aware of excitement seething in the street. A man yelled at him and he reluctantly halted, saw Pat Hall beckoning from his blacksmith shop. There were other men there with the blacksmith. He recognized Summers, the lawyer, and Doctor Lemmon, old-time residents.

They hurried across the street, angry, bewildered, alarmed men. Summers was coatless and was holding on to unfastened suspenders as he ran.

"What's the meaning of this outrageous affair?"

he asked breathlessly. He was a tubby little man with a white goatee and a Southern accent. "The Mexicans have gone mad—thrown our town marshal in jail, suh, and by your orders, they say, suh."

"That's right." Adam spoke harshly, eyes hard, his hand on gun. He was in no mood to waste time with these men. "You've let Newt Berren pull wool over your eyes long enough."

"He's a respectable citizen, suh!" stormed the lawyer. "He's my client. I must protest."

Adam said contemptuously, "You're a pack of fools. I'd rather think that of you than believe *you're* crooked, too."

Pat Hall interrupted another outburst from Summers. He said slowly, "I'm thinkin' Marshall is talkin' sense, Judge. There's been things goin' on that's got me to wondering some about Berren." The blacksmith fingered a bristly chin. "It was Berren spread it 'round that Monte Cline was dead and knowin' all the time that Al Deen had him in jail. Smells awful bad to me."

Doctor Lemmon nodded his bald head in agreement. "I don't understand it in the least, but Pat is right. It smells bad—very bad, and I'm puzzled about old John Marshall's illness and why I am not allowed to see him. I've known John for years, and I've known Adam here since he was a boy." The doctor drew out a handkerchief, mopped his hot, red face. "I certainly side with Adam in this matter," he declared firmly.

"Thanks, Doc." Adam's expression softened, and then, crisply, "You can talk it over with Monte Cline. He's in charge of things here. And you don't need to worry about our Mexican friends. This is their town, too, and they only want a square deal." He stared frostily at the lawyer. "Think it over, Summers."

He left them, a sober-faced group, and clattered along the plank walk to the big livery barn where an armed Mexican lounged in the doorway.

Miguel Estrada had two glowering prisoners in the office, covering them with his gun while another Mexican tied their hands. The prisoners rolled frightened eyes at Adam as they met his bleak look. One of them was the stableman he had left trussed in the manger the previous dawn.

"These two are the last of them," Miguel said with a contented grin. "It is the big cleanup, no?"

Adam gave him an answering smile. "I'm riding," he told the Mexican briefly; and he hurried into the stable.

There were some dozen horses in the stalls. He ran a critical eye over them, selected a rangy, sleek-coated chestnut gelding. He knew the horse and for good reason. A JM animal, and one he had himself broken to saddle. He knew, too, that the chestnut had speed and stamina, which he was going to need.

He heard movements from another stall and took a look, saw a Mexican rubbing down the red bay horse he had left in the gulch below the cave. Severino had lost no time in sending for him.

The man gave him a grin, gestured at the saddle gear slung on a peg. His own saddle, his Winchester in its scabbard.

He carried the gear back to the chestnut's stall, eased on saddle and bridle, and led the horse into the early-morning sunshine. Miguel Estrada was prodding the stableman and his fellow prisoner from the office. Adam halted the procession.

"Any idea where Sam Doan went when he left here with two horses?" he asked the stableman.

The hostler shook his head. "Wasn't on duty when Sam went off with the broncs."

"You know what horses he took, don't you?"

"The gray mare's gone," the man answered sullenly, "and the sorrel he most always rides."

Adam said, "That's all," and Miguel moved on with the prisoners. He muttered in a low voice as he passed, "*Vaya con Dios, Señor Adamito.*" And he added in English, "That *señorita* mooch nize. You find her queek, no?"

Adam nodded. "*Gracias.*" He finished buckling on his spurs, took the Winchester from its leather boot, made sure it was fully loaded, thrust it back into the boot, and swung into his saddle.

He took a look at the sun, now a brazen, shimmering disk above the mountains. Only a little more than twenty-four hours since he had ridden the red bay out of this same barn. He had just left Sam Doan, senseless and hog-tied in one of his own stalls. And now he was following Sam's trail to wherever it led. So much had happened in those twenty-four hours, and he was still following a dark and dreadful trail that seemed to have no end.

The big chestnut was fresh and sensed the urge in the man on his back. Adam had to restrain the horse. No telling how long the miles ahead of them.

He rode steadily for an hour, eyes wary, ears alert, the thought of Fred ever in his mind. It was easy enough to follow the tracks made by the horses that carried Sam and Linda, but as yet he had failed to pick up any sign of the sheep dog, or the killer so ruthlessly trailing him. He had never seen the man and his only identification would be the pinto horse Pop Sidler had said he was riding.

He thought with fierce satisfaction of his brief stay in Dos Ríos. Al Deen and his gang of killers were in jail, and the few decent Americans in the town were now shocked out of their apathy, beginning to realize the sinister character of the man they had respected as a leading citizen. He had not yet met Newt Berren, but his grandfather's words had drawn a picture he could not miss. *A cunning and dangerous man who cloaks his black heart under a mask of benevolence you'd look for in a parson.* He would know Newt Berren when at last they came face to face.

Adam's thoughts raced as he rode, eyes alert on the trail he followed through the chaparral. The pieces were falling into their proper places, fitting conclusively, building a horrifying picture of Newt Berren's activities. The man possessed the mind of a devil. His intentions about Monte Cline were plain enough. When the chosen time came Monte would have been found in the JM ranch house, dead, a gun in his hand, slain in the act of murdering John Marshall.

Adam was sure he had solved the mystery of Monte Cline, why he had been kept alive in the jail. Berren was careful of his reputation as a good citizen, a benevolent and kindly man. He had schemed desperately to cloak his black heart from such men as Doc Lemmon and Judge Summers, and succeeded with diabolical completeness. Once the JM ranch with its miles of range was in his grasp he would quickly put an end to Brazos Jack. He would be in the saddle, and not a breath of suspicion to worry him, put a cloud on the good name he had been so careful to make for himself in the unsuspecting eyes of his fellow American citizens. He had made his one big mistake when he included Linda Seton in his schemes. Adam knew now, and the thought sent a cold prickle through him, that if it had not been for the meeting with Linda he, Adam, would have ridden blindly to his death at the ranch.

He suddenly reined the chestnut to a standstill, eyes intent on the hoofprints where they turned off the trail, and after a moment he swung the horse, rode slowly to where the imprints of shod hoofs led.

Something lay there, half concealed in a clump of sagebrush. Adam halted his horse, his eyes hardly daring to comprehend; and then he saw that what lay there was a dead man—not a girl in yellow skirts.

He got down from his horse, went slowly to the dead man, and as he stared he was conscious of an odd stirring in him. A long-limbed man, with dark red hair, sightless eyes upturned to the blue sky. He bent, scrutinized the face so still in death, saw the scarred lip, and knew that this lifeless thing was Brazos Jack, his distant cousin, offspring of the *fool Marshall girl* who had run away with a renegade half-breed.

Adam drew a long breath, lifted his eyes, saw something lying under a saddle blanket. His heart turned over. It was a man lying there. He could see the legs, the boots. And there were stones, holding the blanket against the wind.

He moved swiftly, drew the blanket aside, and for a long moment he held his gaze on the face he saw there, wondered at the hint of peace that softened the harsh sun-and-wind bitten features. He had a vague feeling that Sam Doan had died proudly, and that in dying he had paid a debt in full, wiped clean a shameful slate.

With a swift motion Adam replaced the blanket, secured it again with the stones. Linda Seton had done this kindly deed. The imprints of her sandaled feet told the story. She had leaned over this dead man, covered him with the blanket, placed the stones.

Adam turned and looked at the outlaw, and he saw the picture of those swiftly passing death-ridden moments. Guns, belching smoke and flame—men dying, dead—and Linda there—seeing these men die, and yet the courage in her holding her steady, not letting her forget a tender thought for the man who had died in her defense.

There was nothing more here for him, except to pick up the trail. The saddle, lying there in the brush, the stripped-off bridle, told him the girl had turned Sam's horse loose before leaving this grim place of death. He stepped into his saddle, swung the chestnut back to the fork.

The signs indicated that Sam's sorrel horse was trailing the girl; and suddenly he saw where she had cut into the chaparral. He followed the tracks, came to the sagebrush where Brazos Jack had concealed his horse.

Adam got down from his saddle and carefully scrutinized the trampled ground. The small neat hoofprints of the gray mare were distinct, and the larger tracks of two more horses. Sam's, and the horse Brazos Jack had tied here.

He returned to the trail, now beginning its descent into the gorge of the Rio Blanco. Three horses ahead of him, the signs said, one of them on a lead-rope and another running loose, straying from the trail to nibble at inviting bunches of grass, then breaking into a gallop to overtake his companions. The horse on the lead-rope would be the dead outlaw's animal. For some mysterious reason the girl had taken him along instead of turning him loose to make his way home.

Another hour brought him to where the trail branched east and west. The west fork led to Jim Oland's ranch some fifty miles away, the east fork gradually worked over to Sombrio Canyon and on to the JM.

Adam halted his horse, conscious of a dismay in him as he studied the hoofprints. He had been hoping they would take the west turn. The signs were all too plain. Linda had taken the east fork, and *that* way led to danger for her.

He wondered if Sam Doan had told her of the trail to the Oland ranch. The fact that Sam had lost his life in getting her away from Dos Ríos was proof he had no intention of taking her to the Marshall ranch. Sam would know that JM was no place for Linda. It was a certainty that he had been heading for Oland's place when the encounter with the outlaw had cost him his life. It was more than likely he had talked to the girl, told her about the Oland ranch and the west fork that led there. Even so it would be easy for her to miss the fork in the darkness, unwittingly take the wrong turn. The horses were JM animals. Sam had bought the gray mare and the sorrel from JM, and the horse Brazos Jack had ridden was a JM. They would naturally head for the home ranch, turn east when the fork was reached. Linda would have no idea which way she was going in that darkness. Filled with gloomy forebodings, Adam swung into the east fork. As yet he had seen nothing to indicate that the sheep dog had picked up the trail, nor had he seen any sign of the man riding the pinto horse.

The trail dropped steeply to the canyon floor. Sunlight dappled the sycamores, drew silver flashes from the creek. Adam kept the chestnut moving at a fast-shuffling walk, his eyes alert, scrutinizing every patch of soft ground they crossed; and suddenly he saw something that made him bring the horse to a quick halt.

He got down from his saddle for a closer look. The imprints in the soft, marshy ground were unmistakable. The tracks left by a fast-running dog on a warm trail.

Adam got back into his saddle and sent the horse into a lope. It was evident the dog had got wind of the girl from the bluffs and cut down to the trail. It meant that if Fred was following the dog he would be forced to ride back to where the trail entered the canyon. It would be impossible for a horse to make a direct descent from the bluffs.

The thought cheered him. There was a chance Fred would give up the chase as hopeless. He fervently hoped so. No telling what might happen if the man overtook Linda. From Pop Sidler's description this Fred was a snake, and worse.

The trail twisted through a grove of close-growing alders and broke into a small clearing. There was grass here, and signs that horses had been grazing.

Adam dismounted. It was almost impossible to pick up tracks in the thick, short grass. The light press of a girl's sandals, the paws of a dog. He was sure, though, that this place had been a camp, a camp without fire or food. Water, yes, in the creek, and the grass for a bed, the dog nestling close for company. Because it was here the dog would find her.

His roving gaze suddenly fastened on a small black object that lay under the wide-spreading branches of a cottonwood. He picked it up, a piece of black ribbon.

Adam stared at it for a long time. A piece of ribbon from her dress. He remembered Carmela's words. *A white waist with little black ribbons on it.*

He put it carefully into his shirt pocket. One thing was certain. Linda had made camp here. She would water the horses at the creek, satisfy her own thirst.

He quickly found the place, a strip of sandy beach, scuffed up with hoofmarks, and among them the clear press of Linda's sandals and the tracks left by the dog.

Adam drank, watered his own horse, and swung into the saddle. He could only follow where the trail led. His fears for her were mounting, for this trail would take her to the JM ranch. She was riding straight to disaster.

He saw from the hoofprints that one of the horses was again on a lead-rope. The thing puzzled him, and he began to search for any possible reason that could make her want to take the dead outlaw's horse along. She must have had some powerful motive.

Something of the truth came to him as he frowningly wrestled with the mystery. Linda knew the horse would make his way back to the home ranch if she turned him loose. She did not want the horse to get back to the ranch. Brazos Jack's fellow renegades would wonder what had become of him, send out a search party.

Adam was unable to repress an admiring grin. The girl was smart, used her brains. If neither horse or rider showed up at the ranch Berren would probably suspect that Brazos Jack had fled the country, alarmed because of Adam's return to Dos Ríos. It was a plausible answer and explained why Linda was taking precautions to keep the horse from returning riderless to the ranch. At the worst she would give Berren something to worry about.

His eyes were keen on the trail ahead, on the watch for additional hoofprints that might mean Fred's pinto horse. Adam began to believe the man had given up the chase as useless. He was not in the canyon, or if he were he was now miles behind, with Adam between him and the girl.

He was suddenly aware of a movement in the bushes below the canyon wall. Something flashed there, the glint of sunlight on rifle-barrel.

Adam swung his horse sharply, heard the vicious whine of a bullet zip past his head as he dropped from the saddle.

The reverberating echoes of the gunshot faded into the distance. He lay motionless in the concealing brush and reached for the gun in his holster. Perhaps he had been a little too sure about Fred not being in the canyon. Fred would recognize him as the man he had seen take Linda across the plaza to Moraga's *cantina.*

The chestnut horse, startled by the crashing report, had started to run at the moment when Adam left the saddle. He circled, headed back toward the trail, came to a standstill a scant ten feet away.

Adam crawled closer to the big clump of buckbrush. The sight of that riderless horse would likely fool the would-be killer. In due time he would want to know if his intended victim was dead. That impromptu dive from the saddle might lead him to believe his bullet had not missed.

He watched the horse, saw the chestnut's ears prick up, and now he heard a stealthy rustle from somewhere beyond the trail. The man was stalking the place where Adam had fallen.

The rustling noise grew louder. Adam guessed he was a novice, or at the least overconfident, a little too sure he would find a dead or mortally wounded man somewhere near the motionless horse.

The chestnut horse showed uneasiness, swung round with a startled snort, halted, and again stared at something he saw beyond the trail.

Adam lifted his gun, and now he glimpsed the stalker, a ferret-faced youth with wisps of blond hair showing under the upcurved brim of his hat. He carried a rifle under his arm and a short gun in lifted hand. The dirty white rag wrapped around his wrist was identification enough.

Adam inwardly raged at himself for the compunctions that kept him from squeezing the trigger of the gun in his hand. This feral creature had attempted to kill him from ambush. His continued existence was a deadly menace to Linda Seton. It was folly to let him get away, and yet he could not force himself to shoot the man in cold blood. The thought was repugnant, against his code.

He continued to wait, and suddenly the decision was taken from him. The youth came edging stealthily around the bush, eyes greedily seeking the man he thought was lying there—dead. His eyes, coldly venomous as a crawling rattlesnake's, fastened on Adam and he froze to a standstill, lifted his gun.

Adam was not waiting any longer. He read the lust to kill in that exultant, grinning face. This boy, not yet quite a man, was a killer more dangerous than any rattlesnake. He pulled the trigger twice, and even as smoke and flame belched from his gun he felt Fred's bullet fan a breeze like the breath of death past his cheek.

He got slowly to his feet, stood there, gaze on the would-be killer. He saw there was still life in him, met the glazing eyes spitting their hate, and for some reason he found himself thinking of Linda Seton's father.

Adam moved quickly, bent over the dying youth. "You asked for it," he said. "You made me do this to you."

"You was too fast for me," gasped Fred.

"The other man wasn't too fast for you," guessed Adam.

"Got him first shot," Fred said, and the sheer delight in his pale eyes made Adam shiver.

"I'm talking about Seton," he said.

"Sure . . . I killed him—" Fred's voice faded, and then with a last gasping effort, "Newt Berren give me this new Colt for killin' him—" He was suddenly silent, and Adam saw that he was dead.

He went slowly toward his horse. He felt sick, shaken to the marrow of his bones by this thing. This blind trail he was following was a trail of dead men. He wondered how many more would die before the end was reached.

18

THE CLOSING TRAP

The sun was already a blinding shimmer in the hot turquoise sky. The glare hurt Linda's eyes. She longed for the shade of her wide-brimmed Stetson.

She was hopelessly lost, unable to locate the west fork Sam Doan said would lead through those folding brown hills to the Oland ranch. She could only keep on, follow this gorge that kept twisting east into the blistering horizon, always hoping to at last find the right trail.

The gray mare showed apathy, drooped her head, laid back pointed ears, and the big sorrel dragged on his lead-rope. The horses did not like it, kept swinging off in an attempt to head the other way. Their behavior both exasperated and reassured Linda. One thing was certain, she was not heading in the wrong direction, toward the JM ranch.

She was tired and heartsick—and hungry. More than twenty-four hours now since she had eaten Maria's *arroz con pollo*. It was torture to even think of that plate of chicken with its rice and onions and tomatoes—the peas and peppers. She toyed apathetically with the idea of trying to shoot a rabbit with the forty-five that Sam Doan had confiscated from the dead Bert. The cartridge belt and heavy Colt had become an unbearable burden, slung around her slim waist, and she had fastened them to the horn of the saddle.

She doubted if she could hit a rabbit with that big gun, and even if she made a lucky shot she had no matches to start a fire. The very thought of trying to eat a raw and bloody rabbit nauseated her.

She thought dully of Adam Marshall. It began to look as if she would never see him again. She would keep on wandering in this remote wilderness until at last she was too weak to stay in the saddle. Someday her bones would be found in the brush. Bones—bleached white by sun and wind, but first there would be buzzards.

Linda shuddered, wrenched her thoughts from the picture. She would go quite crazy if she allowed herself to think of such horrors. Weariness and hunger were dragging her resistance down to zero. She must continue to hold on, not lose heart. Old John Marshall would tell her it was cowardly to give way to despair. *You've got the courage it takes for this country.* He had meant those words.

The thought stiffened her pride, hardened her resolve. She was not going to give up, lie down and wait for death. She would draw on her strength to the last shred, keep her mind clear, her courage bright.

Linda became aware of sudden excitement in the mare, and instantly she was alert. That shape down in the sandy wash ahead, hardly to be distinguished from the clumps of brush, was a horseman, motionless, evidently watching her. She could see the glint of sunlight that caught the rifle in the saddle boot.

She pulled to a standstill, and the horse on the lead-rope, and the loose sorrel, came up on either side, ears pricked up inquisitively. Amigo growled, whimpered uneasily, slunk into the bushes.

More riders emerged from the shadowed gorge, moved slowly through the clumps of mesquite. Linda watched apprehensively. She wanted to believe these more than half-score horsemen were friends, sent by Jim Oland to help his old friend John Marshall. It was possible Jim Oland had heard rumors of trouble at the JM. There were signs that raised doubts in her. One of the riders was obviously ill, leaned forward on the horn of his saddle. Two others were hatless and their heads were bandaged, and one of the horses carried two men.

Linda felt there was something wrong, something that boded her no good. She pulled frantically on the reins, kicked the mare into a lope. The led horse hung back, snapped its rope from the saddlehorn. She was not caring any more about Brazos Jack's horse. She only wanted to get away from there.

Hoofbeats roared up behind her, a horse surged alongside, and a hand reached out to grab the mare's bridle. Linda snatched at the forty-five but the gun was jammed in the holster she had tied to the saddle.

She went limp, stared with dilated eyes at the man's lean dark face. She had never seen him before. The malicious amusement in his hard eyes made her shiver.

More riders clattered up, surrounded her, hard-featured men who slouched in their saddles and eyed her with mingled curiosity and suspicion.

One of the men broke the silence. "Who the hell is she, Tod?"

"Search me, Farg," replied the rustler foreman. He released his grasp on the mare's bridle, added with a semblance of courtesy, "Wasn't meanin' to scare you, ma'am—"

Linda fought off her panic. "I—I'm lost," she stammered.

"Mighty bad country to be lost in," Tod said, still sympathetic. "Where was you headin'?"

Instinct warned her not to tell him she was looking for the Oland's ranch. She said confusedly, "A ranch—a friend's ranch."

Farg was staring intently at the horse she had

led all the way from the scene of the fight in the chaparral. He spoke sharply, "Say, fellers, ain't this the bronc Brazos was ridin'?"

"Sure is," muttered one of the riders. "His saddle, too, or call me a liar."

Tod shifted his look to the horse, and Linda saw that he was suddenly tense. His gaze came back to her, read fright in her eyes.

"Where did you find this horse, ma'am?" he asked very softly.

They were all looking at her, silent, suspicious, waiting for her answer. She forced herself to speak. "I found him—tied to a bush."

"Brazos Jack's bronc right enough," said another man. "This here saddle's got that new stirrup he fixed on couple of days ago."

Tod was suddenly reaching for the forty-five in the holster tangled on her saddlehorn. He looked at it, then sharply at Linda.

"Did you find this Colt gun in the bushes—too?" There was danger in his quiet voice, a threat in the cold gleam she saw in his eyes. And then, as she gazed at him, wordless, her thoughts racing, trying to think of an answer to his challenge, Tod swung his long arm, held the gun out to Farg. "Ever see this forty-five before?" he asked in the same deadly voice.

Farg took his time inspecting the gun. He was the man who had been riding double, and he was on the ground now, a leg held stiffly as he stood there, turning the Colt over in his hands. He lifted an astonished look at the girl, ran his thumb over the scarred walnut butt as if to convince his doubting eyes.

He looked up at Tod, said flatly, "Bert's gun . . . Bert Stager's gun, Tod. I seen him cut these 'nitials with my own eyes . . . loaned him my jackknife when he carved 'em."

Linda sat very still in her saddle. She thought the silence would never end. Her heart was a lump of ice as she sensed the gathering storm in the eyes of the lean dark man crowding so close to her side. She lowered her eyes from the bleak look he bent on her, said in a tight voice she hardly recognized was hers, "You've no right to keep me here, asking questions—"

"Ain't so sure but what we've a right to know how come you got Bert Stager's gun dangling from your saddlehorn, ma'am." Tod's soft-spoken voice sent shivers through her. This hawk-eyed man was no fool, and he was wanting the truth from her.

Linda was not aware that her soft-curved lips were as tight-set as her father's when with swinging saber he had led the remnants of his Confederate cavalry against overwhelming odds. She only knew this lean and dangerous man would get no information from her.

She said again, quietly, and her voice now was clear and steady, "I'm asking you to let me go on my way. You have no right to hold me here, question me."

"Ain't so sure about that, ma'am." Tod seemed never to lift his voice. He was a great purring cat, Linda thought despairingly, and his claws were making ready for the kill.

He was talking to her, smoothly, yet with biting emphasis. "Don't look quite right, ma'am, you having Brazos Jack's horse trailin' with you, and Bert Stager's gun like I found it on your saddle. I sure want to know what's been goin' on." His soft voice took on a rasp. "Somethin' else happened last night. Lost my trail-herd in a stampede. Cain't figger out how come that stampede, and my temper's mighty thin right now, ma'am."

Linda was conscious of an odd stirring in her. She began to vaguely understand. *A stampede....* Thousands of thundering hoofs that scattered men and horses like chaff in the wind. Men maimed—*killed.*

The rustler chief caught her glance at the clustered riders. He gave her a chilly smile. "Yes, ma'am. Some of the boys was hurt bad and there ain't nothin' left of the chuckwagon but wheels and splinters." He was watching her closely. "Yes, ma'am, a mighty queer stampede. I reckon Farg will swear to that."

"I'll say it was queer," muttered Farg. "I sure crave to meet up with the gent that put them cactus thorns under my saddle."

"Farg's horse got to pitchin', started the stampede," Tod explained. "Took us until after sunup to round up the remuda." The rustler's voice was almost a whisper. "Perhaps you can tell us how come those cactus thorns got under Farg's saddle, ma'am."

Linda wondered if her eyes were too bright. She felt she could make a good guess about those cactus thorns. She could tell this man the answer wore the name of Adam Marshall. She was sure of it. Adam had done this thing to these weary-looking scoundrels. He was somewhere close, or had been. The thought made her heart leap.

They were watching her again, waiting for her answer, and it was very still there, and fear raised its head again under the impact of those cold, questioning eyes.

She said feebly, "I've never seen you before, or been near your herd of cattle."

Tod had Bert's gun back in his hand. He stared at it, fastened his hard gaze on the girl. "I ain't likin' this business, ma'am. I reckon we'll take you along with us. Mebbe you'll make up your mind to talk, tell us how come you got this forty-five away from Bert, and how come you picked up Brazos Jack's horse, and this sorrel that's runnin' loose with you."

He looked at the man who had been riding double with Farg. "You can fork that Brazos horse, Slim."

Linda asked faintly, "Where are you taking me?"

Tod gave her his thin smile. "I'm takin' you to my boss, ma'am. I reckon he'll make you talk plenty."

Her anger suddenly blazed. "I won't go!"

Tod said nothing, gave Farg a nod, and the man fastened a lead-rope to the mare. Linda started to get down from the saddle, felt Slim's hands forcing her back.

"Ain't wantin' to rope you," Tod said warningly.

Linda saw it was hopeless. She gave up.

Tod swung his horse back to the sandy wash and rode into a narrow gorge that twisted up through the hills. Farg followed with the mare on the lead-rope. The other riders strung out behind. Linda wondered about the dog, thought she glimpsed his tawny shape gliding through the scrub. She was not sure if what she had seen was Amigo or a coyote. She knew she was being taken to the Marshall ranch.

Despite her resolve to hold onto her courage she was conscious of a paralyzing fear. She knew without being told who the *boss* was. The boss was Newt Berren and he would be at the ranch. The jaws of the trap were closing with remorseless sureness. There seemed no way out—no hope of escape.

She thought of the rustler's talk about the

stampede, found herself grasping at vanishing shreds of hope. Adam Marshall must have caused the mysterious stampede that had obviously played such havoc with this gang of desperados.

Adam—*Adam*. To think of him was a voiceless prayer that brought comfort, steadied her.

19

DEATH WHISPERS

Rosa Baca closed the door softly, stood listening for a moment, ear pressed against the panel, then she went slowly to the bed. Her brown face wore a troubled look.

The old man on the bed saw the anxiety in her eyes. He asked in a low tone, hardly above a whisper, "What is it, Rosa?"

The Mexican woman stole a cautious look back at the door, and with a warning gesture bent close to him. "It is bad news," she whispered in Spanish. "They have brought the young señorita, locked her in a room."

Rage, a hint of fear, flickered across John Marshall's lined face, and he said, his whisper hoarse now, "The damn wolves! So they got her."

"A man watches in the hall, and another of them sits under the tree opposite her windows."

"You have spoken to her?" asked Marshall.

"No, señor—" Rosa shook her head. "Nor have I seen her. I was locked in my room when they brought her into the house. I listened at my door and heard her voice." Rosa smiled faintly. "She said hard words to Berren, and to the others. She is brave, that one."

"Sure, she's brave," muttered the old cowman. "Knew she had spunk the moment I laid eyes on her." He was silent for a moment, brows corrugated in thought. He looked up at the Mexican woman. "I'd like to see her," he said. "Can you manage it, Rosa?"

"I will try—" Her tone showed doubt. "They watch me like hawks, now that Berren is here. He is uneasy, and the look on his face is like a dark thundercloud."

"I want to see her," reiterated Marshall. He was silent again, bending his knees up under the bedclothes.

"Your legs get stronger every day," Rosa said. She glanced nervously at the wide windows. "Be careful, señor. It will be bad for you if they see."

"The shades are drawn," he pointed out.

"The windows are open and sometimes the wind blows the shades. They have not been watching the windows because they believe you are completely paralyzed, but now the señorita is here they watch everything." She shook her head at him worriedly. "So be very careful you are not seen by the man outside the windows."

He frowned. "Looks like I've got to stop being so damn careful." He fumbled under his pillow, slid the Colt forty-five Adam had given him under the bedclothes. "Be more handy," he said with a grim smile.

Rosa's hand lifted warningly. "Somebody come!" She moved swiftly to the far side of the room and began to dust a rocking chair.

Marshall's long, gaunt frame relaxed under the covers, he closed his eyes, made no effort to look at the big bearded man who came quietly into the room.

Despite his huge-shouldered frame and massive postlike legs, Berren could move with the lightness of a cat. After a brief glance at the Mexican woman busy with her dustcloth, he approached the bed, big square-toed boots making less than a whisper of sound.

As Rosa had said, the man's dark scowl showed disturbance in him. His eyes were restless, his majestic serenity gone.

He stood, gazing down at the man in the bed, spoke to Rosa without turning his head. "Any improvement in him? Can he use his hands at all?"

His low whispering voice seemed to make her cringe and for an instant horror dilated her eyes as she looked up from the chair.

"Poor señor mooch seek," she faltered. "I no like thees long time señor lie so still."

Berren's nod indicated that he heard her. He spoke again, his husky whispering voice reeking with venom. "Wake up, Marshall, damn your hide."

The old cattleman's eyes opened, met Berren's

look, and his lips moved, made meaningless sounds.

"I'm not caring if you can talk or not," Berren told him. "Can you hold a pen in your hand, good enough to make your signature?"

Marshall just stared up at him, eyes contemptuous, indicating that he understood the man's purpose.

Berren swore softly and he moved with his quick, gliding step to one of the windows, slid up the shade, and drew the curtain aside. He gestured at a huge tree now visible some twenty yards away.

"Remember that cottonwood, Marshall? That's where you let my father swing until he choked to death. I was only a kid, but I swore that I'd get even some day."

A muffled sob came from the other side of the room and Berren looked at Rosa, dabbing at her eyes with her apron. He said in his evil whisper, "Get out of here, you damn Mex."

Rosa flung a despairing look at the man rigid on the bed, went on stumbling feet to the door, disappeared into the hall.

Berren's malignant gaze followed her until the door closed her out. He began talking again, rasping whispered words that poured in a stream from his bearded lips. "I make my plans well, Marshall. You'd look good, swinging from that tree, but I've different ideas about it. No man shall know that my hand took your life. I am well thought of—a respected citizen and will be among the loudest of your mourners—and the day of mourning will be soon, now—very soon. I'm not wasting time nursing you forever."

He let the curtain fall back and returned to the bed, glowered down at the man under the covers.

"I'm using that tree to swing your murderer. *I'm* going to pull the trigger of the gun that kills you. I won't deny myself *that* pleasure, but we're going to catch a man in the act. That will be our story, Marshall, and we'll hang him from the same tree you hung my father on. You won't guess who the man is . . . you think he's dead, but I've kept him alive because *his* father's hand put the rope around *my* father's neck."

Berren's face was a mask of hate. "You know who I mean now, Marshall, and it's going to be *my* hands that put the rope over Monte Cline's neck."

He turned away abruptly, and in a moment the door closed behind him.

John Marshall lay very still, gaze on the door, his face drawn and haggard, then slowly he drew the gun from under the concealing covers, and as he looked at it his face took on the hardness of granite.

On the other side of the door, Berren stood looking at a man who sat tipped back in a chair down the hall. The man saw him, got to his feet.

Berren approached him, paused, said softly, "You don't need a chair to help watch this door." He leaned down, seized the chair with big hands, wrenched the front legs off with two quick jerks. He flung the pieces down. "If you let that girl escape I'll do the same to you," he said; and he turned the key in the lock, pushed the door open and went inside.

Linda, sitting in a chair under an open window, met his benevolent smile with a stony look. She wondered how she ever could have been deceived by his pretense of kindliness. His eyes never smiled. They were cold slate, all the more inhuman because of their lack of expression.

He went toward her, and now she sprang to her feet, backing away from him with a gesture so expressive of disdain and horror that he halted abruptly.

"You'll have to get used to me," he said in his husky whisper. The benevolence was gone from him now, and he stood there, white teeth showing through his beard in an ugly wolf's grin, big hairy hand stroking the square-cut beard.

Linda said nothing, threw a wild glance at the window behind her. A man lounged outside in the shade of a tree, a rifle under his arm.

"You won't get away from me again," Berren said. He went on, his whisper like the rasp of a saw. "Did you kill Bert Stager?"

She shook her head.

"Tod found Bert's gun on you."

Linda kept silent. She could think of nothing to say.

"You had Brazos Jack's horse on a lead-rope, Tod said." Berren watched her with unwinking eyes. "Did you kill him, too?"

She broke her silence, said contemptuously, "You know I didn't kill anybody."

"Sam Doan's missing," Berren continued. "What do you know about Sam, Miss Linda?"

"You're wasting your time, asking questions."

"It was Sam who killed Bert, got you away," he purred. His eyes probed her mercilessly. "I see, yes, I think I understand what happened. Sam killed Bert, and killed Brazos, but what happened to Sam?"

Linda closed her eyes. What was the use? She said in a tired voice, "Sam Doan was a brave man—not a coward—like you."

He looked at her for long moments, silent, his expression thoughtful, and she sensed he was forming a picture, Sam and the outlaw, smoking guns—two dead men. She had the feeling the picture pleased him.

He was smiling now. "I see," he repeated. "Sam and Brazos shot it out. Simplifies matters for me. I'd have been forced to kill both of them—eventually. Their usefulness was about finished."

He looked her up and down, and a hint of concern showed on his face. "You're very tired

". . . need rest and food. You've had a hard night, Miss Linda." His tone was gentle again, his smile kindly. "I want the roses back in your cheeks, the sparkle in your eyes. I can make you a very happy young woman—when you're willing to listen to reason—be sensible."

Linda lowered her eyes. No good letting him see the loathing in them. She must play for time, do nothing to further enrage this strange man.

She made an effort, forced herself to look at him, conceal her disgust. "I *am* hungry—and—and tired." She let her glance stray longingly to the bed.

Berren nodded. "I think you want to be sensible. I'll send the Mexican woman with food."

"Thank you." Linda made her voice sound grateful.

She watched him go, her heart beating fast, wondered if the Mexican woman might be Rosa Baca. It seemed hardly possible.

She waited in a fever of impatience, heard steps approaching along the hall, heard a woman's voice, a man's gruff answer. The door opened and she caught a glimpse of the guard's scowling face, and then Rosa Baca came into the room, a laden tray in both hands. The door closed.

Rosa placed the tray on a table, turned and looked at her, a gleam of triumph in her dark eyes. "*Habla Usted Español?*"

Linda shook her head. She felt dizzy with relief.

This woman actually was Rosa Baca, Adam's old nurse—his friend.

The Mexican woman went to her, took her hand. "No be frighten, señorita. You remember me, no? You come that day old señor 'ave the str-roke." She smiled reassuringly, patted the girl's hand.

"Yes," Linda said. "You are Rosa Baca. . . . You are Adam's friend."

"*Sí*—" Rosa nodded. "Adamito, my leetle baby." She leaned closer, her voice a cautious whisper. "Adamito come las' night . . . talk weeth old señor." Her eyes glowed. "Adamito mooch smar-rt." She filled a cup from the coffee pot, held it out. "You dreenk, poor leetle one."

Linda obediently put the cup to her lips. The hot coffee tasted good. She smiled gratefully.

Rosa pulled a chair up to the table, gestured for her to sit. There was a small steak on the plate, and hashed browned potatoes, a hot muffin.

"You're very kind," Linda thanked her. This woman's presence enormously heartened her.

Rosa went on whispering to her. "Old señor wan' to see you—" She looked frowningly at the door. "Thees man watch all time."

"Mr. Marshall is—is all right?" Linda asked, anxiously.

"*Sí*—" Rosa smiled mysteriously. "We make beeg treek—no let thees Berren know old señor str-rong man now."

"He can walk again—talk?" Linda's voice was breathless with amazement—relief. "How wonderful!"

Rosa nodded, smiled happily. "You no tell—"

"Of course I won't—"

Rosa's look went again to the door, and Linda guessed she was trying to solve the problem of the man on the other side.

"He won't let me leave this room," she said. "I heard Berren tell that man he would kill him if he let me escape."

"I 'ave plan," smiled Rosa. She tiptoed to another door, opened it. Linda saw a large closet, and men's clothes, boots, a Stetson hat on a peg. This was Adam's room, she suddenly realized.

Rosa beckoned, finger on lips. Linda got quietly from the chair and joined her.

"Thees closet opens into old señor's closet," Rosa told her. "Old señor made it w'en Adamito baby so 'e come queek w'en Adamito cry in night."

She pushed the clothes aside and Linda saw a narrow door so skillfully fitted into the wall it was hardly noticeable.

Rosa slid a catch, motioned her to pass into the big closet on the other side. "I take tray back down 'all," she whispered. "The man no suspect you 'ave gone from room. You wait . . . I come queek—take you to old señor."

Linda nodded that she understood. She bent

low, slid through the narrow opening, was plunged into darkness as the door quietly closed behind her.

She waited interminable minutes, hardly dared to breathe. The closet smelled of a man's things, tobacco, saddle leather.

At last her listening ears caught a faint sound. The door opened, and there was Rosa, beckoning her into the big bedroom. The shades were drawn, dimmed out the sunlight.

Linda went swiftly to the man lying under the bed covers. She sank on her knees, clasped his hand. She wanted to cry, but knew that John Marshall would not want tears. She smiled instead, squeezed his hand hard.

He said softly, "Good girl," and after a moment, "We don't give up easy, huh? We fight when trouble's in the saddle."

Linda nodded, smiled. It was hard to find words at that moment.

"Looks like Adam missed you," the old cowman continued. "He was headed for Dos Ríos to get you away from that town. He didn't know about Berren until I told him."

She found her voice. "It's wonderful to be here—with you—find you—all right again."

"We're keeping 'em fooled," chuckled the old man. His tone was suddenly grave. "Tell me everything, girl, just the highlights."

Linda told him briefly about the affair at the

store, about Sam Doan, the fight in the chaparral.

Marshall nodded, said simply, "Sam died the way a JM man should. I reckon he paid his debt."

"He wanted you to know he was sorry for what he did," Linda said. She went on with her story, told about the encounter with the rustlers, the stampede that had scattered the trail-herd.

John Marshall's eyes glowed. "Means Adam is on the job," he chuckled. He patted her hand. "I reckon it explains why Berren's jumpy now. He knows there's a Marshall gunning for him."

"Adam is like you," Linda said. "He's a fighter."

John Marshall looked pleased. "Was hoping you'd kind of like Adam." His eyes were suddenly wistful. "He—he thinks a lot of you, girl."

She met his look bravely. "I like him—a lot—oh, so very much—"

The old cattleman nodded, his face grave. "I was hoping you'd feel that way about him, girl." He paused, and fire crept into his eyes, and his hand tightened hard over hers. "He'll pick up your trail, girl. He'll be back this way—looking for you—"

A faint whisper of sound came from the hall, drew a low, frightened exclamation from Rosa. She seized Linda's hand. "Queek . . . the closet—"

Linda gave Marshall a despairing look, ran into the closet, pushed deep among the clothes as the Mexican woman quickly closed the door. She dreaded going back to the other room, was suddenly aware it was impossible to go back—*now.* Men's voices in there told her it was too late. Her absence was already discovered.

She heard another voice in Marshall's room, Berren's wicked husky whisper. She pressed against the wall, listened, her heart pounding.

"Where's the girl?" she heard him ask, and the fury in him made her shiver. "She's not in her room."

"*Speak—or I'll strangle you with my own hands—*"

Linda heard a frightened cry from Rosa, knew she could not bear this thing. She groped in the darkness for the door, pushed it wide open.

20

TRAIL'S END

The ditch reached in a straight line from a bend in the creek to the several acres of grass and trees that surrounded the ranch house. John Marshall had built a headgate at its mouth to govern the flow of water when he wanted to flood the grounds. Cottonwoods and willows that had taken root during the long years lined its banks.

Adam crawled cautiously through the tall weeds. Even though his mind was occupied with the grim problems confronting him, he was vaguely irritated by the rank growth in the ditch. It had always been a sacred law of the ranch to clean out the weeds in the late autumn, make the ditch ready for the spring floods. His grandfather would be fretting about it. The ditch was his pet hobby and he took a vast pride in it. One of Adam's boyhood recollections was the first moonlit night he had helped John Marshall patrol the banks, on the watch for holes that could quickly cause a break in the levee if not discovered in time. His grandfather had given him a birthday present of a little red-handled shovel and he had used it well that night, stopping the beginnings of a break. His grandfather had found him, knee-deep in the gurgling flood that was tearing out the soft earth, had stood there, leaning on his own long-handled shovel, watching his panting, struggling efforts, and let him stop the break without trying to help. It was good experience, he had told Adam. It was necessary for a man to learn how to pit his wits and strength against threatened disaster. Adam had felt very grown-up for all his nine years.

It was hot, sticky work, crawling through the rank growth of weeds. The midafternoon sun blazed from a cloudless sky and the air was very still and the gnats pursued him relentlessly, trying to get at his eyes and ears.

At last, crouching there in the ditch, he could see the top branches of the great cottonwood in front of the house. The Hang Tree. A murderer had died on it. Newt Berren's father.

Adam crawled up the bank and lay flat in the welcome shade. He needed to think out his next move. It was going to be difficult, getting inside the house. He had to get in. His grandfather and Linda were there. They needed him and he had to find a way. Now, if ever, had come the moment to pit his wit and strength against threatened and dreadful disaster.

He was certain Linda was in the house. The trail had been plain. She had fallen into Tod's hands and the rustler had taken her to the house, taken her to Newt Berren.

He speculated about Bill Clemm. Bill would not reach Oland's ranch until sundown of this same day. It was close on fifty miles and Oland's men could not possibly make it until much before the following dawn.

Adam grimly put the thought of Oland out of his mind. He could not wait for Oland. He must play out the hand alone, get his grandfather and Linda away before it was too late.

He got to his feet, and was suddenly reaching for his gun. Something was stirring the tall grass, and now he glimpsed a tawny shape—a dog.

The hardness left Adam's eyes. The sheep dog—Linda's dog. For some reason he was cheered, and the feeling of loneliness left him. Here was a friend, a loyal friend.

The dog remembered him, knew too, that this man was a friend. He approached, sniffed Adam's outstretched hand, wagged his tail.

Adam said softly, "We both love her, huh?"

The dog whimpered, turned and moved toward the house, halted, looked back as if to say, "Come on . . . what are we waiting for?"

Adam followed stealthily, saw the dog flatten like a stalking wolf.

The warning was just in time. Adam crouched behind a bush, watched the man standing guard under the bedroom windows with fierce, calculating eyes.

There was only one way to handle this first

obstacle, and now, crawling on hands and knees, he inched closer, reached the concealment of another bush. He waited, wondering desperately how he could manage the remaining few yards, felt the dog press against him.

He continued to watch the man, saw him lean his rifle against the tree at his back and fumble tobacco sack and papers from his shirt pocket.

Adam looked at the dog, motioned for him to move on. The dog seemed to understand his purpose, and tail up now, and tongue lolling, went trotting into the open.

The man muttered an exclamation, stared at him, both hands busy with the cigarette he was shaping. Adam crept closer, lifted his gun. He hated to do this thing, but there was no alternative.

The guard was grinning at the dog. He said wonderingly, "Where in hell did *you* come from?" He thumbnailed a match, lit the cigarette and bent down, snapped a thumb invitingly.

Adam slid toward him, and perhaps the shift of the dog's head, or the rustle of leaves underfoot, warned the man. His hand swooped to the gun in his holster.

Adam was close enough now, and the barrel of his gun caught the man's temple as he turned his head in a startled look.

It was a hard blow and for a moment Adam thought he had killed him. He dragged the limp body behind the bush, assured himself his victim would be unconscious for a long time and that it was not necessary to tie him up.

The dog ran to him, bristling and whimpering, and now Adam heard from the direction of the house a husky whispering voice, and the evil in it sent a cold prickle down his spine, made him think of Rosa Baca's words, *A whispering voice that makes me think of the Evil One who reigns in hell . . . my flesh creeps . . .* Berren's voice . . . and he was there in that room, and Linda was there, and she was defying the man.

Adam was not waiting to hear what she was saying to Berren. He was already running to the window and scrambling through. The dog tried to follow, missed his leap, ran in a circle and tried again, and this time cleared the sill.

Berren was slowly backing toward the hall door, his big hands holding Linda in front of him, and standing by the bed was a gaunt old man in a nightgown, one hand gripping the bedpost for support, and his other hand clutching a long-barreled forty-five and helpless to use it because the girl's body was shielding the man he wanted to kill. Rosa lay sprawled on the floor where Berren had flung her. She was moaning and tugging a knife from inside her dress.

Adam hurled himself across the room, and Berren, loosing his hold on the girl, grabbed a heavy chair and flung it at the man charging him.

Adam ducked, and the chair hurtled across the room, to strike the man who came running from the open closet. He groaned, sprawled his length on the floor. A second man ran from the closet, staggered, and fell with a bullet in his heart from the gun in old Marshall's hand.

Adam was between Berren and the door, now, but Berren was giving him no chance to use the gun still in its holster. His massive arms drew Adam into a bear's hug. Adam broke the terrible hold, but he could not overcome this man's brute strength. As he tried again to get his gun out, he heard a cry from Linda and saw Tod suddenly appear in the hall doorway. The lean, dark-faced rustler's gun was flashing up, and a snarling tawny shape leaped at him from the window, sank sharp fangs into the man's forearm, deflecting his aim as the gun exploded. The bullet intended for Adam struck Berren between the eyes, and he pitched heavily on his face. Tod was screaming curses at the snarling dog and trying to pick up his fallen gun. Bad as he was, the man was no coward. He flung the dog aside and snatched up the gun, but Adam had his own forty-five in his hand now, and the shock of the heavy bullet smashing into his shoulder sent the rustler staggering against the wall. His knees buckled under him, and he slid senseless to the floor.

Adam's look went to Linda and then to his grandfather, clinging to the bedpost, the gun in his hand still smoking. They were all of them dazed by the appalling suddenness of the affair. In less than thirty seconds two men had died, a third lay unconscious on the floor, and a fourth man was groaning under the heavy chair that Berren had hurled toward Adam.

John Marshall broke the stunned silence. "Was kind of looking for you to drop in, boy, but not quite so sudden." He smiled wryly, eased down on the bed. "These old legs of mine don't prop me up any too good yet."

Linda ran to him, the big sheep dog close at her heels. He waved her back. "The show isn't over," he said. "Better shut and lock those doors, Adam."

They could hear the pounding of feet outside, a man's hoarse shout. Tod's outfit was coming on the run to investigate the shooting.

Adam quickly closed the hall door, and Rosa, now on her feet, tottered to the closet door, slammed it shut.

The old cowman said placidly from the bed, "I'll watch the windows." He waggled the big gun in his hand. "Looks like I can still shoot straight." He threw a complacent glance at the dead man lying near the closet door.

The kitchen door was slamming and they could hear more men running up from the bunkhouse. Feet clattered along the hall, and a man shouted Tod's name. Adam recognized Farg's voice.

"What's goin' on? . . . Heard shootin' some place here!"

The doorknob rattled, and a man said, "Hell—she's locked! Don't look good, fellers."

"Kick the damn door in!" yelled a voice. A boot thudded heavily and another voice said, "Need an axe to bust *this* door down. Go git an axe, somebody."

"Yeah!" shouted Farg. "And some of you fellers git outside and try the windows."

The man lying under the chair stopped his groaning. "Only two of 'em in here, Farg," he yelled. "They killed the boss and looks like Tod's dead. Smash the door!" He began clawing for the gun he had dropped when the chair hit him. Linda ran quickly, snatched the gun from his reaching fingers. She leveled it at the man, said sharply, "Shut up. . . . I'll shoot."

Adam gave her an approving look from the door he was watching, and he said quietly to Rosa, "Get that other gun, and don't stand where you can be seen from the windows. Shoot the first man who tries to climb in."

The Mexican woman hurried over to the senseless Tod and picked up his Colt.

The door was shaking under the lusty kicks. Adam and old Marshall exchanged grave looks. Only four of them against probably a score of hard-bitten and desperate scoundrels, and one of the four a young girl, another an old woman. The prospect was far from bright. These men would not hesitate to shoot them down in cold blood.

He motioned for Linda to keep out of range from the windows. She pressed close to the wall, and he saw that her eyes were very bright and that there was no fear in her.

There had been no time for words between them. It was enough just to be together again, and Linda was aware of a great gladness in her, and the horrors of the long night seemed nothing now Adam was here.

The man lying on the floor so close gave her some concern, and she said to the dog, "Watch him, Amigo." The big sheep dog understood, took a snarling stance in front of the rustler. The man was suddenly very still, seeming hardly to breathe.

Men were running along the side of the house, and suddenly a head appeared at one of the windows. John Marshall flung a quick shot, and the bullet lifted the man's hat. He let out an anguished yell, dropped from sight and now there was silence.

The deafening roar of the gun silenced for a moment the battering on the door, which now began to show cracks in the panels. Farg's rasping voice called out, "You ain't got a chance to git out of this house. Ain't more'n two of you, Slim was yellin'."

Adam hardly took notice of what he said. He

was listening tensely, and the sound he heard was the distant drumming of horses coming on the dead run. Others were hearing those approaching hoofbeats, and a startled shout broke the silence outside the windows.

"Hell! There's a bunch of fellers comin' on the jump. I'm gittin' away from here."

In a moment the attackers were in frantic flight for the yard, the hall suddenly empty, the men gone from the windows. Adam could hardly believe his senses. Bill Clemm must have found help much closer to home than the Oland ranch. He stood there, dazed, his smile on Linda, listened to the thunder of those approaching hoofs. He had never heard a sound so welcome.

Guns began to crackle. Adam unlocked the battered door, jerked it open, and ran down the hall. Linda started to follow, saw John Marshall trying to get up from the bed. He was too weak to stand. She hurried to him, and he leaned his weight on her. "I want my pants," he fumed. "Rosa—get my pants—boots."

Rosa padded across from the window, the big gun dangling in her hand. "No, señor!" she scolded. "You do not go outside, so weak like this."

"Get me my pants!" he roared.

Rosa shook her head and her lips tightened. "I stay here with murderers to nurse you all thees long time, now you shout at me because I will not let you go out and have another bad stroke. You are unkind—"

The old man's face softened. He patted her arm. "I reckon you're talking good sense, Rosa." He lowered himself down to the bed and picked up the gun from the covers, and said to Linda, "You run on, girl, go bring me news of what's doing outside. I'll watch this low-down cow thief." His brows bristled at the man lying on the floor.

"Amigo will watch him," confidently asserted Linda.

The dog's tail quivered, but he kept his fierce eyes fastened on the rustler. The old cowman grinned. "I reckon the two of us can hold this prisoner," he chuckled. "You run along, girl. I want news. Sounds like there's plenty action outside in the yard."

Linda ran from the room, the gun in her hand, keeping her eyes averted from the dead storekeeper as she passed him. She noticed that the other man, Tod, was still unconscious, and there was a big red stain widening down his shirt sleeve. She could feel no pity for him. He had tried his best to kill Adam.

A lean man with a tired, brown face stopped her in the kitchen. With a start of surprise she recognized Bill Clemm. He put a hand on her arm, said quietly, "I wouldn't go out thar right now, Miss Linda. Too much shootin' . . . you'll likely catch a bullet."

His eyes were bloodshot, his face streaked with dust and sweat, but there was grim contentment in him. Linda said breathlessly, "You came just in time."

The old JM foreman nodded. "Had a lucky break . . . met up with Jim Oland and his outfit ridin' hell-for-leather to git here."

Linda gazed at him, bewildered, finding it difficult to grasp the fact that she was talking to Bill Clemm. She had thought him dead.

He understood her amazement. "Reckon Adam ain't had a chance to do much talkin'," he drawled. "He run into me, whar I was hid out down in the canyon. Got me a bronc and sent me hightailin' it for Oland's ranch to git help."

"No," she said, "we've had no time for talking, but I'm so happy, Mr. Clemm."

Bill nodded gravely. "Been a tough time for the old boss. He stuck it out, like he always done when thar was trouble in the saddle." His slow, understanding smile covered her. "Seems like Adam left word for Ed Stines in Phoenix he was needed bad at the ranch. Ed's U.S. Deputy Marshal. He run into Jim Oland at the Cattlemen's Association meetin' at Willcox. They got mighty uneasy and that's how come they was headed this way when I met 'em."

"It's a miracle," Linda said soberly.

Bill Clemm grinned, then said solemnly, "I reckon that's the truth, ma'am." He limped toward the hall door. "I'm mighty anxious to see the boss. I'm bettin' my last chip the old longhorn is frettin' plenty—him layin' thar in bed, listenin' to them guns smokin'."

"You'll be good medicine for him," smiled Linda.

Bill Clemm chuckled, and went limping into the hall.

Linda went down the porch steps, leaned over the gate under the towering tankhouse. The gunfire was silent now, and she saw riders herding a group of men into a corner of the corral. The men held their hands above their heads, and she saw that they were prisoners.

Adam and two men stood near the long water-trough, talking. One of the men had a deeply sunburned face and a drooping grizzled mustache. He wore a star pinned to his shirt, and she guessed he was Ed Stines, the U.S. Deputy Marshal. She heard Adam's voice, quiet, contented:

"Monte Cline has the rest of the gang locked up in jail. We're going to have law and order in the Dos Ríos from now on, Ed."

Linda was conscious of a new and wonderful peace in her. They had been so close to the dark brink of oblivion. The bright courage of valiant men had brought blessed peace and security and honorable living to this vast land of wooded hills and lush valleys and painted deserts. Her own country now, for always.

Adam turned, saw her waiting at the gate, the sunlight burnishing her chestnut hair, and he moved quickly toward her.

Thoughts whirled through his mind. There was so much to tell her, so many plans to make. Faithful Catalina Ortiz and her *ranchero* husband. He would send for them and they would run sheep on Linda's land. He had his own plans for Linda. She belonged here, on the old JM ranch, where she could be waiting for him, leaning over a gate, watching him ride in from the range while sunset faded to twilight, and her eyes would have the look in them he saw now. It had been a long trail from that crossing of the Rio Grande, from the shadows of death in Mexico. This was trail's end, and the girl he loved was leaning on a gate, waiting for him.

Adam's stride lengthened. He was in great haste now to reach that gate—the promise that waited there.

Center Point Large Print
600 Brooks Road / PO Box 1
Thorndike, ME 04986-0001 USA

(207) 568-3717

US & Canada:
1 800 929-9108
www.centerpointlargeprint.com